THE MOGUL

Vish Dhamija is the bestselling author of six crime fiction books. He is frequently referred to in the press as the 'master of crime and courtroom drama' in India. In August 2015, at the release of his first legal fiction, *Deja Karma*, *Glimpse* magazine called him, 'India's John Grisham' for stimulating the genre of legal fiction in India, which was almost non-existent before his arrival on the scene. *The Mogul*, a legal thriller, is his seventh novel. Vish lives in London with his wife, Nidhi.

VISH
DHAMIJA

THE MOGUL

HARPER
BLACK
An Imprint of HarperCollins *Publishers*

First published in India in 2018 by Harper Black
An imprint of HarperCollins *Publishers*
4th Floor, Tower A, Building No. 10, DLF Cyber City,
DLF Phase II, Gurugram, Haryana – 122002
www.harpercollins.co.in
2 4 6 8 10 9 7 5 3 1

P-ISBN: 978-93-5302-024-8
E-ISBN: 978-93-5302-025-5

Typeset in 11/14 Bembo at
Manipal Digital Systems, Manipal

Printed and bound at
MicroPrints India, New Delhi

The pharisees challenged him, 'here you are, appearing as your own witness; your testimony is not valid.'

JOHN 8:13

PROLOGUE

9 June

Nine Bridges Resort

Jeju Island, South Korea

Prem Bedi was on the first tee at the creak course—for the front nine holes that posed challenges in shape of stone walls, dry streams and shrubs. Since he was the guest, his host and business associate Mr Sung-min Lee had given him the honour of teeing first. Hyun, the caddie, a young lad of twenty-five, had already briefed Prem that it was 380m/Par4; a straightforward course that only the distance made Par4. Prem could visually determine as much, but he let Hyun take pride in his job. A fine drive between 175-200 metres would be splendid if Prem didn't go out of bounds. The green was 28m wide, so to get on it in the second stroke would be simple enough.

Prem Bedi had been an enthusiastic golfer since the age of eighteen, when he first accompanied his father to The Bombay Presidency Golf Club in Mumbai, some thirty-five years ago. And while he had stayed an amateur, he didn't really need Hyun's explanatory spiel. Nevertheless, he appreciated the Korean hospitality. Hyun was one of the guys on the course who was bilingual and as such he also played the role of the interpreter between Prem and Sung-min Lee camps.

At fifty-three, Prem Bedi was five-feet-eleven and lean, with once perfect salt-and-pepper coif slicked back from a sharp widow's peak that he had once shaved off completely but then grown back.

Prem's father had abandoned his ancestral zamindari and moved to Mumbai before the Partition, but he carried the genes and sharp features of the men that came from the erstwhile British-India Punjab. Prem's mother, Rani Devi Singh, was the heiress of a small princely Jat state near Benaras, in Uttar Pradesh. Consequently, Prem's appearance was a handsome balance of rustic and regal, and because of his Jat ancestry, he had powerful cousins in high places, and openly supported the Jat lobby. Members of his extended family were politicians and ministers in State Governments in Haryana, Punjab, UP and Rajasthan.

Prem's father—Pran Bedi—had set up cotton looms in Mumbai's Lower Parel area in 1931. It remained a medium-sized operation till 1947, when most cotton mills encountered a substantial setback. During Partition, the majority of the long-staple cotton-growing farms went to Pakistan, while the mills remained in India. The irony was lost on no one.

As other mills' business started incurring losses since importing cotton was prohibitively expensive, Pran Bedi was thrown a lifeline.

Rani Devi Singh's father, the Raja Sahib, came to the rescue, and with a substantial cash injection from him, Pran Bedi got the thirty-plus owners of the mills together and offered them loans in lieu of stake in their businesses. He wagered that, in time, the industry would recover. He was right, and with twenty-five per cent stake in thirty-five mills, when the tides turned, Bedi was rolling in gold.

From those humble beginnings over half a century ago, the textile mills paved way to shipping, then banking, retail and telecoms. The conglomerate went public in the late seventies, but the majority stake remained within the family trust.

The media loved Prem Bedi and branded him a Mogul. He was the sole trustee and largest shareholder of Bedi & Sons, which had a market capitalisation of over 200,000 crores. He owned companies in the Indian subcontinent, the Middle East, the Far East, North, East and Central Africa, Australia and New Zealand. Most of these companies were publicly traded; some were privately held or were partnerships. And Prem Bedi was the third-richest man in the country.

Prem's drive from the first tee was straight, but it landed shorter than he would have liked: 130m.

Lee hit a fantastic 195m.

'Wow, Mr Lee,' Prem said, looking at his adversary.

Lee and Prem were accompanied by their legal advisors for a four ball match. Prem was here to secure a twenty-five per cent stake in one of the microchip manufacturing companies that Lee controlled. In return, Prem was offering him that percentage in his retail business of 400 shops across India. It was a win-win deal. However, Lee wanted a higher stake, and Prem wasn't conceding. Neither man needed to negotiate: yielding a slightly higher percentage wouldn't have bankrupted either, but the power play was about egos.

The teams were at par on the third hole.

Prem and his legal advisor Tej Malhotra had arrived at Seoul the day before and had stayed at the Ritz-Carlton. Lee had flown the guests in his personal Cessna Stationair to Juju Island. The pilot, the golfing foursome and Hyun, filled up the six-seater.

At hole six, Lee and his advisor Peter had a four points lead.

At the seventh and the smallest hole in the creek course—136m/Par3—Tej Malhotra's drive went straight into the water next to the green.

Lee and Peter were now six points ahead.

At the eighth hole, Prem, visibly restive at the looming defeat in the first nine, teed off rather ridiculously. No loft, no distance, the ball landed a mere 90m when it should have an easy 190. Exasperated, he thumped the driver hard on the ground; it hit a hard buried rock on the side and splintered; the head totally detached from the body.

'I'm so sorry, Mr Lee.' Prem said.

Lee smiled and said something in Korean, which Hyun translated as, 'It's only a game, Mr Bedi. You have another ten holes to cover up, don't worry.'

Tej Malhotra looked guilt-ridden. Team Lee's lead had primarily been due to Tej's sloppy performance.

'I'm sorry, Prem.' He made a glum face.

'It's only a game, Tej.'

Hyun translated the little banter for Lee and came back with Lee's riposte: 'That's the spirit. I will gift you a new driver when we get back to Seoul.'

'Thank you.' Prem picked up the remains of his driver and put them in one of the wastebaskets by the side.

After the ninth hole, the party broke for lunch, and ordered iced teas and lobsters. Prem felt his iPhone vibrate in his pocket. He ignored it for the sake of etiquette. The faint buzzing continued for five rings before it stopped.

The waitress cleared the table and left them with the dessert menus.

'What time do we start again?' asked Prem.

'Let's have coffee and move.'

Prem's phone vibrated again. The purr was audible to all at the table.

Lee said something.

'Please take the call. It might be important if someone's trying a second time,' Hyun translated.

Prem apologised and pulled out his iPhone but it had stopped ringing by then. He noticed both the calls were from an India number but other than the country code, which was Mumbai's, the number was blocked. 'Strange.' He showed it to Tej.

'You want me to call the office to check, Prem?' Tej offered.

'Yes, thank you. You call the office, but first, let me check my voicemail.' But the caller had left no message. 'Very strange for someone to call me twice, get to voicemail and not leave a message.'

Tej excused himself and stepped away from the table to make the call, while Hyun translated the exchange.

The waitress returned with their coffees.

Tej stood away from the table, waiting for someone back at the Mumbai office to answer. Tej Malhotra had been the legal advisor to Bedi & Sons for the most part of the past decade. He was initially hired to advise on financial matters, but he was now a close confidante and advisor on everything Prem did – professional and personal. A trustworthy friend and golf companion, he was only six years older than Prem.

Although golf had brought them closer to each other, the two of them also enjoyed similar music, watching cricket and social drinking. But the similarities ran deeper, all the way to their roots. Tej's father had migrated from the same region in Punjab, albeit after the Partition. Both men were now single. Prem Bedi had had a divorce about twelve years ago; Tej was a widower with two children – his daughter worked for a clothing company in Italy and his son was a small-time criminal defence advocate starting on his own after a few years with a renowned firm.

Prem glanced at Tej and he could see that something was amiss. His friend's face was the colour of a ripe tomato; nevertheless Prem sat and waited. Finally, Tej cut the call and returned to the table.

'The news isn't good, Prem,' he said.

Lee whispered something to Hyun. 'Do you gentlemen want us to take leave?'

'If you don't mind …' Tej said.

'No,' Prem said. 'What is it, Tej?'

'Prem, your wife … I mean, your ex-wife, is dead.'

For a few seconds, Prem was still. Then he swallowed hard and tried to regain his composure. 'So, why are you so upset? Even I haven't seen her in the twelve years we've been divorced. And you didn't know her at all. Sure, it is a sad untimely death; she would have been forty this year, but—'

'She was murdered,' Tej blurted.

Lee asked for immediate permissions and the Cessna flew out of Jeju Islands at 5.12 p.m.

One the flight, everyone was silent except Lee, who was on the phone with his office, making arrangements for his staff to check out both his guests, pick up their baggage and transport it to Seoul International Airport. There was a Korean Air flight departing Seoul at 8.30 p.m., and he had organised two first-class seats on the same.

TEJ MALHOTRA

5.20 a.m.

We were told that our flight from Seoul International Airport was delayed by fifteen minutes due to air traffic. It eventually took off three hours later than its planned departure. I wasn't too concerned as any delay only helped us arrive in Mumbai at a saner hour. We were now hovering over Mumbai, waiting to be cleared for landing.

Ever since I broke the news of his ex-wife's murder to Prem, there had been little conversation between the two of us. Prem looked subdued; he had retracted into some kind of a shell. Shock? Perhaps. It couldn't be grief. It isn't like he had been in love with Rea; in fact, he had explicitly stated that he didn't care about her, not after the acrimonious divorce almost twelve years ago. I wasn't part of his life then, but thanks to the media, the details were no secret. When he married Rea Khanna, he made news. Their divorce, unsurprisingly, made headlines.

But the unlikely couple's marriage had lasted longer than what the media had predicted. He was thirty-two and she was nineteen when they first met at a charity ball. An eight-month courtship had led to a marriage that lasted eight years, before finally ending.

Before this, I had never seen Prem concerned by what Rea did or where she lived, or whom with. However, her death seemed to have shaken him. He was visibly upset. And this was when he didn't even know the complete truth – that it had been a double murder. Rea had been found dead at her Pali Hill residence in Bandra, along with her current husband Mahesh Desai, the big time loud-mouthed journalist who she had left Prem for. I had tried to give him all the details I got from that call, but he had refused to come aside even for a moment during the lunch with Mr Lee, and what with all the rush to get home, I hadn't gotten a chance since. And I didn't have the heart to tell him everything during the flight after I witnessed him withdraw into his own world. Prem had declined the champagne and gone straight for the hard stuff. I knew he loved a drink or two of Single Malt, but this was the most he had ever consumed in my presence.

It was 5.36 a.m. when we finally landed. The morning light welcomed us through the fissures in the accordion vestibule that connected the aircraft and aerobridge. Perhaps I should have taken Prem aside and briefed him of the entire incident as we walked out, but I didn't think he had sobered up enough to receive the details.

We crossed Immigration, took the escalator down and walked towards the baggage carousel. Quietly, like two strangers travelling together, we picked up our overnighters and golf kits and walked into the arrival lounge.

Nothing. It was then that it struck me. The media must have known about the murders by now, but they had no information regarding Prem's arrival by this flight. He had originally been booked for two days later. And since I hadn't asked for a separate airport pick up for him, no one here knew he was returning today. My driver saw both of us, rushed forward, doffed his white cap and immediately took our baggage.

'Thanks, Tej ...' Prem turned to me. His voice didn't waver. I guess he had an accelerated ability to process alcohol.

I looked at him questioningly.

'For keeping the plan of our early return under wraps. If you had so much as told the office to send my driver, the media would have followed him here.'

Prem wasn't dumb. He had instantly grasped why his driver Ganesh hadn't come to the airport like always. Then again, if he were dumb he wouldn't be one of the most successful businessmen in the country.

'It's something you would have done for me too,' I responded. 'Do you want me to just drop you at your place or would you like me to be around with you for a while?'

'It would be great if you stayed, but suit yourself. If you need to go home for a while, you can always return in the afternoon. I'm not going to the office, and I am certain sleep will give me a wide berth.' He made a half-hearted attempt at a smile.

'I need to talk to you anyway, I'll stay back. I've got clothes for another two days that I had packed for our travel.'

'Thank you.'

'Stop embarrassing me, Prem. I'm your friend. Isn't this what is expected of friends?'

'You're right. So what is it you need to talk to me about?'

'I'll tell you when we get home. Just relax for now.'

I told my driver Mani to take us to Prem's residence at Altamount Road. Like Mumbai and many other places in

India, Altamount Road had been rechristened Barodawala Marg some time ago, but everyone still called it by its erstwhile name. With the vertical expansion of Mumbai, most of the large stand-alone bungalows in the vicinity—Nepean Sea Road, Carmichael Road, Malabar Hill—had been bought and brought down by property developers, giving way to high-rise apartments. Amidst these skyscrapers, only a few old-world mansions remained, and one of them had been in the Bedi family since the '40s.

Prem closed his eyes and serenity spread over his face. I couldn't tell if he was sleeping or just relaxing, but it didn't seem wise to disturb him by making calls, although I had over two hours to kill in the twenty-kilometre drive, and I desperately needed to get a picture of the situation on the ground. I had called Mumbai from Seoul around 4.00 p.m. Korean time, which was 12.30 a.m. Mumbai, and it was now 7.00 a.m. here. By the time we got anywhere near Altamount Road, it would be past nine, almost an entire day since we got any news.

The traffic got worse as we hit the morning rush hour, but Mani soldiered on. I was sure he had heard the news and picked up on our uncomfortable silence.

As we turned left from Pedder Road, I put my hand on Prem's shoulder to wake him. I then called his caretaker at the bungalow to inform him of our imminent arrival. The last thing I wanted was to be held up outside the large brown gate, answering to a crowd or posing for pictures. Prem—he had confided in me once—had experienced living his life like a goldfish in a crystal bowl, and had known the pleasures and pressures of being in the limelight.

As expected, I counted at least five cameras and about nine people hanging around the gates waiting for them to open. As the pneumatic gates rolled open on the inside on their huge metal casters, Mani honked the crowd away and slipped into the drive. The gates closed over people shouting questions about the recent killings.

11.20 a.m.

'You can tell me everything now. I'm as prepared as I'll ever be,' Prem said, as we sat down in the small veranda outside, after we had showered and changed.

Prem's old, yellow mansion had a wooden portico on stilts in front, which carried his personal study on its roof, and similar, but much smaller, wooden loggias stretched all around the first floor that hung out to create permanent awnings for the Victorian wraparound veranda. The building was sufficiently covered on all sides by thick trees that had been there in the 5,000 square metre plot for over fifty years. Even a hawk-eyed sleuth couldn't get a single picture of anyone inside. In the daytime, two security guards at the gate made it virtually impossible for someone to get in uninvited. And at night after the guards and other house staff left—except the caretaker and his wife, who stayed in the outhouse behind the main building—Prem was all by himself, and the CCTVs and electronic surveillance took over. He believed that electronic surveillance was better than a human one, since electronics didn't doze off. The fortress was impregnable twenty-four/seven.

The caretaker had called the cook and cleaner too, now that Prem was back in town. Coffee was served, and breakfast was on its way.

'Rea was murdered, as you know. But that's not the whole truth ...' I began, breaking the silence.

He nodded, listening intently.

'Rea was murdered along with her husband ...'

'Mahesh?'

'Yes, Mahesh Desai. Both were offed in their Pali Hill house on the night of the 7th. The following morning we flew out.'

Prem nodded again, as though reminiscing. The Pali Hill house at Bandra was another detached property that had belonged to the Bedi family, but as part of the divorce settlement the court had ordered it to be handed over to Rea. She had, after all, sacrificed her modelling career in her youth for Prem. She was twenty-eight when the divorce happened, and by then had gotten accustomed to a life of riches and independence. As such, her advocate had convinced the judge that it was impossible for her to stay in an apartment where she would be a subject of sneer and gossip by other residents. Prem didn't want to part with the prized property—it having survived the developers' onslaught when even detached properties of film stars had been sold—but he was mature enough to understand her perspective.

'Have the police found any leads?' he asked.

'No idea. I was told that they aren't releasing any information to the media at the moment. Why don't you call Police Commissioner Saxena?'

'He's not in the country. Besides, I don't think we need to pull strings for something like this ...' He let his last sentence hang there, waiting for me to refute his statement.

I didn't.

I knew that Prem calling the police commissioner would mean he needed a favour, which I knew he didn't want to ask for.

'Why are they being so discreet about murders? Normally they go out with a brass band and publish more info than required,' he wondered aloud.

'That's what is worrying me,' I sighed.

'Why are you worried?'

'What if—'

'What if, *what*, Tej? Out with it, what's troubling you?'

The breakfast arrived then. Poached eggs on toast. The way Prem noshed them highlighted how much he needed some greasy food after the heavy drinking on the flight.

'I don't know … what if someone plans on setting you up?'

'How would anyone do that? I have had no communication with Rea for twelve years. More importantly, why would someone do that? What's in it for anyone now?'

'I guess you're right. I'm just paranoid because I care.'

'I know you do.'

'Did you still care … about Rea?' I asked finally.

'Twelve years is a long time, Tej. At first I was bitter, like any other cuckolded husband, particularly because she was flagrantly cheating on me, not even being coy. When I confronted her, she had the audacity to take the divorce to the court, the public, knowing well how it would harm me.'

I understood the tacit reason. Prem being the more well-known of the two, all dirt would stick harder to him. Even to this day, Rea was posthumously being referred to as ex-Mrs Prem Bedi and not as Mrs Rea Desai. The media didn't want the public to forget that she had been important, once upon a time.

'I guess it was only natural that my love morphed into hatred,' Prem carried on. 'Something I didn't want to talk about or think of too often in the early days. And not to mention her second husband Mahesh Desai, who ran a smear campaign against me in the name of journalism; he wrote long op-eds accusing me of tax evasion, business malpractices, bribing government officials, you name it. He ultimately got tired of wasting ink on me when I did not react or sue him for slander, which in retrospect I should have. Or maybe his editors stopped seeing merit in Mahesh taking out his personal resentments in public. Whatever the reason was, it stopped, and even that news is more than decades old. To be honest, I was at a stage where I thought I had become indifferent, but this shock has broken that illusion. So to answer your question – at some level … I guess I cared.'

Though his voice didn't break or quiver, I could see his eyes glistening with unshed tears. I decided to change the subject.

There had been no further news on the murders. The local channels were still playing the same footage of some local Bandra Police ACP Dutta standing outside Rea's Pali Hill residence—the front door behind him open and people in white paper suits going in and out and the ubiquitous police yellow tape barricading the entire property. He was talking to the media about the double murder: *'We were called at about ten in the morning, the day before yesterday, by Mahesh Desai's brother who, in turn, was informed by the victims' driver, who had reported for duty but on ringing did not get any response from the house. After finding both the cars parked, the driver waited fifteen minutes before he called Mr Manish Desai, Mahesh Desai's brother. Mr Desai rushed to the Pali Hill residence and on arrival discovered the corpses of Mrs Rea Desai and Mr Mahesh Desai. That's all. I have no further information to release at this moment, so if you'll please excuse me ...'* he walked away from the camera.

You could hear the crowd in the background asking:

'How were they killed?'

'Was anything stolen?'

'Any leads so far?'

And ACP Dutta kept repeating: '*No comment, no comment ...*'

Lest they forget, the scroll on the screen below reminded the viewers that Rea Desai was noted businessman Prem Bedi's ex-wife, and had had a rather nasty divorce with the Mogul twelve years ago. And that Prem Bedi was not available for comments.

Why Prem Bedi would want to comment or sit for an interview regarding the repugnant episode was beyond me.

8.30 p.m.

'Do you want me to stay over or go home?' I asked Prem as we sat having tomato and coriander soup on the twelve-seater dining table; he at the head and I on the chair to his right.

'Go home and rest. So will I; we have work tomorrow.'

'You want to come to office tomorrow?'

'Of course. I cannot let work suffer any longer. I only returned because I wasn't sure if anyone on Rea's ... I mean Mahesh's side of family would take responsibility of the last rites since Rea, like me, was an only child, and her parents are long dead.'

That was Prem in a sentence.

I had known *of* him for over three decades, though I only came to know him personally some eight years ago. Prem Bedi was sincerely magnanimous. I know plenty of phoneys that fake generosity for brownie points; Prem did virtuous work only for the right reasons. As I was now a close associate, I knew how many charities he funded anonymously. Not for some hogwash like corporate responsibility or to save taxes like some others. He more than once narrated to me that his father had, from his early age, impressed upon him the lion's analogy: *'A lion hunts not only for itself; it has to provide for all the other animals too, after its own hunger is sated.'* With his marriage terminated eons ago, and him having no heirs, he honestly believed in the maxim and bestowed both money and time upon charitable causes. I had been one of the very few lateral hires into Bedi & Sons; most of the employees there had been with Bedi & Sons since the beginning of their careers. Employees didn't quit because the upsides included the generous salaries, and loans in times of genuine requirement, like birth, sickness, weddings and deaths. More importantly, the feeling of being part of one large family, the Bedi family, kept everyone happy and invested.

When Prem said that he had returned in case he'd be needed to perform the last rites for his ex-wife and her husband, with whom she had cheated on him, I was reminded of his finest quality. Everyone knew that Rea had leeched more money than she deserved at the divorce, and Mahesh Desai had slandered Prem in the media. But despite all of this, Prem wouldn't leave her side at this last minute.

The dinner was served. Grilled fish with potatoes and some kind of beans. Not my kind of dinner, but Prem was conscious of what he ate.

'When do you think the police will release the bodies for cremation?'

'I'll check first thing in the morning,' I offered.

But it wasn't meant to be.

As we sipped at our coffees after dinner, the nine o'clock bulletin came on air. Though the young poker-faced female reporter standing near the yellow tape recited it in a detached monotone, the news was disquieting:

'The Bandra Police investigating the double murder of Mrs and Mr Desai's at their Pali Hill residence has now released further information on the gruesome killings. The police spokesperson informed that initial autopsy reports have revealed that the murders occurred at least eight to nine hours before the bodies were discovered, which puts the time of death on or a little before midnight of June 7. The victims' detached house has been ransacked. However, it is difficult to assess what has been stolen from the property at this moment. The police have made a public appeal to anyone who has seen, heard or noticed anything unusual in the area, such as suspicious persons or vehicles. In short, any anomaly should be reported. Currently it appears the police have no leads to follow. An anonymous source has disclosed to our special correspondent that death in both instances was caused by head injuries, specifically blunt force trauma, likely inflicted by a cricket bat or a golf club.'

Golf club—the mention of it made me shudder. I looked up to see Prem shaking his head in disgust. We both recognised the implicit slant this might take in the coming days. Prem was a longstanding member of the prestigious Bombay Presidency Golf Club; a lot of local and national magazines that had covered him over the years had identified him as a patron of the game. Something told me this was going to blow up in our faces.

'A hit from a cricket bat should be quite different from a golf club,' I finally said, after Prem muted the television. The newsflash had ended and the weather girl was on.

'How do you mean?' he turned to me.

'Wouldn't the size of the dent on the skull indicate whether it was a cricket bat or a golf club that they were hit with?'

'Pure speculation. I always find it suspicious when an *anonymous* source tips off a special correspondent with crucial details. This is just the media fuelling the fire.'

'I don't have a good feeling about it.'

'It is what it is; we'll take it as it comes tomorrow. I'm sure it will turn out to be a robbery-turned-homicide if the place, as they said, has been robbed. I suggest you stop worrying and have a good night's sleep. I'll see you in the morning at work,' Prem responded.

TEJ MALHOTRA

The entire landscape had transformed overnight. It was as if I had gone to bed on a beach in Mauritius and woken up in the middle of Siberia. Local channels had been covering the murder story non-stop.

The double murder headlined all national dailies, with the story spilling over to the local pages. Several angles and opinions, and copious mention of Mrs Desai being ex-Mrs Bedi had been slipped in. They had nothing to report on *how* or *what* or *who,* but saw that a victim related to a man of Prem's stature meant sensation, scandal and ultimately, sales. Though Bedi & Sons could operate profitably without Prem running day-by-day affairs, his unceremonious association to these murders was sure to affect the businesses negatively. Contrary to what people said, not all publicity was good.

What caught my eye was that, at some point in the night, the police released a formal bulletin, confirming the weapon was indeed a golf club. And if that had been the only thing they had officially revealed, I wouldn't have been so wobbly in the knees. The investigators, using electrostatic dust lifters, had recovered a shoe outsole impression on the stone step right outside the main door. Considering it had rained heavily on the eve of the murders, the investigating teams were inclined to think that any residual prints before the downpour had been washed away. The police surmised that this print was presumably left behind by the perpetrator who exited using the front door and maybe, in his or her haste to flee the scene, did not realise the recklessness of stepping on stone rather than jumping on to the lawn, which would have retained no prints. The police had evaluated the shoe print and they were looking for comparisons. They had already eliminated the *knowns*: Mr Mahesh Desai's shoe size did not match and neither did he have any shoe in his wardrobe that matched the outsole impression retrieved. The driver, who was first to arrive in the morning and got suspicious when the Desais did not open the door, had been ruled out too, and so had the gardener, who could have been the only other possible visitor early in the morning before the driver had arrived at the scene. Manish Desai had been cleared too.

The police was withholding information regarding the details on the type, brand, and pattern of the impression under the pretext that the forensic agents were further analysing it for any clue on the height and weight of the owner.

However, they had released the shoe size.

It was size eight and a half.

That was what made me dizzy. I knew Prem's shoe size was also eight and a half. The only two pieces of information released by the police so far pointed towards my friend.

I looked at the newspaper for five minutes, probably the longest five minutes of my life.

Three of the directors called me in succession before I got into the shower. They could have got together and called me from the conference room instead, since the conversation I had with each was almost the same. They had read the various news and editorials and drawn whatever conclusions they had, but they didn't voice them. The calls were to show support and concern for Prem:

'Is he alright?'

'How has he taken the news?'

'Tell us if any of us is required at any time…'

I had to plead that they not make an event of the matter by showing up at Prem's residence. The best thing they could do was to leave Prem alone, as he was doing fine, but needed some time to think and reflect. I assured them that the only reason Prem wasn't coming to office was to avoid the media.

Mindful that Prem would have seen the news too—either in the morning dailies or on a permanent scroll at the bottom of the screen on the local channel—I deliberated if I should call him or just drive to his residence instead of adhering to my routine of proceeding to office directly.

I lived in a two-bedroom apartment in Worli, about five kilometres from Altamount Road. I could quite easily take a slight detour en route to our office at Cuffe Parade. I looked at the time: 7.22 a.m. Knowing that my driver had already arrived on duty, I finished quickly with my shower before taking the decision.

But Prem beat me to it. I had two missed calls from him.

When I called back, he told me that he had read the morning papers and watched the local broadcast.

'What do you think?' I asked. I wanted to know if he had the same palpitations that I was having since then.

'It sounds like an open-and-shut robbery-homicide case, what's there to think?'

Maybe I was over-thinking things, catching merely what my subconscious was telling me to. 'Robbery…?'

'Yes. It is briefly mentioned in the papers on the third page, and even the morning seven-thirty bulletin stated that the safe in the bedroom had been broken into and whatever was in it has gone missing.'

'Oh, I totally missed that.' I sifted through the newspaper till I saw the small addendum to the main story on the front page. 'Oh yeah, I see it now.'

'See you in office then.'

'Are you still thinking of going to office?'

'And why shouldn't I?'

'Uh, only because we were meant to be out of the country for the next few days so I thought you might want to take it easy. Maybe return to work on Monday.'

'You've been behaving a bit strangely since yesterday. Is something still bothering you?'

'Why don't I come over and we can talk?' If I were to have a discussion about my concerns, I'd be more comfortable having it face-to-face.

'You're most welcome. I suggest you leave now and we can have breakfast together before going to office. Does that work for you?'

'Sounds like a plan. I'll leave here in the next fifteen minutes.'

Was I hallucinating? Was I the only one who was putting unnecessary pieces into a puzzle that didn't even exist? Whatever the case was, I couldn't shake my bad feeling about it.

When I arrived at Prem's residence, he was already dressed for work – a charcoal-coloured suit with his usual crisp white cotton shirt. He very occasionally wore a tie; usually when he was meeting clients.

'You were right,' Prem said after the pleasantries. He pointed towards the television. A young man with a devil-gifted set of mean eyes was animatedly talking to the cameraman: '*I am telling you it is Mr Bedi behind these murders, he should be brought to justice … my brother and his wife were always scared of him …*'

I looked at Prem, who smiled and pressed mute.

'Who is he?' My mouth was agape.

'Meet Manish Desai, Mahesh Desai's younger brother.'

'What is his problem?'

'I don't know. I didn't even know Mahesh had a younger brother till the murders happened. This man has been talking to media and trying to convince them that I murdered Rea and her husband.'

I slumped into the sofa.

'And he's not the only one …'

'What? Who else has been saying that?'

'Well, you have been cagey since yesterday, like I mentioned over the phone.'

'I'm only trying to anticipate the events, Prem. I don't like the fact that the murder weapon has been identified as a golf club and the shoe outsole impression recovered from the doorstep is sized eight and a half. That's two discoveries revealed so far by the police and, sorry to say, both of them point to you…'

'I'm touched that you remember my shoe size. There are … what, eighteen million people in Mumbai? Even simple maths should tell you how many adult males play golf and wear a size eight-and-a-half shoe. And that is only taking into account the golfers. But you don't have to be a golfer to have access to a golf club.'

He had a point.

'What about Manish Desai? What is his beef with you?'

'Only he knows. As I said, I didn't so much as know about his existence till now. I have no idea what his brother or his sister-in-law told him about me. I can't imagine why they'd have been talking about me at all.'

'So you agree now that my paranoia isn't exaggerated?'

'Quite frankly, I don't, Tej. I still can't see any merit in the whole argument; it doesn't matter what you fear or what this little brother is yelling himself hoarse about on television. The police will find some evidence ultimately, and they will name the suspects and apprehend them. Brother Desai here is enjoying his fifteen minutes of fame. Some rags will catch him, maybe pay him to do an interview and then it will fizzle. It's a week's worth of hot-selling news, that's what I think.'

It could only be one of two things: either Prem wasn't cottoning on to the fact that shit was about to hit the fan, or he had understood the implications, but he didn't want to get ruffled before it happened.

'Look, just hear me out,' I attempted one last time. 'Forget the golf club and the shoe size for a second. If Manish Desai has already started pointing fingers at you, don't you think the police will look into it and pay you a visit?'

'I'm happy to oblige. What will they find? Yes I have golf sets—how many, even I don't know. Yes, I obviously own shoes; all of them sized eight and a half, because that's the size that fits me … I can't see why any of that should unsettle either of us.'

'I'm sorry, Prem. I think you're right, maybe I'm overreacting.'

'Let's have breakfast then.' He switched off the television. 'It's quite embarrassing to see some guy making such a fool of himself, if you ask me.' He obviously meant Manish Desai.

We barely sat down at the table when my phone rang.

'It's Maya, let me take this.'

Maya had joined the company only two years ago, replacing Prem's previous secretary, who had retired. She was *his* secretary, so why was she calling *me*?

I got up and walked away from the table.

'Good morning, Maya.'

'Good morning, sir,' Maya's voice was tinged with fear. 'The police … the police are here, sir.'

'Calm down, Maya, what is it? Who's come there?'

'One ACP Ranjeet Dutta … wants to see Mr Bedi …'

My mind went into overdrive: ACP Dutta from Bandra Police, the one who was on television, and who was heading the investigation. I feigned confusion; I didn't want to let on that we had been following the local news and knew of the man.

Although I had expected a call from the police, I hadn't thought of what the course of action, if any, should be when they eventually called. Subconsciously, I had wished all along that I was wrong. Maybe the first salvo had hit quicker than I had anticipated, but it was all happening now. The tension was fuelling my anxiety too.

'What does he mean he wants to see Mr Bedi? What is it regarding?'

'It's regarding Mrs Rea Desai. He says he needs to talk to Mr Bedi.'

'Give me a minute,' I said and put her on mute. Then, turning to Prem, I asked, 'The police want to have a word with you. Do you want me to make an excuse?'

'Why should we avoid them? But let them come here. I don't want the police visiting my office.'

'Okay, we'll talk after his call,' I concurred, and then told Maya, 'Could you put ACP Dutta on the line, please?'

'Good morning, Mr Bedi,' ACP Dutta sounded courteous.

'Good morning, officer. I'm not Prem Bedi. I'm his business colleague and friend, Tej Malhotra.'

'My apologies, Mr Malhotra, I thought I was talking to Mr Bedi. Could I speak to him, please?'

'Of course, officer, what is this regarding, if I may ask?'

'It's regarding the recent murders of Mrs and Mr Desai, which you might have heard of.'

Like I didn't know; like everyone in the city didn't know.

'Why should their murders make you want to speak with Mr Bedi?'

'Unfortunately, I can't talk to you about that, Mr Malhotra, at least not on the phone. I just had a few routine questions for Mr Bedi …'

'Fine, ACP Dutta, I can appreciate that. However, Mr Bedi isn't coming to office today. Would it be at all possible for you to come by his residence?'

'Not a problem, Mr Malhotra. I'll take his address from Miss Maya here ...'

'Should we say … around four?'

'Is it not possible for me to see him right away?'

'Well, you said it was merely routine questions so I gave you the first available free time in his diary. Is it urgent?'

'No. It's okay. I'll see him at four.'

'See you then.'

Click.

'So…?' Prem asked.

'ACP Ranjeet Dutta wants to talk to you about Rea and her husband's murders.'

'And you called him at four, I heard that. I also heard you say I'm busy …' Prem raised his coffee mug to show. 'Busy having coffee with Tej Malhotra.'

'Yes.' I came back to the dining table and sat down. 'We need a lawyer present for the meeting—'

'A *lawyer*?' he intonated like I'd mentioned some disease. 'What do we need a lawyer for?'

'I want the conversation legally recorded. I don't want any *I-said-you-said* later, just in case.'

'Just in case, what?'

'Just in case we need to go to court for anything, later …'

'But you're present here, and you're a lawyer.'

'I think it would be better to have a third party present, not me. I'm technically your employee.'

'Oh, so why don't you call Rohan?'

Rohan, my son, exuded confidence and the impression of being in complete control, even though he was still a novice. Only a few months ago, he had chucked a well-paying job at one of the biggest legal firms in Mumbai to start his own one-man legal practice as a rookie advocate.

'No, I was thinking we should call his old firm, Dadawala & Partners.'

'But why? If all we need is a legal record of the conversation, why do we need to bring in a big firm? You know who needs big and famous criminal defence advocates? The guilty – which I know I'm not.'

I debated for a while that Rohan might not be able to handle the pressure, because he hadn't yet represented anyone since he'd gone solo. But Prem was adamant.

'Okay, I'll call Rohan, but if it is more than routine questioning, you have to promise me that we will call Mr Dadawala himself.' I said, finally giving in.

'We shall talk about that later. End of discussion. Now, would you call Rohan, please?'

I pulled out the mobile from my pocket and dialled Rohan. I thought of his smiling face: my son looked quite like me, just a bit taller. He had taken my hair, long and wavy; but he had taken his mother's paler skin tone, which suited him. I loved him.

ROHAN MALHOTRA

Well, this was odd—a call from Dad in the middle of the week.

Dad and I generally spoke over weekends, but we made it a point to meet at least once a month unless, of course, he was travelling. I lived in Juhu with my wife, Urvee, and my daughter, Pia, who would be three soon. Dad knew I would be in the car at this time, dropping Pia off at her playschool. Her mother, a science teacher at a local school here in Juhu, usually left for work early.

'Hi, Dad, all well?' I answered over the Bluetooth in my car. I had dropped Pia and was headed towards my office in Lower Parel, which had come to be known as Upper Worli. Hip!

'Hi, Rohan. I'm fine, how are you?'

Something in his voice told me that this wasn't a courtesy call. I couldn't put my finger on why or what sounded different, but there was an element of frenzy in his voice.

'I'm doing fine, Dad. Is everything okay?'

'What are you doing this morning? Any appointments?' He hadn't answered my question. Something was off.

'Nothing I can't put off for something urgent. What is it?'

'I can explain if you could come to see us … now.'

Us?

'Who're you with and where?'

'I'm with Prem … Prem Bedi, at his residence and I will be grateful if you could postpone your other appointments for the day and come here straightaway.'

'Please. You don't have to be "grateful" for anything, Dad. I'll be over in a bit. What's bothering you, though? You sound preoccupied.'

'What time can you get here?'

I had just crossed Chatrapati Shivaji International Airport on my left and was approximately twenty kilometres from Altamount Road; I glanced at the time in the radio panel of the car: 9.43 a.m. With Mumbai traffic at its peak, it would likely take me about an hour. 'Should be there by eleven.'

'Thanks, Rohan. What car are you driving? I'll let the security at the gates know you're coming.'

'I'm in my white Jetta …' I gave him the details and disconnected the call. Dad didn't need to give me the address, I had dropped him to Mr Bedi's residence a couple of times, though it had always been a *drive-in-drive-out*. I had never been invited in. To be fair, I had never had any business with Mr Bedi nor he with me. Dad had never spoken about Mr Bedi's family to me. All I knew about him came from media coverage.

I couldn't understand what Dad had called me to Mr Bedi's residence for. I mean, I had read about the events of the past couple of days and, like anyone else, I knew some dirt was headed Mr Bedi's way, but what could a rookie like me help with? I hadn't handled a single criminal case since I had quit my job. And Mr Bedi could afford any damn advocate in India. So why call me? Especially since Dad had a degree in law and, from what I'd read, so did Mr Bedi. Between the two of them they had more than what I could possibly offer. No, this had to be something else, some insubstantial case on the side. *Would I mind if it was a small case?* Yeah—if I were insane.

I had wanted to be associated with Mr Bedi for more years than I could even count. Years ago, I had wanted to bring Mr Bedi's business into Dadawala & Partners. It would have increased our billings and the size of my annual bonus cheque. And since I had started flying solo, even one big client like Mr Bedi would be enough to keep my kitchen fire going forever. Any business for him, however small, would be huge for me.

I tried calling Urvee to tell her, but it went straight to voicemail. She must be in a class.

Fifty minutes later, I turned into Altamount road.

Even from a distance I could see the crowd outside his residence. There was a virtual pandemonium at the gate. The circus had begun with people from the media: cameras, microphones, television vans, all jostling for a chance to be closest to the gates. The uniformed guards had been briefed about my arrival; they let me in, the rest of the mob out.

The house was a mansion … beautiful, glorious. I could throw in half a dozen other adjectives and still not do justice to the property. It looked like someone had painted it yellow only yesterday. It shone bright, with no moss or cracks. There was no car in the carport, but I didn't think it wise for me to park there. I drove past it and parked behind Dad's car. Mani, his driver, saw me and stepped out of the car. He smiled and asked for my car keys, just in case the vehicle needed to be moved.

I walked to the door and dinged the bell. Dad had told me more than once that Mr Bedi was a good man, but I still braced myself to expect a rich, pompous, maybe even arrogant, aristocrat.

The guy who opened the door was in uniform too. Like Nestor—the tall and bald butler who worked for Captain Haddock in *Tintin*. So this was how old-moneyed royalty lived.

He shut the door as I stepped in and led me through the broad black-and-white tiled foyer into a large room, which I guessed was a formal sitting area. The floor was white marble, faded to a pale cream with time but it still shone; the room had an antique wool and silk carpet in teal blue with some Persian design. The furniture was Victorian and the furnishings were clearly worth more than my annual income.

'Please be seated. Sahib will be here to see you in a minute. Could I bring you something in the meanwhile?' Nestor asked.

A shot of chilled Russian vodka would be great. 'Cold water, please. Thank you.'

I downed the glass of cold water the moment he brought it and asked for a refill. That was when Mr Prem Bedi walked into the room, followed by Dad.

'Hello and many thanks for coming over at such a short notice, Rohan. I'm Prem Bedi,' he stretched out his hand.

'H—hardly a bother, sir. Good morning, very nice to meet you.' I had seen Mr Bedi on television, in print, but never in flesh. The first sight of him was electric. I had never been in the presence of someone as distinguished as the man who stood in front of me now. Somehow, he made my confidence dwindle, and suddenly I needed to pee.

'Thank you, Rohan.' Dad's voice, and his presence, thawed away some of my uneasiness. It had always been the case since my first day at school: if Dad was around, everything was all right, or soon would be. And all these years later, his role in my life hadn't diminished.

'How may I be of help, sir?' I asked Mr Bedi.

'First, please stop calling me "sir". Call me Prem, like your dad does.'

'That's not possible, Mr Bedi. I don't think I could call you by your first name.' I liked the way my words rolled out, polite yet firm.

'Alright. Mr Bedi is fine, but *sir* sounds a bit too much.' He smiled. 'Why don't you sit down?' he gestured towards one of the ornate winged chairs in the room.

The second glass of water arrived and though I wanted to gulp it down too, I took small sips. Élan.

'We want an advocate to represent Prem this afternoon,' Dad began, and went on to tell me about some ACP Ranjeet Dutta from Bandra Police Station, who was due to visit Mr Bedi the same evening for some routine questions about the recent double murders at Pali Hill. He explained that there was no cause for concern, but they wanted an advocate to be present at the time so that everything was legally chronicled for records.

'Would you be willing to take the job?' Mr Bedi asked.

'Of course.' It sounded straightforward to me.

'That's good, because your dad has been fretting since yesterday.'

I looked at Dad, who kept a poker face.

'Nothing to worry, Mr Bedi. I'll just make a few calls to get the contract in place before four.'

'And you don't have to give me a generous discount, a token will be fine.' Mr Bedi smiled. 'Stay here as long as you need to, use the phone and the desk. There's a fax, in case you need some documents sent across to or from your office. And feel free to press the buzzer next to the desk if you need anything else.'

'Thank you, Mr Bedi.'

Mr Bedi left the room; Dad stayed behind.

'Everything okay, Dad?'

'I have an eerie feeling about this whole thing. I'm not sure you've followed the news but, as yet the only two pieces of information released by the investigating officers are that the murder weapon was a golf club and the shoe impression recovered from the murder site is sized eight and a half; both things connect Prem to the scene …'

A chill went down my spine.

'Are you saying Mr Bedi was there, at the murder scene … ?'

'On the contrary, I think someone is trying to frame him.'

'Why would someone do that?'

'I wish I knew. The only thing I've seen on the telly is this guy Manish Desai—the deceased's brother, pointing fingers at Prem.'

'What if it's true?'

'It cannot be.'

'Why not?' I didn't mean to sound abrupt, but couldn't help myself.

'I've known Prem for eight years.'

'Dad, I am sure you are right, but …'

'No buts, Rohan. Should the police give any indication to suggest that they have anything worthwhile to prosecute Prem, I'll call in Mr Dadawala personally. You don't have to worry. I'm not going to push you into something you're not ready for, and certainly not a case that impacts Prem's life.'

That was reassurance and a rebuff in a single sentence. I knew this case was too big for me to cope with, given my lack of experience, but it stung that my own father had little confidence in me. But I shook the feeling off and nodded. Dad had Mr Bedi's and my best interests at heart.

I sat at the desk and called my office. I spoke with my office assistant—since I had just started my own practice, I worked out of a small office in the business centre and there was a pool of assistants provided to us—and told him to send me the contractual forms I needed. If I was to be Mr Bedi's advocate, it was legally required that the contract be in force *before* ACP Dutta arrived, or else I'd be just another advisor or a friend. The police could ask friends and advisors to leave Mr Bedi alone when they questioned him; and they would be well within their rights to do so.

What the police could not do was ask a legal advocate, retained by the client for the specific purpose, to leave the room when they came in for questioning. I also asked my assistant to inform everyone that I was not to be disturbed unless it was an emergency, and certainly not between 4 and 6 p.m.

While I waited for the required papers to arrive, I called Urvee and told her that I was not in the office today, but at Mr Bedi's residence working for him. With five years of being married to an advocate, she knew that asking '*why*' would never get her an answer. The nature of work I did for my clients was strictly confidential. I shared what I could and she appreciated that.

The fax started rolling out of the machine within thirty minutes. I read the contract to check if everything was in order. It was a basic one that stated that the client, Mr Prem Bedi, had appointed me as his advocate for the purpose of being present at the time of the said initial enquiry and advise him on the proceedings. Nothing more. I filled in the details I knew: name, address etc., and called Dad on his mobile for the others. After I filled in all the details, I pressed the buzzer and Nestor was there to carry the papers in for the client's signature. When he came to return the signed documents, he informed me that Mr Bedi and Dad were waiting for me for lunch.

Lunch? Me? With Mr Bedi? Wow!

After lunch, we had coffee in the veranda and chit-chatted about everything other than the case for a while. Mr Bedi and Dad intermittently got calls on their phones and slipped away to attend to them. I guessed their business was an ocean compared to my small one-man shop. And in today's time one didn't need to be in the premises to be running an empire. Moreover, with the local channel telecasting the footage of the murders nonstop, constantly reminding viewers that the victim was ex-Mrs Bedi, personal calls from his friends and associates were in full swing too.

I didn't know what the ACP would ask, but I could hazard a guess and I wanted to ask Mr Bedi some questions ahead of time. I looked for a quiet moment and waited for him to sit down when he walked back after taking a call. 'Mr Bedi, I need to ask you some questions so that we are all on the same page when ACP Dutta arrives.'

'Go ahead.'

'The outsole impression found at the scene of crime is size eight and a half, and I believe you wear that size. Am I correct?'

I knew that they might have already discussed these things before, but I had to ask nonetheless. 'Yes.'

'We still don't know what kind of shoe it was, but just for my information, how many pairs do you own?'

'I don't know the exact number, to be honest. Most shoes I own are in the house, maybe some at the office, a few in the car. And certainly a few pairs in my locker, at the golf club—Bombay Presidency, in Chembur.'

If someone were to ask me the same question, I had two pairs of formal shoes—one black, one tan; a pair of trainers for when I went jogging or accompanied Urvee to the gym, a pair of casual leather slip-ons and one pair of bathroom slippers, and they were all stacked in the bottom shelf of my cramped wardrobe in my equally cramped Juhu apartment.

'I see. And how many golf sets do you own?'

He looked up as he tried to recall the exact number. 'Eight, maybe nine. I'm not sure.'

'Are all of them here, at home?'

'No. I should have five or six here, one in the car and a couple at the golf club.'

'One last question, Mr Bedi. Is there any club missing from any of these golf sets?'

'I can't think—'

'Yes,' interrupted Dad, his countenance was suddenly startled. 'Prem broke a driver while we were at the Nine Bridges in South Korea recently. Remember, Prem?'

'Oh yes, one club is missing that I know of.'

'Where is it now?' I probed.

'I dumped it there; why would I carry a splintered driver back?'

Shit. I just about stopped my fist from slamming the table. That wasn't going to be easy to explain to ACP Dutta.

'Is that a problem, Rohan?' Mr Bedi asked.

Are you kidding? The police have identified the murder weapon as a golf club and they are coming to question you. And you have one golf club missing from one of the many sets you own. And you're asking me if that's a problem?

I managed: 'Could you ask someone to retrieve your broken club from wherever in South Korea and parcel it to us?'

'Why?'

'Because the missing club *will* make the police suspicious. It could mean that it was dumped because of blood evidence.'

'Do you think I'm guilty?'

'No, of course not. But it doesn't matter what I think, it's what the police might think, Mr Bedi.'

'I'll call Mr Lee to see if he can send someone to get it picked from where Prem dropped it, though I wouldn't pin my hopes on it. I'm sure the authorities would have had it removed and disposed off.' Dad dialled and walked away from us.

'Thanks,' I said. I didn't know what for, though.

TEJ MALHOTRA

I calculated the time difference as I stepped away to call Mr Lee. 3:30 p.m. in Mumbai meant 7 p.m. in Seoul. I didn't think it was too late to call.

As I looked for Mr Lee's number on my mobile phone, I was peeved at myself for having overlooked the missing golf club until Rohan had asked about it.

'Hello, Mr Lee, this is Tej Malhotra from Mumbai, India.'

'Wait,' he said. I knew why. It had totally slipped my mind that conversing with Mr Lee required an intermediary to translate. I wondered if he had one around at this moment. A few minutes passed by but they felt like eternity, what with my mind going into turmoil.

'Yes.' It wasn't a human voice that responded; it was a machine. Mr Lee had an electronic interpreting software.

'Mr Lee, hello from Mumbai, I'm Tej Malhotra.'

'Hello, Mr *Mall-Hot-Ra*,' the raspy electronic response came after a few seconds of lag. It felt like I was communicating with one of the members of the eighties German band *Kratwerk*.

'I have a favour to ask, Mr Lee.'

Silence. Then I heard the Man-Machine say something in Korean. I waited.

'Sure, please ask. What can I do for you, Mr Mall-Hot-Ra?'

I explained in a circuitous manner if he could ask the authorities at the Nine Bridges Resort to recover Prem's broken golf club and, if they found it, could he get it couriered to India, please?

It took a while, but he comprehended the request and promised to do whatever he could to get it picked up. Of course, there was no guarantee that it hadn't been destroyed, he clarified.

I looked at the time on my mobile phone as I ended the call. 3:56 p.m.

The ACP could be here any minute. What if he asked to see all the golf sets?

It was easy to deflect him for now: *Did he have a search warrant?*

If and when he came back with the search warrant, it was simple to say that Prem had only five golf sets at home. Who would know if I took one of the sets away and dropped it in the Arabian Sea at night?

God! I wondered why my mind was working that way.

I prayed that Prem hadn't done something stupid. Deep down I was scared as I walked back to where Prem and Rohan sat.

ACP RANJEET DUTTA

Bureaucracy is funny until you see just how comical politics can get. On the surface everyone declines that they ever engage in politics within an organisation but everyone does their best to associate themselves with those in power. In my years of service, I'd witnessed careers made and destroyed. I was an IPS officer, currently an ACP—Assistant (not Additional) Commissioner of Police, due for a promotion, which would, most probably, be out of this state. It could be Delhi, but I had no assurances. And that was the dilemma. If I went after Prem Bedi and he turned out to be innocent, I could kiss my career goodbye. If I chased Bedi and he was not innocent, I might get a medal now but it could well be my swan song when I moved to another state where Bedi had political connections—I'd better be prepared to sell peanuts on the pavements. Whereas, if I condoned Bedi, the current government in this state could make my life so miserable, I might as well forget about the promotion. Complicated? Welcome to my world.

Until now I had nothing that implicated Prem Bedi in the murders. I knew he played golf; everyone and their unborn child in Mumbai knew Prem Bedi played golf, so if someone wanted to incriminate him it was their best shot. I stopped by a few shoe shops during my investigation, and found out that the most common shoe size for an adult male in India was eight or eight and a half. It could be totally random that the person who offed Mrs and Mr Desai wore a size eight-and-a-half shoe. It took my informers less than thirty minutes to find out Bedi's shoe size. They called three shoe stores that stocked élite shoes and voila! If someone wanted to frame Prem Bedi, they'd done their homework well by hiring someone who wore the same-sized shoe and then determinedly ensured that they left a print behind. Best part was that they didn't need to find a murderer who had a shoe size of eight and a half; they could simply implant the shoe print there on the way in or out without wearing the damn thing.

I had been out for two days straight since the murders, with little sleep and and a blinding headache when I turned into Altamount Road. The constable driving my jeep had his hand on the horn to disperse the crowd and thread into the gates.

Prem Bedi sat in the veranda with two other men. One was old, the other one about my age. I could have told you they were father and son even before they were introduced to me. The son was broader and taller than his father, but only slightly. Father wore glasses, son didn't. The three of them stood up as I climbed the two steps and walked towards them.

'Good afternoon, ACP Dutta. I'm Prem Bedi, and this is my friend and colleague whom you spoke with this morning, Tej Malhotra.' I shook hands with Messrs Bedi and Malhotra. 'And this is my advocate, Rohan Malhotra.'

Did he just say advocate?

'Good afternoon, gentlemen.'

We had barely sat down when a uniformed butler appeared with cold water. I took out two 500 mg Paracetamol tabs from my pocket and popped them in with the water. 'Just a little headache,' I explained, although nobody had asked.

'How can I help you?' Bedi began.

I looked around. Did he really think I wanted to ask him questions with two other men present? If it had been anyone else—an individual with less significant persona or social standing—I would have been stern, maybe attempted intimidation from the word go, but I stopped my authoritative self. He, of course, twigged my predicament.

'As I mentioned, ACP Dutta, Tej is a long-time friend so if *you* have objections, I can ask him to wait inside. Rohan Malhotra is my advocate, so he has a right to stay with me during any or all conversation.'

So I had heard it right first time, Bedi had already lawyered up. Did it make any sense to ask his friend to leave? If he wanted his friend there, what concern could I have, considering this was only a customary enquiry?

'It's only some routine questions. I am happy either way but I hope you understand that some of the questions I might ask could be of a little personal nature … maybe intimate even.'

'I am too old to have any inhibitions, ACP Dutta. Please begin.' Bedi smiled, looked at the two gentlemen who nodded their consents too. 'But before that, would you like me to request some coffee or tea for you and Mr Constable there? Why is he standing there, he can come join us.'

Was he for real? I had expected a rather belligerent man shooting expletives that I had dropped in to ask him questions when I had zilch evidence.

'He's okay there, but yes coffee would be great.'

Bedi had a remote buzzer. The uniformed butler named Damodar Singh was called and coffee was requested. *Requested*, not ordered, I noticed.

'Yes, ACP Dutta, I'm all yours now.'

'Mr Bedi—first of all I am sorry about your ex-wife. But I understand you weren't on talking terms.'

'Correct.'

'When did you last see Mrs Rea Desai or Mr Mahesh Desai?'

'I honestly don't remember, maybe ten … eleven-twelve years ago.'

'Oh, it doesn't really matter then if it was that long ago. So you did not have any interaction with either of them recently either in person or over phone or through some third party?'

'None whatsoever.'

I had wanted to be precise but thorough. I didn't have a lot of time to squander on what I believed had been one man's quest to malign Bedi. But Bedi had disappointed me by having an advocate present. Maybe it was merely a precaution, this smartass move. But in my experience, it was a typical tactic of those guilty and ergo, I decided to rattle the trio a little.

'Did you have any burglary or break-in in the past two or three months?'

'No, why?'

'Mr Bedi, the whole world knows you are a golfer, and we also checked your shoe size. I was wondering if one of your golf clubs or a pair of shoes were stolen by any chance …'

'Not that I am aware of.'

That didn't make sense. Wouldn't he know if his shoes or golf clubs had been pinched? I squinted and he took it as my incomprehension.

'I mean I don't keep a count of my shoes, and I have more than a few golf sets I haven't used for years, so I guess it's impossible to tell if one club from any of them has gone missing.'

Really? I was sure he had checked this after watching the news, but I resisted my temptation to say as much. I did not want to disconcert him just yet and I didn't have enough evidence for a search warrant. Another pointer and I knew I would be back with a brass band.

'Fair enough,' I said softy. Any break-in would have been noted and perhaps reported regardless. 'Mr Bedi, can you think of any person or persons who would possibly want to harm Mrs or Mr Desai, any bad blood you were aware of?'

'I can't think of anyone who would want to hurt Rea. I don't know about Mr Desai; he wrote inflammatory editorials and slandered people, so if he managed to ruffle some feathers that he shouldn't have, I wouldn't know. I guess it would not be a bad idea to speak with those he wrote about recently…'

'Why only recently?' My research had shown that Mahesh Desai had disparaged Bedi too in the past.

'It is what I'd do. I know he wrote a lot of unwanted junk about me, but that was more than a decade ago. In my mind, that's done and dusted. People normally react to things happening in the present or what's happened in the past six-seven months, while the hurt is still fresh …'

'What about the theft at their residence?' Tej Malhotra jumped into the discussion.

'We don't know what was stolen, but there is a safe locker in the house that's been broken into. We don't know what's missing, except Mr Manish Desai's word on television that there was cash, jewellery and expensive watches in it.'

'So is it a burglary gone wrong or a vendetta? It can't be both,' Malhotra said.

'Well, it can. A vendetta settled and made to look like burglary? Or whoever was sent to settle a score decided to be a bit enterprising and broke the safe.' Either of the scenarios I mentioned weren't unheard of.

For a while, there was silence in the veranda as all three of them seemed to ruminate on what I'd just said.

'When will the bodies be released?' Malhotra asked.

'I'm not sure. Maybe in a few days—why?'

'Prem thought he might be required for the last rites, as Rea had no relatives.'

'I think that won't be necessary, as Mr Manish Desai has the first claim on both his brother and sister-in-law.'

'I understand that,' Bedi said graciously.

'Just one more question, Mr Bedi, and please don't misunderstand me, but I have to ask this – where were you on the night of seventh and the early hours of eighth this month—the night of the murders?'

'I was here at home on the night of the seventh, packing for our morning flight on eighth to Seoul.'

'Where you alone?'

'Yes, I live alone.'

'What about the guards at the gate or and employees that work here? Could anyone corroborate your alibi?'

'Unless I am out at a social gathering or travelling or have guests at home, I can't provide an alibi for any night in the last ten years. You could ask the caretaker; he lives in the outhouse behind the main building. He would know if someone came and went out of main gate, as it is alarmed.'

I sat for another twenty minutes, finished my coffee and talked about everything except the case. Part of the reason for my visit was to appraise Prem Bedi. Of what I had seen of Manish Desai on television, the guy was abrasive—a young, wounded, stern adversary, a total antipode of Bedi. This man who sat in front of me gave the impression of complete calm. I couldn't look through the façade. Maybe he was genuine, maybe he was not. He certainly didn't *look* like a psychopath who could one day wake up in the morning and decide to murder his ex-wife and her husband—far from it. But I couldn't be certain. Moreover, what had I expected? The divorce happened twelve years ago. It would have actually made me cringe if I had found him sobbing like a school kid.

'Could I ask you for a favour, ACP Dutta?' Bedi requested.

'I don't see why not.'

'Could you get the whole media circus removed from the gate, please? I don't want to be incarcerated in my own home. It's a nuisance.'

'I can't promise, but I'll try.'

Before I left, I told them I'd be in touch if anything came up, and that they should call me if they thought of something they wanted to tell me—the usual police jargon. Rohan, the advocate, hadn't spoken a word the entire time, but he got up to walk me to the jeep.

'ACP Dutta, I have one question before you go.'

'Go on.' The guy seemed reasonable. I can't explain why, but sometimes you meet someone for the first time and you know the guy is genuine.

'Have they identified what golf club it was?' he asked.

'I don't know much about golf. I wouldn't even know what kinds there are, honestly.'

'Broadly speaking, it could be a driver or an iron or a putter.'

'Uh-huh, I have no clue ...'

'Would it be possible for you to call me and let me know when you find out, please?' He pulled out a visiting card and handed it to me. It carried an address in Lower Parel. So he wasn't some top-shot advocate from a Rolls-Royce firm, just a rookie trying to get into the big league.

'I'll see what I can do.' It was best to be non-committal at this stage. I didn't know what he was after, so why make a promise in the dark?

'Thank you, ACP Dutta, have a good day.'

I sat in my jeep and we drove out. It struck me then—why hadn't Rohan asked me this in front of the other two men?

MANISH DESAI

I knew my story. I had practised it for days now, said it aloud in front of the mirror a million times till it passed the acid test. I had started believing it myself. Most people missed the point—if you told a lie often enough, it did not become the truth, but it appeared to be the truth. And that's all that was required. People believed in appearances.

I was ready with the arsenal. I had vowed not to let my brother's death be in vain. I couldn't care less about that gold-digger, Rea. No disrespect to the dead, but she was having an affair with my brother before she had divorced her sugar daddy, Bedi. How unscrupulous was that? I was twenty-five then and she was twenty-seven. Good God! She was gorgeous and fit and filthy fuckin' rich. I remember my brother telling me stories of their rendezvous at various hotels, in numerous properties that Bedi owned across Mumbai. They even made it in my apartment and I kept that sheet on the bed for days, imagining her rolling in it. The girl was insatiable, my brother had told me. I knew that my brother wasn't the first one she had slept with. Bedi, she admitted, was too old to give her what she needed and hence, she began screwing younger men barely two years into her marriage. Unfortunately for her,

Bedi found out about her extracurricular activities. Everyone recognised Rea as Mrs Bedi then and thus, it had been only a matter of time before the idylls of Rea Bedi got to the ears of Prem Bedi.

She was conniving, no doubt about it. Despite having been caught cheating, she was the one who conned him, made him pay through the nose, as they say. He tried to settle, but she wouldn't give him an easy way out. She knew that taking him to court would get her the maximum mileage. I had been part of some of those discussions. I can still remember how she'd sometimes wear those short dresses, how her toned and bare legs would move and tease me so that I could hardly concentrate. Rea knew exactly what Bedi was worth; she, Mahesh and I deliberated and planned. But she was the one who gave the performance of a lifetime—the weak and neglected wife who was forced to seek companionship outside marriage because Bedi was hardly ever at home. *Poor thing. Unloved wife.* Mahesh played his part by penning editorials about Bedi, portraying him as a two-faced, unscrupulous businessman who had inherited everything—a playboy. But none of that stuck. However, Rea and Mahesh still managed to wring the rich bastard dry at the divorce.

But it was time for my plan now, and I was confident that I would win outright where Rea and Mahesh had only marginally succeeded. And so far, it all seemed to be going my way.

Rea had once mentioned she had a life insurance policy worth fifty crore rupees. She remembered that the premium for the first few years was paid by Bedi and then the balance was paid by the interest on the premium already paid. I hadn't entirely understood, and back then I hadn't cared.

However, I knew the endowment was due sometime this year, which was beneficial for me for two reasons. Firstly, with Rea dead, along with my brother—I was sincerely sad about his death—I happened to become the sole beneficiary. Secondly, with an endowment due, it gave Bedi a motive for murder—he didn't want her to reap the benefits of the endowment. And then the gods had been so kind to me that whoever killed my brother and his wife used a golf club, and if that wasn't enough, the murderer had mercifully left a shoe imprint that was the same size as Bedi's. If Bedi went to prison for the murders, and if he hadn't revoked or altered his will since his divorce, Rea's endowment money would come to me. Nevertheless, one thing troubled me—where were the Pali Hill property documents? The property was worth millions and I was the only legal heir to it, but I couldn't find its damn ownership papers. There was nothing in the safe …

No one knew that I was the one who had broken into the safe. When I got there after Mahesh's driver called me, I opened the house since I had a spare set of keys. The first thing I did after I emptied my guts was to go around the house to see what had gone missing. And even if no one believes me when I say this, at that time it wasn't for financial reasons. I simply wanted to establish who the murderer could be, based on what had gone missing. I noticed that everything valuable, like watches, jewellery, cash and other sundries had not been taken from the house, and then it struck me—my brother's residence had a safe locker cemented into the wall behind the bed. I knew where the key to that locker was, and I knew where I could find a pair of gloves in the house. I opened the locker—used the meat knife to make it appear like someone had jimmied it—and removed stacks of cash and jewellery. But I found no papers. I deduced they would all be in the bank locker that I had no access to. At least, not yet.

I dumped the jewellery and the kitchen knife into the Arabian Sea that night and kept the cash. I was smart enough not to let any evidence remain on me.

In retrospect, I realised I had been rash and unwise. With the burglary added to the murders, it took the suspicion away from that hussy's sugar daddy. But it was done now.

I had been invited to talk about my agonising story on the local channel's talk show, *Chat-One2One* in the afternoon, and then I had plans to go down to Bandra Police Station to meet some senior officer and tell him my heart-wrenching story.

I met Alisha, the show's hostess at their studio in Chembur.

The plan was for me to narrate my side of the story—a David taking on Goliath. Alisha briefed me that there had been a change in plan. My interview wasn't being broadcast live but instead, would be telecast that evening. I would be on television, *primetime*. It would be a thirty-minute show, with first five and last five minutes needed for hostess' introduction and summary and another ten sold to advertisers. I would be on telly for ten minutes.

I started solemnly, told the audience about the pain of becoming an orphan again, since my elder brother and his wife were my only family. Anybody who'd see me, I imagined, would be moved by seeing my hurt—my eyes welled up, throat constricted. I even looked away and bit my cheeks on the inside like I was trying extremely hard not to break down on camera. When I felt I had done enough to garner public sympathy, I started the crusade against Bedi and that got my hostess interested.

Alisha: Why do you think Mr Prem Bedi would even want to kill your brother and his wife?

Me: Because he is evil. This is how he's operated all his life. My brother tried to expose him but Mr Bedi bought people to stop him.

Alisha: Do you have any evidence … ?

Me: Evidence of what?

Alisha: Evidence of Mr Bedi having bribed anyone to stop your brother from telling the truth?

Me: Men like Mr Bedi don't leave evidence, you should know that. They never do anything themselves; their orders are carried out by people who can never be traced back to them.

Alisha: But Mr Bedi's divorce happened twelve years ago, why would he indulge in something appalling so late in the day?

Me: Because Rea had an insurance policy which was due for endowment later this year.

Alisha: I didn't know that. Tell us about it.

Me: Rea told Mahesh and me that a big endowment was due this year—

Alisha: How much?

Me: I have no idea. I had no interest in their money then and I don't have any now, but I could find out …

I closed my eye like it stung.

Alisha: I'm sorry to be asking you such questions.

Me: It's okay, Alisha. But for people like you, monsters like Mr Bedi would go unexposed.

Alisha: So you think Mr Bedi got rid of your brother and his ex-wife because of this big endowment policy?

Me: Of course. Rea had mentioned that when she had spoken to Mr Bedi recently he vehemently disagreed to let her have a paisa from that—

Alisha: Why did she speak to him?

Me: I have no idea. I don't know why she had to call him, but I believe that is what must have sparked the whole planning on his part. And I guess the only way he could stop her from having her own money is by killing her … and along with her, my brother too.

I pulled out a tissue from my pocket; this was a class act, this was what I wanted the public and police to remember. Alisha asked me a few more questions and that was it.

Sometimes less is more. I had made my point. I had made an appeal to the public conscience. I just prayed that the judge—whoever should get the case when it went to the court for hearing—was watching my sad story.

Unfortunately, the second part of my plan had to be deferred. I didn't want to go to the police station just then. I wanted to visit the police after this interview had been aired. I wanted them to be jaundiced by this before they met me.

ROHAN MALHOTRA

I walked back to the veranda after seeing off ACP Dutta. He was around my age, thirty-ish, and we both stood at around six-feet. He was a lot better built, though. And he was pleasant looking, with acquiescent features where nothing stood out harshly to distract from his friendly face.

Mr Bedi and Dad seemed engrossed in a business conversation, so I said bye, thanked them and left for home. I didn't see any point in driving all the way to my office to merely pick up the post. I doubted if I had any further role to play in Mr Bedi's case. I couldn't imagine why the police would want to question him again. And if the police did come by the second time, it would be for something more serious, and my dad had already warned me that if it did get serious, he'd be hiring someone more experienced. My role for the day was done. I could forget about it and move on. I hadn't been paid for my day's work yet, but I knew Mr Bedi wouldn't dodge me for a paltry sum.

As I didn't have the case anymore, I didn't feel uncomfortable discussing some of the day's proceedings with Urvee at dinner. I told her about the Bedi mansion, the uniformed butler—Damodar Singh aka Nestor, the ACP's visit. Later, she left to put Pia to bed and I went into the room I used as my home office. I had a case I had to read about: a landlord who had served notice to his tenants, but the poor tenants—husband, wife and three kids with only the husband (Ramdeen) working for a meagre salary as a shop assistant—had nowhere to go. Ramdeen had been in the same tenement for ten years now, and hadn't defaulted on rent even once. The landlord had demanded a big hike in the rent, which unfortunately Ramdeen couldn't afford and hence, the squabble and the court case. These were the only kind of cases that came my way since I had quit Dadawala & Partners. Most of them never went to trial. Somewhere along the long continuances and ever-shifting court-dates, both parties negotiated through advocates and compromised, and I got a measly sum for the whole exercise. Crap life, but I worked on several of these at one time, and they all added up to a decent sum at the end of the month. With Urvee bringing in her salary too, we were comfortable, though it wasn't a luxurious life. Therefore, my yearning to work on any case Mr Bedi threw at me. The bigger the better, but beggars couldn't be choosers. I read Ramdeen's case notes, references, medical records: It was a sorry affair.

The little twenty-inch flat-screen telly was on in the background while I worked and the all-too-familiar name of Mrs Rea Desai caught my ear. I looked up to see Manish Desai talking to some girl on a chat show. I froze. He was a despicable creature.

What an idiot, I thought as I heard him talking nonstop garbage. He was openly vilifying Mr Bedi and, unsurprisingly, the hostess was encouraging him by asking provocative questions instead of stopping his interview halfway through and asking the dimwit to leave. But this was what the slimy local channels thrived on—sensationalism. I wouldn't have been at all surprised if the channel had prepped him for it and the motivated monkey had just gotten up and started cartwheeling. Was he on drugs? Did he even realise who he was playing against? Of course I understood that he must be going through some emotional trauma and I could sense a hint of genuine loss, but what was his game? What was his grouse with Mr Bedi?

If I were more than a speck on Mr Bedi's radar, I would have urged him to file for defamation against both the muttonhead Desai and the channel. But I was astute enough to appreciate that Mr Bedi's hands were tied on the issue. If he displayed any signs of becoming defensive, it would only open doors for other channels to host such altercations.

As the brief chat concluded, I thought I'd better call it a day. I switched off the lights and walked out of my study, my mind segued into the missing golf club. I had waited all day for ACP Dutta's call to confirm what specific club was used to hit Rea and Mahesh Desai, but he hadn't called. Was the club left behind at the golf resort in South Korea because ... ? No. I didn't think so. What motive did Mr Bedi have to dirty his hands with the blood of people who no longer mattered to him? Dad had assured me that there was no relationship there. No feelings, not even a hint of hatred. And I could grasp that it was difficult for any feelings to persist after twelve years of separation.

Urvee had gone to bed trying to get Pia to sleep. I didn't have the heart to wake her up only to ask her to come to our bedroom, so I simply switched on the air-conditioner and waited for the room to cool down a bit before I could sleep.

As I lay down and closed my eyes, Manish Desai's words floated in my restless brain. He had mentioned some insurance policy that was due later in the year. However, even that made no sense whatsoever. Insurance endowments went to the person(s) already named in the policies. They did not go to ex-spouses. In any event, Mr Bedi wasn't short of money; he wouldn't commit murder, not even for a large sum. And, if Rea died—especially in the circumstances she had—how could he benefit? If anything, he would have expected the shit to come flying towards him. I made a mental note to check about the insurance policy Manish Desai had brayed about on the chat show before I drifted off to sleep.

When I woke up in the morning, Urvee had just come out of the shower and looked amazing. She was a beautiful woman, petite, with a chiselled face, long legs and shoulder-length tresses. I wanted to get up and grab her but I knew she would be in a rush to get to school. Once she had left, leaving me with a coffee, I yawned and stretched and made it to Pia's bedroom to gently wake up my angel and get her dressed for her playschool. I called up Dad twice before leaving home but the call went straight to his voicemail.

He called back when I was driving to my office, exactly the same time as yesterday, and I was precisely at the same spot as I had been when I took the call twenty-four hours earlier. That was how monotonous my life had become.

'Hi, Rohan,' he started.

'Yeah, I wanted to tell you about Manish Desai's interview last evening on—'

'Who in Mumbai would have missed that?' He let out a snigger.

I felt stupid. I should have known that he and Mr Bedi would have seen and discussed the interview already. They didn't need me telling them that it was on last night.

'Just one more thing, Dad,' I changed tack. 'It wouldn't be a bad idea to ask Mr Bedi about the insurance policy that nutjob was talking about. I'm happy to drop by this afternoon if you need any documents read.'

Do I sound desperate to get a foot in that door?

'Yes, thanks for reminding me. I'll check that first thing.'

He said nothing about me being required there … back to Lower Parel to sort out Ramdeen's mess.

'No worries, Dad. And thanks for thinking of me yesterday.'

'You're welcome, though it wasn't me. Prem asked for you.'

My hopes rose again. Mr Bedi asked for me? *Me*?

'Thank him, Dad.'

'Will do. Bye.'

MANISH DESAI

Rewind, play, rewind.

I watched my performance five times the next morning. Awesome. Then I practiced my next spiel another three times. It was fair to assume that ACP Ranjeet Dutta, the lead on this investigation, would have watched my interview the evening before. Acquainted with a policeman's training to remember details, I couldn't afford to fail or falter now. There could be no discrepancy in the baseline story: my unfortunate brother, my hapless sister-in-law, my tormenting bereavement …

Bandra Police Station is on Hill road, about two kilometres from my brother's Pali Hill residence. I wished only Rea had died and my brother had come into fortune. Mahesh was an unnecessary romantic, and had gotten into hot waters many times because of Rea. The woman was a clinical nymphomaniac. Bedi hadn't met all the guys she slept with behind his back, and when he had, his stature prevented them from telling him that his wife was amazing in bed. But it was different with Mahesh. He was a commoner, and got into altercations, even fist fights about Rea. Mahesh believed she wasn't sleeping around behind his back; that she had moved on from her past mistakes, but I never accepted it, no matter how hard she pretended. Poor Mahesh! But this wasn't the time to feel sorry for him. This was the time to nail Bedi.

I was ushered into a small room when I got to the Police Station. The usual décor welcomed me: pictures of Mahatma Gandhi and Pt Nehru adorned the walls that had old paint cracked in several places. The visitor chairs were hardwood and ACP Dutta sat behind a large desk.

'You wanted to see me,' he initiated after the pleasantries as I sat down across him.

'I wanted to check on when you'll be arresting Mr Bedi?'

'Do you have anything to say besides what you narrated on television last evening, Mr Desai?'

'Not exactly …'

'How old are you?' He grinned. *He grinned* like he was cracking some kind of a joke.

'I'll be thirty-eight this year, why?'

'So in all those years have you ever come across a "not-exactly" that translated to a "yes"?'

I was furious. I'm sure my face turned red; I couldn't see it but I felt like I was standing in front of a steam iron in full flow. I realised my abrupt question on the arrest hadn't gone down too well with the ACP, so I uttered a meek 'No.'

'So let me ask you again. Do you have anything that puts Mr Bedi even near the scene of crime?' He passed that mirthless smile again, son of a bitch.

'Not at the moment, but—'

'So you don't have any evidence now, but you think something might turn up, yes?' He interjected.

'That's precisely what I meant to say, ACP sahib.' I suppressed my anger.

'And you want me to arrest an innocent person based on your belief that some evidence might turn up in future?'

'But you can surely question him,' I urged.

'What makes you think we haven't done that already?'

'I'm sorry but I didn't read or hear anything about that.'

'That's because we've got rules and procedures to follow. We do not speak or televise an ongoing investigation. We only release what's required to be told to the general public.'

'But I am not general public, I'm the bereaved brother—'

'And therefore I just informed you that we've questioned Mr Bedi.'

'I'm sure he said he is innocent. Anyone would say that.'

'While I can feel your pain, here's the truth, Mr Desai. We already have the double-homicide case filed. We are currently investigating it from all possible angles. In all probability, it looks like a random home invasion gone wrong, but that's not to say we won't be looking at other motives …'

'I am telling you the motive is the insurance policy that Mr Bedi was after. Rea told me she had spoken to him and he told her in as many words that he'd kill her if she tried cashing the money.'

Did Rea mention that? Or did Mahesh? Or did I just make it up? How could the ACP verify?

'So what you are saying is that Mrs Rea Desai actually spoke to Mr Bedi?'

'Yes.' I think I sounded confident.

'Was that conversation in person or on the telephone?'

'I don't know. How does that matter?'

'Well, if they met somewhere, someone might have seen them together. Mr Bedi is a recognisable face, Mrs Desai also made it to the headlines, albeit over a decade ago, but still if someone had seen them together, and, knowing the couple had a nasty divorce, maybe they'd remember. It would help if we knew where they had met and roughly when.'

'What if they spoke on telephone?'

'Get me proof of the conversation … Forget it, I can get the records from the telephone companies. If there is even one call to or from Mr Bedi to any phone in your brother's household, or their mobile phones, it should be easily traceable. Leave that to me. Anything else?'

'Have you found the shoe or the golf club?' I soldiered on.

'Not yet, but as you know, the search is on.'

'Have you searched his house?'

'Whose house?'

'Obviously Mr Bedi's house. If you find a shoe that matches the print found at the crime scene or you find the golf club that has blood evidence, you don't need to look at telephone records.' I persisted, 'I've told you he had a serious motive.'

'On what grounds? It's not easy to procure a search warrant on a hunch …'

So at least he had a hunch. All I needed now was to fertilise it a bit more.

'I am willing to give it in writing as an affidavit that I have reasonable doubt that Mr Bedi had a strong motive to kill my brother and his wife—you can quote me as a source. I'm sure that can facilitate a search warrant, don't you think?' I could sense that the cogs in his brain had started to turn. I had read all about affidavits in the last few days. They are nothing more than a written voluntary statement of fact sworn and made under oath or attested by someone authorised by law. 'I want the murderer convicted and penalised, whoever it may be, ACP sahib. If it's unlikely that it's Mr Bedi, it's best to be certain. Search and have him cleared before moving on to another suspect. I won't let my brother and his wife be denied justice.' Okay, I knew the last sentence wasn't necessary, but it couldn't harm.

'Let me know if you want me to draft an affidavit, please.' I pressed on.

'Do that and send it to me,' was all he said and then stood up to let me know that the meeting was over.

I had no interest in hanging around either, but I still wanted to give a parting shot. 'When can I visit my brother's residence?' *And do absolutely fuck-all there*, but obviously I didn't say that.

'Give us a few more days, the investigators are still in and wouldn't want you contaminating the scene any more than you'd already done before we got in.' He said it politely, but his words were scathing.

'No worries, ACP sahib. Thanks for your time, and you'll hear from me soon.'

We shook hands and I walked out, and then drove to *Dhobi Talao*. I had a very old family friend who had his office near the Court of Small Causes there. An affidavit, for however important a statement, is still a minor contract. I wanted to get it ready as soon as possible, return to Bandra Police Station and personally give it to that smartass ACP Dutta before he changed his mind or progressed on some other line of enquiry.

ACP Dutta didn't come across as a friendly police officer. I needed to do some digging to find some other officer—preferably higher in rank than the ACP—who was either more sympathetic or more corrupt. I'm not a bona fide bastard, but fifty crore rupees was a lot of money. Yes, I had known the value of Rea's insurance payout all along. I could guarantee, maybe write another affidavit, that for that large an amount, half the world would have done exactly what I was doing.

TEJ MALHOTRA

I went to the office. Prem had finally taken note of my advice and agreed to stay at home. 'Under protest,' he had said jocularly. I was happy that he was maintaining his sense of humour even under these circumstances.

The ACP had been polite when he had turned up for the routine enquiry, but with the nefarious Manish Desai bouncing his theories around like crazy balls, I was sceptical if the ballad of Rea and Prem would be forgotten anytime soon. It was best that Prem stayed out of the public eye to avoid anything unsavoury.

I informed Prem's secretary, Maya, that her boss would not be in office for a few days. I didn't want to provide any explanation other than Prem feeling under the weather. I also specified that she should communicate to the rest of the employees that Prem wasn't on vacation. Though it was unprecedented, he was working from home, and he expected that the staff to carry on as usual, like they did on occasions when he travelled. If there was any kind of crisis, Prem had instructed that they were to call me.

I had to attend a director's meeting at noon—Prem decided he didn't want to dial-in if he wasn't attending in person—so I got down to preparing for it. The directors, unlike Maya and other junior staff, were curious about what was going on, and how long would it take for Prem to return. They showed genuine concern for Prem, the business and, evidently, their own futures. So I succinctly recounted for them the visit by the police to clarify certain details. It was nothing more than routine questioning. They didn't look thrilled, but appeared satisfied with my clarification nevertheless. Well, that was the best I could offer. They were free to doubt me and choose to jump ship. I had bigger worries on my mind. Maybe I cared for Prem more than I cared for the business. I gave clear instructions to everyone at office that under no circumstances should they call Prem to discuss this matter.

I picked up some files that Prem had asked me to, left the office at three and went back to my friend.

Thank the Almighty! The ACP had been successful in clearing the carnival outside Prem's main gate. I eyed two cars parked on the other side of the road, striving to be blasé, but I noticed the cameras even so. Well, if the ACP had been unsuccessful in shooing them away, there was nothing I could do.

Prem was pleased to see me. Well, he was under a kind of house arrest, so all visitors were welcome.

'Did you hear from Mr Lee?' I asked. I hadn't got a call back from him so I wondered if he had called Prem directly.

'No.'

'I wish we had known about Rea when we were at the golf course …'

'What are you thinking about, Tej?'

'Honestly, I am too numb to think. However, what was that Manish Desai talking about on television last night? What insurance policy?'

'He indeed jogged my memory. He was correct. Rea was insured.'

'And …' I waited.

'We had taken insurance policies of fifty crore rupees each, two years into our marriage, so the endowment is due later this year; that much is correct.'

'But surely you cannot benefit from her insurance, considering you guys were divorced?'

'Wrong. We had an addendum to the original contract that no matter what happened, neither of us could change the beneficiary in our own policy. Hence, the contract remained in force even after the divorce. Rea would have received fifty crores at the maturation of the policy, like I will do later in the year. But her death means that I will now receive a further fifty crores. I might receive it earlier as it would now be paid off as an insurance claim.'

If you had sliced my veins at that moment, I would be dry; my blood had curdled and stopped flowing. This had *menace* written all over it. I knew it was only a matter of time before the police found out about the supplementary clause in the insurance and investigated it. Prem was sitting on a time bomb, so the serenity on his face baffled me. Why wasn't he concerned or rankled? The golf club, the eight-and-a-half size shoe outsole print, being the solitary beneficiary to a fifty crore insurance payout … if it were me, I'd be popping Imodium tablets to stop my stomach from losing it.

'Why didn't you two jointly speak to the insurance company to change that at the time of the divorce?'

'Because, for one, we stopped talking altogether and two, that wasn't an option. The premium was all paid upfront in the first two-three years, so we could either let it mature over its twelve-year lifespan or make it void and lose the investment. I thought it was wise to let it go on.'

'Why did you have such a clause in the first place?'

'Remember we were newly married and very much in love. When we took out the policies the divorce wasn't envisioned. I didn't get married to end up a divorcee.'

In the eight years that I had known Prem, this was the first time he had spoken about his marriage. I shed my role as a business colleague and decided to hear him out as a friend, to let him unload whatever he had been living with because I knew he didn't have many close friends he could have shared this intimate account with.

'What happened then, Prem, how did it all go so wrong?'

'We were happily married for two, maybe three, years. Rea was an unfettered being, and that is what attracted me to her in the first instance. However, I can't say she was solely to blame. My dad passed away and I was pulled into the business as there was no one else, and as time progressed, we drifted apart and the love, it got eroded. We should have split then, but we didn't, and the relationship festered. We carried on despite the fact that I knew she was sleeping around with other men. It was hurtful and embarrassing, to say the least. But I kept the façade of marriage going regardless of the many confrontations at home. Then I started getting approached by men with compromising photographs of her, blackmailing me, asking for money in exchange or they'd let the photographs slip to the media ...'

I could sense his pain. He had drifted far down memory lane, and those memories couldn't be pleasant. But I didn't stop him.

'The worst part is, every time we discussed this, she seemed to enjoy it. For her it was a way of mocking me. Why? I didn't know then and I'm not any wiser now after all these years.'

'You mean she knew the various men were taking pictures of her …'

'Yes, but that's not all. I hired a private eye and guess what he returned with?'

'What?'

'She was involved in the entire racket. The money that the men extorted from me was being split between them and her.'

'No way!'

'I still have the report from the investigator somewhere in the office, if you want to see. He had photographs to support everything. That's how venomous she had become, that's how ugly our relationship had turned.'

'And then you filed for divorce?'

'I didn't have any alternative left. I mean, my wife was not only sleeping with other men, she was also getting herself snapped having sex with them and then blackmailing me for money. And she made it bitter. I could have refuted everything she said but at the end of it all, who do you think the public would have made fun of? Me—I was the one couldn't keep my wife from …'

'Did you never ask her to stop, to return?'

'Tej, no doctor can help a patient who does not want to recover. She didn't want to return. I can understand one mistake, but this was a serial offender we are talking about … anyway, let's talk about something else.'

'I'm sorry. I knew about everything, but I had no idea it had gotten this bad.'

'Except for one of my cousins, Veena, who came from Delhi to be with me during the time because I was terribly down, no one knows the entire history. That reminds me—I got a call from Veena this morning. She's flying in tomorrow to be with me. She is my first cousin, but we are very close because we studied together for some time. I would love for you to meet her.'

'I certainly want to meet her, but may I suggest something, if you don't mind?'

'Go on, my friend.'

'We should speak to Dadawala & Partners tomorrow morning.'

'Why? I am not guilty, I can tell you that, and hence I have nothing to worry about. If the worst came to the worst, we can always ask Rohan—'

'Rohan is my son, but he isn't the best advocate in town. We have two strong pointers towards you, and we have the insurance disbursement coming to you. Irrespective of how innocent you are, the police will consider fifty crores as a reasonable motive. Why do you want to play Russian roulette with three bullets in the chambers?'

'Because there are three empty chambers still and I believe in justice. God's justice, this country's justice. And it's the righteous thing to do. Do you think I'm not being honest with you?'

I had no answer to that question. Only God could bring sanity to him before it got too late. Which era was my friend living in? The wolves had started circling and he was talking about righteousness. I actually wanted to meet Veena now—maybe she could save him, maybe she could pester him into calling Mr Dadawala.

'What's your plan for the evening?' he asked.

'Nothing.'

'Stay for the evening then. We'll have a few drinks and get some good Rogan Josh cooked.'

'I'm sold.'

ROHAN MALHOTRA

I went straight to Ramdeen's file when I arrived at the office in the morning. The court had scheduled the date of the hearing for the end of the month and neither Ramdeen nor his landlord's advocate had approached me with any sort of compromise. That wasn't anything unusual, as many such cases got settled only at the eleventh hour. But this time, my attention was flickering. I had to read every line twice; my commitment was dwindling as I went through the hoops while thinking about the possibility of associating myself with Mr Bedi somehow. I knew that if I could forge any alliance with him at this time, my days of handling the likes of Ramdeen could be behind me. In any other scenario I would have called up the client I had worked for the day before to check if all was okay and that if I was required for anything else, but with Dad over at Mr Bedi's place, I didn't know how to approach matters. I couldn't just call up to ask where to send the invoice. They say, once you get a foot in the door you're half-way there. Not in my case. I had more than one foot in the door yesterday and now I was struggling to even walk through my current cases. I knew well enough that only two kinds of advocates ever made it really big here in Mumbai—either you were pedigreed—your father or grandfather started a law practice and you got your degree and went to work in the established family firm—or you chanced upon a life-changing case like Mr Bedi's. The rest of us existed on the periphery. My problem was that I was far too ambitious to keep doing what I was doing.

I sat there in my chair, sighing, sipping bad coffee, staring at the file and wondering how I could create an opportunity to return to Mr Bedi, when my phone rang.

'Hello, could I speak to Mr Rohan Malhotra?'

'Yes, Advocate Rohan Malhotra speaking. Who's this?'

'ACP Ranjeet Dutta, we met yesterday ...'

Why was he calling me? Then I remembered I had asked him about the golf club and given him my card, but I did not want to exhibit any enthusiasm.

'Of course, ACP Dutta, how may I help you?'

'How secure is this line?'

That got my pulse racing. What was so covert that he needed a secure line, and why did he want to tell *me*?

'It's fairly secure. You can tell me anything.'

'Good. Mr Malhotra, what I am going to tell you is strictly off the records. Is that okay with you?'

How could I agree to keep something under wraps before I knew what it was?

'You're putting me in a tricky situation, ACP—'

'Just call me Ranjeet on the phone, please. It's best you don't mention my designation.'

'Right. As I was saying, you're putting me in an awkward position, Ranjeet, making me agree to something without knowing the significance of the information you're about to give me.'

'If I didn't have your client's interest at heart I wouldn't have made this call, believe me. I am happy to disconnect now if you want …'

No.

'Okay, I promise to keep this off-record.'

The prelude out of the way, ACP Dutta came to the point. 'I am under a lot of pressure from the top to move fast on the Desai double-murders. Our top brass is eager to make the point that law isn't different for the rich and powerful. However, I don't think your client Mr Bedi is a suspect, at least not yet. Anyway, Mr Manish Desai was here this morning, spouting nonsense before he left to procure a signed affidavit to state he has reasons to believe Mr Bedi had a solid enough motive to murder his brother and sister-in-law.'

'Surely that alone cannot be sufficient for any court proceedings.'

'Correct. But you should know cases with even weaker evidence have been filed in our courts if the right influence from the top is exerted.'

'I know, but what is Manish Desai getting an affidavit for?'

'Based on that affidavit, he might bulldoze the police machinery to obtain a search warrant for Mr Bedi's properties. If that happens, I'll start with his house at Altamount Road.'

'You can't do that. You just told me you don't believe he is a suspect …'

'And I also told you that this conversation never happened, remember?'

For a few minutes I didn't know how to react.

'Are you there, Rohan?'

'Yes … yes, I'm here, just thinking.'

'That's why I called you. As his advocate, I thought I should let you know that I can stall the search warrant till tomorrow morning at best, so you need to act now.'

'What am I supposed to do? I mean, if you bring in a search warrant, I can't quash that unless I know it in advance, and you've warned me that I cannot make this conversation public. You've virtually tied my hands.'

'Search warrant isn't what I am concerned about, but if you, as his advocate, know about anything that can turn up in the search, which can steer this case into something more sinister, I want you to be prepared, that's all.'

'You mean—'

'I don't want to talk about it any further. I'm sure you can understand why.'

'Thanks for the heads-up, Ranjeet.'

'There'll always be time to pay me back, Rohan.'

'Thank you.'

'Keep the thanks for now. Only time will tell who needs to thank whom. See you tomorrow morning.'

ACP Dutta had been my manna from heaven. He was extremely soft-spoken, unlike some of the policemen I had met over the years, and I had seen some real pieces of work. He had treated me with respect and dealt with me like I was Mr Bedi's defence advocate. He had forewarned me of the search warrant, he had specified to me which property he would go to first, he had also indicated that the search could turn ugly—which I knew would, what with the missing golf club, which, I knew, could be construed as sufficient grounds to arrest Mr Bedi.

I sat and pondered what I had learnt in the law classes back in the college.

Setback: according to Indian Penal Code (IPC), murder was deemed a non-bailable offence. *Furtherance:* bail wasn't a matter of right here, but nothing stopped the accused to apply to the court; it was the judge's discretion. Criminal Procedure Code under Section 497 allowed the admission to bail in non-bailable cases specially if there were reasonable grounds for believing that the accused was not guilty.

Republic of India followed Common Law—based on past judgements and court decisions that had decided the fate of earlier, similar cases. My mind segued into course of action that I should take immediately: Anticipatory bail. Was it even possible on a murder charge? I vaguely remembered some cases from my college days. I sifted through my law books till I came upon one such case: POKAR RAM VS. THE STATE OF RAJASTHAN AND ANOTHER ON 17 APRIL 1985. The accusation against the defendant was 'offence of murder' under IPC Section 302. The defence advocate had presented compelling circumstances to prove that the primary and the only object to arrest the defendant was to injure and humiliate him. And the Sessions Court Judge, Jodhpur, had granted anticipatory bail. Hey presto!

Mr Bedi's arrest, too, would do nothing more than humiliate him, as the very foundation of the accusation was propagated by the ulterior motive of Manish Desai. Similar to the 1985 case—where the Sessions Judge might have blinked if there had been a firearm involved—there were no firearms involved in the murders of Rea and Mahesh Desai. It could work. It all depended on the judge now.

I deliberated calling Dad, but my self-respect prevented me. Call it extolling myself, but I knew I could handle this. Moreover, if I called Dad, I would break ACP Dutta's trust, and if that wasn't enough, Dad would call Dadawala & Partners immediately, removing me from the game altogether. Why would I want that? After all, ACP Dutta must have believed in me to call me; he could have called my dad but he didn't. This was my chance on the grandstand and I wasn't passing it on.

I decided to keep Dad and Mr Bedi out of the loop till I had something tangible in my hands. In any event, the conversation between ACP Dutta and me was confidential and he couldn't just turn around and say he had already forewarned me. He wasn't going to make any more calls, so if it wasn't for me, Mr Bedi and Dad were unaware of the situation anyway. I was only extending unbidden help. What harm could I do? None. What could I do to help? A lot. Mr Bedi could get anticipatory bail in case the tide turned against him, and if all went well, I would be living a dream from then on. Worth the gamble.

I called up the Mazgaon Court to check which judges were in session so I could pick the one I had some rapport with. My search came up lucky. Honourable Mr Alok Sheroy—Ad Hoc Assistant Sessions Judge, City Civil and Sessions Court, Bombay, was in the court, and he had a twenty-minute window in his diary at 4 p.m. that I booked through his associate. I didn't give him any details except that it was an extremely urgent issue. I had been in Judge Sheroy's court thrice as an assistant advocate when I worked at Dadawala & Partners. I had once presented a point at trial and he had seemed impressed. When I started my own practice, he had called to congratulate me and wish me luck. He said he saw a spark in me and that he would one day like me to argue a case in his court. Maybe the time had come. My perception of Justice Judge was that he was a straight and simple man who didn't fancy frills or theatrics in his court. For him, there was only one truth—the one that was evidenced in the present, and not promised in the future. I knew he would look into my eye and ask: do you think he's innocent? He didn't need to, but he would, and if I faltered, Mr Bedi could forget the bail application.

I started putting the docket together to present to Judge Sheroy in four hours' time.

I worked for two hours straight before I went out for a stroll to prepare myself for what could be the most critical meeting of my life. If I pulled this one, I knew I would be made for life. ACP Dutta called again; he needed a favour of sorts, so I picked up one *vada-pau* from the nearby hawker, wolfed it, and then got another one in a thin clamshell box and walked back. Most of the fellow advocates in the building were swatting flies too, waiting for the next big client. I decided to have impromptu discussions with some within the building to gauge their views—obviously without mentioning that I was representing Mr Bedi in an anticipatory bail hearing. Some of the other advocates knew my father was an associate of Mr Bedi and there seemed little point in approaching those as I reckoned their views would be jaundiced. But some didn't and I wanted to know what they supposed.

'He's guilty as hell. If not him, then who?' one said. He had a point: if not him, then who? Could it really be a burglary gone wrong? Could it be a coincidence that a guy wearing size eight-and-a-half shoes just walked in with a golf club and killed Rea and Mahesh Desai? What was the probability of a double coincidence? Not zero but not much better either. But this theory wasn't something I wanted to recite to Judge Sheroy.

I met a few more but got nothing worthwhile, and then I found the diamond-crusted nugget.

'I can't imagine someone nursing a grudge for twelve years. If he wanted to knock her off he would have done it a lot sooner, don't you think? I would, if I were him,' one of the senior advocates told me.

The statement was brilliant, the statement had conviction, the statement could be assertively repeated in first person as it dripped with confidence: '*That's what I would do.*' It challenged the judge to ask himself the same question: what would you do? Of course, if I wanted to kill someone, would I wait for twelve years?

I left my office at 3.15 p.m.

I was ushered into Judge Sheroy's chamber at exactly 4 o'clock.

I left his office at 4.14 p.m.

Judge Sheroy had been happy with my performance.

People always whined about how anything could go wrong in a minute. Conversely, everything can also go right any minute, but people never mention that.

I sat in my car, switched on the air-conditioning and let the cold blast hit my face. I was perspiring like a pig in a mire—part-heat, part-anxiety. I had been in the trenches for so long that what I had just achieved seemed surreal. I had obtained an anticipatory bail for Mr Bedi.

I looked out of the windscreen to see newspapers at the nearby vendors. Every possible newspaper on the shelf was talking about the case. Updates on the double murder were side-lined by pictures of Mr Bedi—guilty or innocent? I could empathise with them. After all, scribes weren't gods, they were humans too. They knew diddly-squat at the moment and sat on the fence and waited. Mr Bedi's arrest would have provided them the opportunity to go out guns blazing against him, but I had killed their joy before they even knew it existed. I smiled and put the car in gear.

I had left Mazgaon Court around 4.30 p.m. and driven straight to Altamount Road to sport the greatest feat of my life so far. It was a distance of mere 4.5 kilometres, and here I was, at 6.45 p.m., still stuck in the bleeding traffic near S. Mohani Chowk. I called Urvee and, without divulging the intricate details, told her about my grand achievement. She couldn't believe it. She wanted to know the complete story from beginning to end—who, how, what—and I reassured her that, whatever I could, I would articulate it better when I got home, face-to-face.

'What time will you come home tonight?' she asked.

'I'm going to see Mr Bedi at his residence and I should be with him an hour max, then I'll drive home.'

Disconnecting the call, I rang Dad to check where he was. I wanted him to be at Mr Bedi's residence when I walked in with the papers. But I didn't want to give the surprise away. I wanted to see his face. I knew he would be proud of me, his son.

'Hi, Dad.'

'Hey, Rohan, how are you?'

He sounded like he was already a couple of drinks down.

'Fine, Dad, I just wanted to check if everything's good with you and Mr Bedi?'

'Oh yes, Prem and I are at his place, having a few drinks.'

I had already guessed that from your tone, I wanted to say, but I heard Mr Bedi say something in the background. Then:

'Prem says why don't you join us for a drink if you're somewhere in the vicinity and not doing something important. Just one drink, in case you're driving.'

Game. Set. Match. I was in.

'I was planning to drop by anyway. See you in a bit, Dad,' I responded and quickly cut off the call before he could ask why.

The traffic started moving and I eventually turned right into Altamount Road at seven. That was almost two hours and thirty minutes in the car with anxiety surging and the bladder threatening to burst. The gates opened and I drove in past the carport, stopping behind my dad's Mercedes.

I stepped out of the car and walked to the house. I had every reason to be proud and I could feel my gait pronouncing it as I was let into the house by Nestor.

'Hello, Rohan,' said the Mogul, his left hand holding a crystal tumbler with an amber liquid in it, his right hand stretched out to shake mine. 'Tej and I were having a small party tonight, and I thought you should join us. I hope we are not impinging on your personal time.'

Wait till I tell you what I have for you, you might make me the chief guest.

'That's really nice of you, Mr Bedi, I have something to tell you—but you'll have to excuse me as I need to go to the toilet …'

'What's your poison?' he asked when I returned.

'I'll have whatever you're having.'

I hadn't realised that Damodar hadn't left the room. Mr Bedi looked at him and he didn't need to be told anything.

'What do you like your Scotch with, sir? Water, soda or ice?' Damodar asked.

'Straight for my boy,' roared Dad before I could even consider the options.

'Now tell me.'

I waited for Damodar to arrive with my drink. Mr Bedi stepped forward to clink his crystal with mine, and said cheers. I reciprocated. From the corner of my eye I could see Dad raising his glass as a toast.

I took my first sip and let the whisky travel down my throat, warming me up as it descended. Then I got talking. I spoke for about twenty minutes—Damodar replenished my glass once in that time. Then I pulled out the paper with Judge Sheroy's signature and offered it to Mr Bedi to check. He read it and passed it on to Dad. Mr Bedi kept his whisky down and applauded loudly. Dad followed. I was delighted, but I passed a shy smile, pretending that I was embarrassed by the praise being showered.

'That's my son,' Dad spoke first. I could see his eyes welling up with pride, but it was Mr Bedi who gave me a bear hug first.

'Thank you, Rohan. Tell us about it all over again, from the beginning,' Mr Bedi requested, and then turned to Damodar. 'Open another bottle, and ask them to set the table for three. Rohan will be dining with us tonight.'

I couldn't decline the offer.

I called Urvee sometime around 9.30 p.m. and let her know I would be getting late. She was concerned about me driving in the state I was in—maybe my voice gave it away. I assured her that someone would drop me or I'd take a cab. By the time we finished dinner, it was eleven. Mani drove me home in my car, and Mr Bedi's driver followed us in Dad's car so they could return after dropping me. I don't remember if I saw Urvee or if she was already asleep in Pia's room. I went to the bedroom and crashed on the bed without removing my clothes.

When I woke up in the morning, I had a splitting headache. The room was still spinning, the slivers of sunlight penetrating through the curtains into my bedroom were blinding me, my mouth was dry like a camel's foot, my tongue felt heavy like it had been injected with lead and I felt like I would throw up any moment. I was a social drinker, and with Pia so young, we had hardly socialised in the last three years. I drank a beer or two in a month. I couldn't remember when was the last time I had drunk so much that I had woken up with a hangover of such severity. Shit! I crawled, literally crawled, to the kitchen, fearing that if I stood up, I would fall. I put the kettle to boil and raided the fridge. I had a glass of orange juice, and then another one till the kettle boiled. Then I had coffee, black. I repeated the orange juice–coffee combo till there was no juice left.

The kitchen clock announced that it was 9.44 a.m. Urvee had left for the day. It took me a lot of effort to stand still without holding on to something. Then I saw the post-it note on the refrigerator. It was from Urvee, saying she had looked forward to spending the evening with me to celebrate but she understood I was held back for work at Mr Bedi's residence. She had taken Pia with her as it was Friday, so Pia had an early start and early finish and could return with her mother.

I realised that the spectacular job I had done yesterday would be wasted if I wasn't at Mr Bedi's home when ACP Dutta arrived with a search warrant. I popped in some analgesics, took a long shower and changed. Savvy enough to realise I couldn't drive, I walked out and took a cab.

ACP RANJEET DUTTA

If Rohan Malhotra required something from me, I needed something in exchange. Wasn't that the point of barter? Certainly, I wouldn't engage in filth, but asking for something I needed couldn't hurt, especially when I had conferred a huge favour on him already.

'Hi, Ranjeet,' he chirped when I called him.

'Hello, Rohan. I hope I didn't catch you at a bad time.'

'Not at all, what can I do for you?'

'Are you alone?'

'Yes, I'm going back to the office to work on something, but we can talk,' he said. I heard the noise recede, like he was walking away from where he was and looking for some quiet corner.

'Hopefully this will be a quick one. Listen, I know I spoke to Mr Bedi earlier in Mr Malhotra's and your presence, but now I need to speak to him alone …'

'Is he a suspect by any chance?'

I could sense the alarm in Rohan's voice.

'You know police procedures, Rohan—everyone is a suspect until they are cleared, so I won't lie. At least theoretically, Mr Bedi had the motive—some old animosity—and you can't deny that …' I waited for him to accept with some kind of an audible *sigh*, but nothing came, so I continued, 'I need to interview him either in the presence of another police officer or on tape for record.'

'Why not with me present there, at the least?'

'He's not a suspect, why does he need a lawyer present?'

Though Rohan remained silent, I could perceive the gears in his brain turning, processing what my words meant. He knew, despite the fact that there was no evidence as such, there was nothing to stop Mr Bedi from being brought in for questioning to a police station. I bet he didn't want that. I wagered Mr Bedi wouldn't want that either.

'Could I speak to him and confirm, please?' he eventually asked.

'Sure, I'll wait for your call.'

I knew he was going to call his client straightaway.

Rohan called back in twenty minutes. Mr Bedi was willing to see me in an hour.

I left for Altamount Road immediately. I didn't want to include anyone in this conversation with Mr Bedi. I had a cassette tape mini-recorder. Notwithstanding the world around us having changed, the digital recording devices were still not acceptable to record witness or suspect interviews. I presumed that was largely due to the number of manipulation techniques and software that were announced every day.

Mr Bedi was in the veranda, having coffee. Exactly in the same chair, in the same place I had met him the last time. He was alone. He called for a coffee for me and we settled down. I highlighted some of the questions might be a repeat but I had to ask them as I hadn't recorded the previous interview. He gave me a nod.

I switched on the recorder and placed it on the table between us. I articulated his rights, the place, date, time and the people present at this interview.

'Mr Bedi, where were you when you came to know about the murders of Rea and Mahesh Desai?'

'I was in South Korea at a golf resort called Nine Bridges.' He named all those present with him at the time. 'Two days after the murders …'

'How did you know the murders happened two days earlier?'

'Well, I didn't know that at the time, but when I saw it on telly—it was you, I think, who was talking to media outside the property on the morning of tenth of June, I calculated the date of the murders.'

'How did you find out about these murders?'

'I had two missed calls from a Mumbai blocked number, and Tej called my office to check what had happened. He was the one who gave me the news. Someone from your department must have called my office, I reckon …'

'I was the one who had called you. The call was made through our police exchange and hence the number wouldn't have been displayed. And I didn't think the message was apt for voicemail. What happened then?'

Mr Bedi gave me a succinct account of them flying to India only hours after the news of the tragedy and arriving in Mumbai the next morning.

'You told me earlier, you never saw Mrs Rea Desai since your divorce twelve years ago. Is that correct?'

'To the best of my knowledge; it could be eleven years—but it's definitely longer than I can remember.'

'Never met her?

'No.'

'Never spoke to her directly or on the telephone?'

'No.'

'Never communicated with her through some third party?'

'No.'

Mr Bedi didn't blink. He didn't have to think. He didn't seem to be making it up, he was quite clear.

'Mr Bedi, did you know Mr Mahesh Desai?'

'No, not personally, but I did know *of* him.'

'Ever met Mr Mahesh Desai?'

'No.'

'Ever spoke to him on the telephone?'

'Never.'

'He never called here?'

'Not to the best of my knowledge, but …' He stopped.

'Sorry, Mr Bedi, you were saying …?'

'You must know that Mahesh was seeing Rea even before we divorced, so if he called our residence back then, I wouldn't know.'

There was no way to dig that up, and no need either.

'Did you ever visit the Pali Hill residence of Mrs and Mr Desai when they lived there?' I threw in a curve ball here. He had said he had never seen Rea or Mahesh in all those years, but he hadn't said anything about visiting their home.

'No, never.'

His expression stayed apathetic, and I decided to move on. His confidence spoke volumes of his innocence—that, or he was a consummate actor.

'Mr Bedi, would you know why Mr Mahesh Desai ran a smear campaign against you and your business practices?'

'I wouldn't know. He's the only one who could have answered that question.'

'Don't you think you got extra coverage because you were Mrs Rea Desai's ex-husband?'

'Maybe, but I honestly can't say for sure.'

He didn't voice a single ugly syllable against his ex-wife. Maybe it wasn't in his blood. He appeared to be someone who could control his emotions.

'Would you know if anyone wanted to harm Mahesh Desai?'

'No.'

'If you were to guess?'

'ACP Dutta, guessing, speculating and building theories to catch to the suspect are part of your job. I couldn't do that even if I tried.'

The cassette ended. I switched sides and asked him some more questions. But I got nothing of consequence. But at least I had everything on tape, should he change his statement later.

'Would it be okay if the caretaker of your house shows me around and explains the electronic surveillance system, the locking and unlocking of gates?'

'I don't see any issues. Do I need to be present?'

'Not at all.'

He called Damodar, who escorted me into the house to talk to the caretaker. I spent another hour exploring any inconsistency in the narrative or any overrides to the electronics. Zilch.

According to crime manual, one of the most significant motives seemed absent. Mr Bedi didn't need any more money than he already had, so why would he murder anyone? And honestly, it wasn't normal or simple for ordinary people to just kill another human being. However notorious and hideous the act of murdering someone sounded, it still required a lot of strength. Most people couldn't maintain normalcy when they witnessed a dead body. Mr Bedi, however distinguished a businessman he was would still be counted as green when it came to murder. Even if I stretched my imagination and believed that he had offed two people in cold blood, there was no way he could have so cleanly escaped from the scene that the entire investigating team could find no clues.

TEJ MALHOTRA

I had slept in one of the guest rooms at Prem's place the previous night, but I was an early riser, regardless of what time I went to bed. Prem was not up yet, but I sat in the veranda, sipping coffee, enjoying the gentle breeze, the incessant chirping of the birds and the sweet smell of summer flowers. The serenity was only interrupted by the phone calls I received.

It had become a kind of routine now for one or the other director to call me first thing in the morning. Maybe they all colluded in office, and decided that was the best time to catch me alone. Maybe they got together later and discussed my morning summary.

I noticed how their concerns had skewed a bit. In the initial days most of them called to check on Prem. Now, the unrest was more about the business:

'The stock price might not be sustainable in the long run … all eyes are on us.'

'What about the annual board meeting in April?'

'The annual board meeting is ten months away', I wanted to yell, but restrained myself.

I politely listened to their concerns. All of them were genuine. They were concerned about business … and Prem. I assured them that things would go back to normal soon.

Rohan had done me proud last night. He had beaten my expectations in many ways. As it so often happens to all fathers, I had always imagined him as my little boy, but he must have unmistakably exuded gravitas for ACP Dutta to trust him and alert him of what was coming, albeit surreptitiously. And Rohan had been astute enough to appreciate that when the police came to search, the missing golf club in one of Prem's sets would be noticed, and things would go downhill from there.

Despite my numerous requests I had failed to convince Prem to give me the golf set that he had carried to South Korea to take away and bury for good.

'Do you still doubt me, my friend?' he had asked in frustration.

That quelled all my arguments. He was adamant that all would be right because he was innocent.

As I sat sipping the morning coffee, I went over my questions for ACP Dutta—*Had they found anything burgled so far?*

Any suspects?

Which specific golf club was used to commit the murders?

I hadn't realised that Prem's driver, Ganesh, had left for the airport early morning to pick up his cousin. Veena must have left real early from Delhi. I stood up as the car stopped in the carport and she got out. The familial resemblance was striking. She could have been his sibling, only shorter. She must have been five-feet-seven, slim with a boyish frame, but outstandingly elegant. I knew she was almost same age as him, but she had a touch more silver in her hair than Prem, and she hadn't coloured it, which added to her appeal. Dressed in a short cream-coloured raw-silk kurta, pale-blue nylon slacks and *Jodhpuri jootis*, she looked straight out of a portrait of some erstwhile princess, which she was.

'You must be Tej.' She walked towards me.

'Yes, Veena ji.'

'Veena is enough. Is Prem still sleeping?'

'Yes, we had a late night. But I'm sure he will be out anytime now.'

'Let him rest. I'll join you for coffee in the meanwhile.' She sat down, while Ganesh carried her bags into the house.

We sipped coffees, exchanged pleasantries about her flight, about Mumbai, about everything for a while. Both of us knew why she was here, but we weren't sure if we wanted to touch upon the despicable topic just yet.

'Prem is a caring guy, has always been,' Veena started, when the silence between us became awkward. 'He would have never told you that his mother did not like Rea, but being gracious that she was, she didn't make it an issue. If her son was happy, she accepted it. She died of cardiac arrest when she found out about her son's failing marriage. She didn't say anything, but he knows what killed her—the pain of watching her only son live a life of shame.'

The sudden eruption made me uneasy. Prem had recently told me about his marriage, but he had, for some reason, not mentioned anything about his mother.

'The only part I do not understand is why did he bear it for so long?' I asked.

'For the sake of his mother. He didn't divorce Rea, thinking it would all iron out at some point, but that woman was rotten.'

Unlike Prem who, except once, had never opined about Rea with an indecent adjective, Veena was candid.

'Can I ask an honest question?'

'Only if you want an honest answer.' Veena looked me in the eye.

'Did you ever think Prem could kill her?'

'Back then yes, with his bare hands, especially when she dragged him through the nasty divorce. Now, after twelve years, not a chance. At least, I don't think so. But I haven't met him in the last three years. You've been closer to him in the recent years. What do you think?'

'No. For three reasons.' I collected my thoughts. 'Of what I know of him, he is just not the kind to murder. I haven't seen him angry in the last eight years I've been with him. Not once, and believe me, there have been occasions where if it was someone else, they would have lost their top. So, to lose his marbles over something that happened twelve years ago seems extremely unlikely. That is my view as a friend. As a rational man, I can conclude that he couldn't possibly have been there physically, and three, even if we ignore all else and blame him for the murders, do you think he's stupid enough to kill them with a golf club? And then leave a shoeprint on the step? He has a degree in law and he runs one of the biggest business empires in the country; if he had done it, he wouldn't have left a shred of evidence. Forget ACP Dutta, even Sherlock Holmes wouldn't have found a clue. Trust me.'

'I agree. So why is that woman's brother-in-law trying to frame Prem?'

'No idea. My hunch is that either he masterminded the murders and planted spoors to point towards Prem for only one reason—fifty crore rupees, or maybe it is simply a brilliant coincidence that he wants to exploit, now that the opportunity has presented itself. If Prem gets convicted, he obviously doesn't get the insurance disbursement. But does Manish Desai get it as the only legal surviving family member? I don't know.'

'Could we not talk him out of spewing nonsense at the media?'

I had thought about that myself. 'If we approach him with an offer of discussion, he might blow it out of context, like he's done with everything else so far. Even if he comes to the table, I wouldn't have any confidence that he'll do what he agrees with us. And don't forget, trying to get in touch with him might make us look weak, and that's the last thing we want to do when we know Prem is innocent.'

'I just wish it all goes away soon. I don't want any more problems for him. He's suffered a lot by making that one single mistake of getting married to that godforsaken woman.'

We fell quiet again.

Someone was framing Prem. And I didn't think that idiot Manish Desai had the brains to have planned this manoeuvre. I mentally scanned for any business skirmishes Prem had had in the last few months. Who could benefit from Prem's disappearance from the scene? However hard I tried to think, the list only contained one name: Manish Desai. But to think he could have killed his own brother was a stretch even for him. The size of the shoe print found could have been a mere coincidence, but the golf club had me thinking. Maybe the burglar was smart enough to know about Prem and his predilection for golf. Still, if the police suspected that the murder was for vendetta and followed only that line of enquiry, the real culprit would get enough time to get away with the loot.

'You know, we studied together in London.'

I furrowed my eyebrows. I remembered Prem saying something about them studying together, but not clearly.

'Oh yes, we were both packed off to England to study when we were eighteen, to be in college together. Our parents thought it was a good way to strengthen familial ties—young and alone in a foreign land, you come to know your family, and trust and take care of each other. When we returned after five years, we were closer than real siblings could be.'

'Wow. That's great.'

'The last time I stayed with him for the longest time was when he fell seriously ill.'

'Prem was seriously ill? When was that?'

'I think it was a year … no, maybe a couple of years after his divorce.'

'What hap—?'

'Hey, Veena, my little sis.' Prem walked out then.

'Bhai …'

The cousins hugged and stayed in the embrace for a while.

Before they could sit down, the gates opened and ACP Dutta's jeep drove in, followed by a cab with Rohan in it.

ACP Dutta was in crisply ironed khaki uniform with his tan shoes polished. Exactly like last time, but unlike his previous visits, he had two sub inspectors with him, who got down from the jeep while he waited for Rohan to pay his cab driver and walk up to him. From where we were, we couldn't hear the words, but it seemed like they exchanged friendly hellos before the ACP handed Rohan a paper, which Rohan only glanced at. Then Rohan, followed by the ACP, walked up the steps towards us.

'Good morning.' Rohan's eyes were red. He was clearly hungover from the previous night.

'Good morning, Rohan and ACP Dutta,' Prem said. 'Meet my cousin, Veena—she flew in from Delhi. Got here this morning.'

'Good morning, ma'am.'

'Mr Bedi, ACP Dutta here has a search warrant for all your properties, and he would like to start with this one,' Rohan announced to all of us.

Prem and I had known about it since last evening, after Rohan's visit, but we weren't supposed to show that we knew.

'You've seen the document?' Prem asked Rohan.

'Yes, Mr Bedi.'

'Then be my guest. Do you guys need me to accompany you to every room?'

'No, Mr Bedi, I will accompany the search team.' Rohan looked at the two sub inspectors.

'Thanks. I'll ask someone to take you around the house.' Prem buzzed and Damodar appeared.

Rohan and the two policemen followed the butler into the house.

'And you can join us for coffee, ACP Dutta.'

'I don't see why not.'

Our conversation started with the mundane and general but, as expected, eventually moved to the case. I asked if the

ACP had any suspects. Nil. I asked if he knew which golf club was used to murder? He said that the post-mortem report hadn't specified it in the first round. He assured us that he had asked the same question and was still waiting for the response. The police had rounded up all known miscreants in the area who had ever been booked on break-in or larceny charges but no article stolen had been recovered. The police informers had come up empty too.

'Is there some truth in what Mr Desai has been talking about?' ACP Dutta asked.

'About what—he's been talking about a lot of things ...' I asked.

'About the insurance policy?'

Prem told ACP Dutta exactly what he had narrated to me. But it had a different reaction on the ACP than it had on me. Perhaps his deduction from Prem's account made him a tad suspicious, perhaps it just solidified Prem's motive in his mind. He didn't know Prem well enough to recognise that he was totally devoid of greed. For him, money was hardly a motive at all.

The conversation ran dry after an hour.

Another hour passed by. Coffees were replenished. Veena went in for a shower and returned. Prem disappeared inside for a while. ACP Dutta excused himself to go in and check on his team. Breakfast was served. We sat and ate it in the veranda.

The two sub inspectors and Rohan finally came out around 1.30 p.m. Rohan came and sat with us while ACP Dutta walked to his officers who stood at the main door. He returned to us after ten minutes with a solemn face.

'Mr Bedi, while the boys did not find any shoes that gave away anything, do you know that one golf club is missing in one of the seven sets that are present in your house?'

'I know. One of the drivers; it broke on my recent trip to Korea.'

'I was there when it happened,' I jumped in. 'In fact, we didn't know about the details of the tragedy while we were there and didn't realise the significance of the golf club then, but I've asked our contact in Seoul to recover the club from the trash and send it to us.'

'And is there any chance we can examine that club soon?'

'I don't know. I mean, they have to track it down first.'

'So they don't have it in their possession yet?'

'As I said, I've asked them to recover—'

'Sorry, I missed that.' ACP Dutta was looking uneasy. Maybe he was having doubts about Prem.

'What is it that you're thinking, ACP Dutta?' Rohan asked.

ACP Dutta turned and gestured his men towards the jeep, where they went and waited. 'I don't know,' he started, 'the missing golf club could be construed as evidence tampering … don't you think?'

'That the missing golf club is the one used as murder weapon isn't an evidentiary fact, ACP Dutta,' Rohan said confidently.

'That is an acceptable interpretation too.' ACP Dutta scratched his chin. 'However, I'm in a dilemma here.'

'Feel free to express yourself,' Rohan said.

'Honestly, if you ask me, I'd happily go with your interpretation, Rohan, until we come across some real evidence, but this case hasn't been an ordinary one from the start. My supervisor and I don't have a highly understanding relationship, if you know what I mean, and the media and one member of the victims' family haven't stopped talking since. Let me see how I can go about this. I'll keep you posted,' ACP Dutta spoke to all of us but he looked directly at Rohan.

'You mean, you can actually make an arrest on something that flimsy?' I asked.

'Mr Malhotra, you know as well as I do that we have made arrests on even weaker evidence, or on the sheer lack of it.'

'Well, let me make the decision easy for you, ACP Dutta.' Rohan finally pulled out the paper he had been carrying since yesterday. 'I have an anticipatory bail to enlarge Mr Bedi on the grounds that the arrest is being made on unsubstantiated evidence. It clearly points out that an arrest cannot be made if there is lack of evidence that can prove him guilty. The missing golf club is just that, isn't it?'

ACP Dutta took the paper and read it once, twice. Then he allowed himself a smile. 'Totally acceptable,' he said, pocketing the piece of paper. 'How soon can we get the broken golf club back?'

Rohan looked at me.

'I don't know. I'll call Seoul again today. But wouldn't it be easier if you could ask the pathologist who performed the autopsy to identify which particular golf club was used as the murder weapon?'

'That will be my next visit after I leave from here, Mr Malhotra, don't worry.'

'Thank you, ACP Dutta.' Prem, who hadn't spoken for a while, got up as it was evident ACP Dutta was finished here. 'When would you like to visit my office?'

'Tomorrow?'

'May I request you to be discreet, please?'

'You can count on that, Mr Bedi.'

'Thank you once again.'

ACP Dutta finally walked to his jeep, followed by Rohan. The two spoke in soft whispers, standing away from the other policemen, before the ACP got into his jeep and left.

ROHAN MALHOTRA

As I walked back after seeing off ACP Dutta, I was a bit uneasy. A lot of what-ifs hopped around in my foggy brain, which was still recovering from the previous night. The excitement of being an advocate for Mr Bedi was subdued by the complications it seemed to carry. My predominant worry at this moment was how to approach him. I had jumped into the fray and managed to get an anticipatory bail for him, but this looked far from over. The way it was going, it wasn't far-fetched to infer that this case could go to court. If ACP Dutta got another morsel of evidence, besides the missing golf club, he'd be obligated to take his investigation to the public prosecutor, who wouldn't miss the opportunity of filing the case against Mr Bedi. Would I represent him then? Or would all my smart work till this point be swept aside with Mr Bedi hiring Mr Dadawala? I was getting increasingly anxious, and on that short walk from the jeep to the veranda, I decided I had to show some confidence. I could do this.

'Thank you, Rohan,' Mr Bedi said when I returned.

'We need to talk, Mr Bedi.' Yes, I surprised myself. My voice held no nervousness.

'Of course.'

I looked at Dad, then at Mr Bedi's cousin.

'There isn't anything to screen from them, is there?' Mr Bedi asked.

I shook my head. There was nothing I was going to say that they couldn't be around for.

'I think we should be prepared for the worst, Mr Bedi. By that I mean that this case might get dragged into court before we know it.'

'What makes you think that?'

'For one, the missing golf club will be the first hurdle. I doubt if Mr Lee will find the broken one. Then, with you being the insurance beneficiary, the police will be in their right to suspect that you had a motive—' I stopped when I saw Dad fidgeting in his seat, like he wanted to stop me right there, but Mr Bedi looked at him and then gestured for me to carry on. 'We have one missing piece of evidence, and a strong motive, and not to forget the matching shoe size. ACP Dutta—however friendly he has been so far—will have to speak to the public prosecutor very soon. We are covered by the bail, but that does not stop them from filing a case.' I finished.

'Based on?' This question was from my father.

'We don't know what we don't know, Dad, and that is the challenge. So far the police haven't released any information that points in any other direction …'

'Hmm …' Mr Bedi didn't say anything more. *Hmm*? What kind of a man said 'hmm' to a looming accusation of murder?

'Will you represent me?' he finally asked.

'You want me to be your defence advocate should the charges against you be brought up in court?'

'Yes, is there a problem?'

'No.'

'Yes,' Dad charged in. 'Don't get me wrong, Rohan. You've done a fantastic job with the bail, but, quite frankly, you don't have the experience to represent anyone in a murder trial. I don't doubt your capability, but I worry about your inexperience.'

'Tej, this will be one of the easiest cases for Rohan to try, with lots of exposure.' Mr Bedi said.

'How will it be easy?' Dad asked.

'I am innocent and I know that. No one can find any evidence against me, as I haven't been near that Pali Hill bungalow in over a decade. How can the police possibly find any proof that links me to the scene of crime?' Mr Bedi was reassuring.

'Still ...'

'Come on, Tej, be positive. Rohan will represent me. And then he always has us. You and I have degrees in law, and Veena, too. That's four qualified people.'

Veena nodded her approval. 'I agree with Prem. The guilty should worry, not the innocent.'

'Get the paperwork ready, Rohan. I appoint you as my defence advocate, should this murder trial go to court.'

'Could I speak to you in private as your advocate, Mr Bedi? It'll only take a minute,' I requested.

Dad looked at me sternly.

'Of course.' He looked at Dad and Veena ji—both of them got up and went inside.

I let a minute pass to let the two get out of earshot. Then I pulled together all the confidence I could and asked, 'Mr Bedi, as your defence advocate, I need to know if you are, in any way, guilty of the murders of Mrs and Mr Desai.'

'I'm glad you asked. Do you know who hires big advocates and firms to defend themselves—those who are guilty. That's exactly what I told Tej. I am one hundred per cent innocent and, therefore, absolutely comfortable with being represented by you. While I maintain a calm façade, I am conscious that I'm being framed. I don't know why and I don't know by whom, except that Manish Desai is raging a campaign against me.'

'Thank you, Mr Bedi. I'll get all the paperwork ready.'

'Was that all?'

'Yes.'

'And don't worry about the fees.'

'Of course not.'

I wanted to ask how much, so I could update Urvee, but I restrained myself. My dad was nearing retirement, and he still made more money working for Mr Bedi than Urvee and I made together. I could always ask Dad later for an expense account to keep things moving. As they said, there was a time and place for everything.

ACP RANJEET DUTTA

As we drove back from Mr Prem Bedi's residence to the Bandra Police station, I tried to call Dr Donald D'Souza. Dr D'Souza was one of the leading morbid pathologists, and while he abhorred murder and any violent death, he lived and breathed to dissect corpses. Bald by choice, tall and gangly, he was fifty, a bachelor and smoked like a steam engine. I had a suspicion that he chain-smoked only to escape the putrid odour of death that lingered around him all through the day. I had worked alongside him for the past four years, ever since I got transferred to Mumbai, and I remembered the first autopsy I attended with him—he had told me that he was the only medium via which the dead could tell their tales. I'd found that quite dramatic.

I got through to Dr D'Souza's office but was told that he was in the operation theatre with a victim brought in from Chembur this very morning. I knew he never took phone calls during post mortems, notwithstanding the fact that his patients could hardly be offended by the interruption. His assistant told me he'd only be free at five. It was Friday and I had to see him today. The missing golf club was all we had yet. Meeting Dr D'Souza was therefore urgent, though I didn't know if he could actually determine from the shape of dents on victims' skulls what golf club it was.

As we drove to Bandra, my team members, who had searched Mr Bedi's apartment, told me that they had gone through all available golf sets and shoes with the UV lights and luminol spray but couldn't find any trace of blood or any other body fluid that could incriminate the owner. They had searched everywhere, including the caretaker's quarters behind the main building, but had found nothing.

Rohan was right—I couldn't convict someone based on a missing piece of evidence. Speaking of Rohan, some people could construe I was a dishonest police officer who let the alleged accused's advocate know what my next steps were going to be in advance. I wasn't. You could say that I was saving my ass by condoning a powerful and influential man, but that would only be half the truth. I was an ambitious police officer who had, by experience in the force, learnt to sit on the fence till the last minute, and at this juncture in this case, I didn't know which side to jump. Thus, I was performing a Mr Nice Guy for Mr Bedi and his advocate, and simultaneously looking for the truth. And if the truth came out with evidence against Mr Bedi, so be it.

When I got to my office, I had a message waiting at my desk telling me to call my boss, DCP Dilip Mathur. I despised Mathur and the feeling was mutual. He was from the State Police cadre and I was an IPS officer. He was DCP at forty-five, and my next promotion would make me his peer at thirty-two. He loathed all IPS officers, not just me. However, I found him disgusting because he was a bare-faced pussy hound, and I was told his wife had left him for that reason. He had bullied my predecessor into rounding up young hookers for him. Mathur would get drunk, tie them up and sodomise them—sometimes he kept them chained all weekend. Who could they complain to? And though I had refused point blank to feed his feral libido, I was still a wimp for not making a formal complaint against him for rape and torture. Like most other people in the world, I had ignored the undesirable.

I looked at the message at my desk and wondered what had prompted the bastard to seek me. We didn't normally meet alone. I had closed more cases in the last four years than he had in his entire life, and I wasn't accustomed to taking useless orders from him. But disregarding a written instruction from a superior would be considered intentional contemptuous behaviour, a break in procedure that bureaucracy abominated and penalised. I wasn't going to grant Mathur that joy.

When I walked into DCP Mathur's office, the first thing that hit me was the scent; it was a concoction of roses and horse-piss. He looked up as I got into his office and smiled. His hand reached for his thin pencil moustache. I followed his eyes and spotted Manish Desai sitting there with a young woman in a short skirt; it took me no time to comprehend what had transpired. Manish Desai must have heard about Mathur's weakness for girls and he was there to negotiate. He had obviously failed to impress me much, except for the affidavit that resulted in me getting a search warrant. He wanted Mr Bedi arrested, and that hadn't happened yet.

'Good afternoon, sir. You called for me.' I purposefully ignored Desai. If he had shown discourtesy of bypassing me to see my boss, I had no reason to extend civility anymore.

'I'm sure you've met Mr Manish Desai and his girlfriend, Sonia …'

Girlfriend? Yeah, right.

'I've met Mr Desai, of course. Hello, Miss Sonia.'

'Hi.'

Run while you can, I wanted to tell her.

'So what have you got for us now, Mr Desai?' I took over the conversation before DCP Mathur could speak. 'We've only just returned from the search of Mr Bedi's residence.'

'Did you find anything?' Desai sounded eager.

'I don't have to tell you that but I will. We found nothing.' I did not want to reveal the information regarding the missing golf club. This man, I knew, would run to the media and wouldn't stop whinnying till every newspaper, rag and television channel ran the news.

'That is strange—'

'What's strange about it? Just because you and your family have had some history with Mr Bedi does not mean that he killed your brother and his wife in cold blood,' I said sternly without raising my voice. 'May I request you to let us run our investigation according to procedure rather than come here every day to waste our time?'

'I was only trying to help. As a matter of fact, I just told DCP Mathur that I remembered, after we spoke yesterday, that Rea Desai had actually met Mr Bedi personally.'

I had to give it to him; he was a proficient liar. After he had left my office yesterday, I had ordered all telephone records for the Desai residence telephone and their mobiles. There was no call to or from Mr Bedi's office, residence or mobile. I suspected that after he had told me that Rea Desai might have had a *supposed* conversation with her ex-husband realized that I'd ask the telephone companies for their records, he got the jitters. He was now back-pedalling from the earlier alleged telephonic conversation to a meeting, which could well have been equally imaginary.

'I thought you said they might have spoken on the telephone.'

'As I said, it completely slipped my mind that Rea had told Mahesh, who confided in me, that Mr Bedi and she had met. I guess I'm still in too much of a shock from the murders ...'

Well played, asshole!

'So it wasn't Rea who told you directly? She told your brother, who *confided* in you?'

'That is correct.'

'So when and where did the two meet?'

'You mean Rea and Mr Bedi?'

'No, Santa Claus and Mandrake, the magician. Of course, Mrs Rea Desai and Mr Bedi; who else would I be interested in at this moment?'

'I don't know where or when exactly.' He looked up like he was recalling something. He was an admirable actor. 'Mahesh told me about it a month ago, so it should be a little before that time.'

'And what exactly did he *confide* in you?'

'That the two had met.'

'And ... ?'

'He said they had met regarding the insurance endowments that were due this year.'

Manish Desai was gunning for Mr Bedi, no doubt about it. I needed to ascertain soon that if Mr Bedi was removed from the scene, who would become the beneficiary of Rea's share of the fifty crores? The insurance company, obviously, wouldn't reveal this information to me unless I had a court order. I cursed myself for not asking Mr Bedi; he might have known and, maybe, divulged the information to me.

'So that's it? You don't have any specifics about the conversation or the meeting, except that they spoke about the insurance?'

'That's it. I'm telling you Mr Bedi is behind this, just arrest him.'

'Where did the two—Mrs Rea Desai and Mr Bedi—meet?' I was getting used to ignoring his waffle.

'He didn't tell me that. It wasn't important at the time so I didn't bother asking. It's only now that I remembered it so I thought I should inform you.'

What a model citizen!

'So you don't know where Mr Bedi met your sister-in-law, you have no idea what conversation they had when they met, except that your brother fed you some crumbs about insurance, and you want us to go arrest Mr Bedi?'

'We will definitely look into this, Mr Desai,' DCP Mathur interjected. I had seen him intermittently eyeing Sonia the whole time and I guess the blood was gushing to between his legs now. It was getting to four o'clock and the poor girl had no idea what she had signed up for.

'Thank you, DCP Mathur. I'm really grateful that we have officers like you who listen to the bereaved relatives ...'

Manish Desai was such a phoney piece of shit.

'You're welcome, Mr Desai.'

Suddenly, as if Manish Desai got some inspiration, he turned to me. 'You said you did not find anything implicating

Mr Bedi in the murders at his residence. Have you searched his office and other properties?'

'We will, of course, search them too.'

'If you don't find anything, that should not exonerate him; he might have disposed of the murder weapon and the shoes.'

'Are you an advocate, Mr Desai?' I was annoyed now.

'No, but it does not take an advocate to—'

'Listen to me,' I interposed. 'Listen carefully, as I will not say this again, but I'll make it simple. This is my investigation, I'm running it and I have closed more murder cases in Mumbai than anyone else. I do not, I repeat, *do not* need your constant advice on what should or should not happen. So unless you have some evidence that isn't bare-faced bullshit, I strongly recommend that you stay away from me and the investigation. I understand you have lost family members and we, the police, are doing whatever we can. I cannot turn a blind eye to all other possibilities because you hold a grudge against one man in Mumbai.'

He looked agape. DCP Mathur was astonished at my firmness too. As if I cared. If he as much as raised a warning eyebrow at me, I had decided I'd follow him after this meeting and see where he took the girl and then whip his ass the next day.

'Now, if you would please excuse me, I have work to do and I'm sure so does DCP Mathur. Have a good day.' I walked out.

At 4 p.m., I called Dr D'Souza's office again. They told me he hadn't come out of the theatre yet. I requested them to tell him to either give me a call the next time he took a smoke break or wait for me at the centre since I was coming there. I called up forensics again to check if they had recovered any hair, body fluid, blood, skin residue or anything that could provide us with any further clues to the identity of the killer. They said that they were still analysing the material and promised to send me a detailed report before 8 p.m. that night.

Then I left to see Dr D'Souza.

Perhaps the autopsy suite was initially established in Byculla to complement the courts in Mazgaon, though no one was sure, and if there was some history, it was now lost. However, JJ Post Mortem Centre was one of the leading centres in Mumbai. I knew it would take me forty minutes to an hour, depending on traffic, to get to Byculla and I did not want to take any chances. We ran into traffic, but my driver took a diversion from the other side of Mahim and we got to Byculla a minute before five. Dr D'Souza was still in the theatre, but that was okay. I had been into that theatre for my cases a number of times and there was no reason why I couldn't go in now. I donned the white paper overalls, put on a face mask and walked in.

Though the odour of death permeated the air, a much stronger smell made me queasy the moment I stepped in. I could see Dr D'Souza supervising the stitching up of a female corpse.

'What brings you here?' he asked as I approached him.

'The Desai murders.'

'If I'm not mistaken, I sent the report yesterday itself.'

'I know, but I wanted to clarify something.'

'Give me five minutes.'

He whispered some final instructions to his assistant, washed his hands, binned his mask and gestured me to follow him out from the rear exit where, I knew, he'd light up immediately.

'What is it you're after, Ranjeet?' He said, exhaling a plume of smoke.

'You confirmed in the report that the murder weapon was a golf club, right?'

'Yes.'

'How did you verify that?'

'The indentation on the skulls. Both victims were hit by the same weapon. It was blunt, long-handled and metal. By process of elimination we knew it wasn't a hockey stick, hammer and the likes, and were in a conundrum till we saw a parallel-striped imprint—on one side of the gashes in both victims—that is typical to the face of a golf club. We then closely examined the other side of the laceration and it had marks of the cavity that the golf club has at the back of the face. We brought in some samples and presto, it matched the dimensions and the angle, which confirmed it was a golf club. As a rule, I don't confirm anything in a report that I am not a hundred per cent convinced of, but why do you ask? Do you doubt my judgement?'

'Not in the least, Dr D'Souza. I'm terribly sorry if it came across like I was challenging it. That wasn't the intention.'

'No offence taken, my boy, none whatsoever, but I can sense that something's bothering you. What is it?'

'I'm wondering that if you brought in samples of golf clubs, will you be able to somehow confirm what golf club it was?'

'What do you mean what golf club? You mean do I know the make or brand? That will be—'

'That would have been my second request. But at the moment what I'd like to know is what club was used. I was asked the same question and I drew a blank, so I did some research on the internet. There are different clubs for different strokes. The three most popular ones are—irons from numbers one till nine, drivers which have thick heads, and putters. All of them have different angles, shapes and strength, if that's any help to you.'

Dr D'Souza looked at me as blankly as I must have looked at Rohan when he had asked me the same question.

'I do remember the shape, but I wouldn't know …' he took the last drag of his second cigarette, exhaled and stubbed it in the nearby ashtray. 'However, I'll look at the photographs and notes we have on file. We've also kept those golf clubs so I could compare the indentations and angles on the victims' skulls once again.'

'When can you do it?'

'First thing, Monday morning. Call me after ten.'

'Sounds good to me, Dr D'Souza. I'll owe you one.'

'Well, if everyone in the Mumbai police department paid all that they owed me in the last twenty-five years, I'd be a zillionaire today.' He laughed, and I laughed with him.

My driver brought me back to the Bandra office by 7.30 p.m. I got in and made myself a coffee and waited for the forensic report. I wasn't going anywhere. I wasn't married, I didn't have a girlfriend at the moment, and I was not a skirt-chaser like DCP Mathur who, I reckoned, would be screwing Manish Desai's so-called girlfriend at the moment.

The forensics obliged me earlier than they had promised. They had unearthed nothing that I did not already know. No DNA of anyone other than the two victims and those who were known visitors to the place, had been found—Manish Desai's presence was established all over the house, including the main bedroom where the dead bodies were discovered; the gardener's DNA was found only in the living room and the kitchen, the maidservant's and cook's in parts of the house too. Nothing else was recent enough to be suspicious. However, a salient point of the report caught my eye. The team had observed that there could have been two perpetrators instead of one. They found that the size and material of the gloved hand on both the inside and the outside doorknob was different to the gloved hand that had broke open the safe in the house. They could identify that with the material of the glove—there was a print from a latex surgical glove on main door, and the other pair was cotton. They offered two possible scenarios—either it was two individuals that had jointly committed the crime, or the single offender had changed gloves. The last page said that they were still looking into this and this wasn't the final report.

I closed the file and pondered.

Why would a killer change gloves halfway through the job? Did he end up ripping the first pair somehow? If he accidently slit them, what was the probability that he had carried a second pair in his pocket? But why would he do that? For what benefit? I wasn't thrown by this discovery, although it was a bit confounding. I thought for a long time, forming and shredding theories. Then it hit me. The first pair of gloves couldn't have been discarded because the marks on the inside doorknob could only have been put there after the crime had been committed and the person or persons were exiting the house. So then, this could be a two-person job. But I had no further data to advance my theory. I wasn't willing to even entertain the notion that two random men broke and entered the same house in succession on the same night and neither was aware of the other. That was the least possible scenario. The burglary angle looked all too convincing now.

And Rea and Mahesh Desai had become collateral damage. Pure and simple.

ROHAN MALHOTRA

'What do you mean you didn't discuss the fee?' Urvee couldn't believe I hadn't agreed on a fee for defending an accused in a murder trial, and I could hardly blame her for losing it a bit.

'There's a time for everything, babe.' I tried to sound magnanimous, but intrinsically, I agreed with her. It hadn't been my smartest move.

'Don't you *babe* me!' she fumed.

'The case might never go to court ...'

'All the more reason to know what you'll be paid if it doesn't go to court.' Then after a pause, she added, 'Does that mean you don't get paid at all?'

'I didn't mean that. It's just that he's asked me to be on standby for the time being, just in case ... and I've got the contract signed.' That was the truth; that was all I had done after leaving Altamount Road. I faxed the papers and got a return fax all, signed. 'So it isn't like Mr Bedi would run away.'

'What if he loses the case? Who'll pay you?'

'What? He can't lose. The police don't have any evidence.'

'Mr Advocate, do you think no innocent person has ever been convicted in this country?'

She had a point.

'What if you simply get outmatched by some big prosecutor?' Urvee pressed on.

'Huh?'

'You say the police don't have any evidence. What evidence do you have that Mr Bedi didn't do it, other than your dad's blind trust in him?'

I had no response. Her question only worried me more. *What if* Mr Prem Bedi got convicted? *What if* he was really guilty? *What if* I got no fees at the end of it all? *What if* my future had nothing in store but handling cases like Ramdeen's?

I thought about calling Dad, but what would I say? That I needed an expense account? I had never let him know that my legal practice was only paying the bare minimum.

'Rohan, Rohan … are you listening to me?'

'Yes, sorry, I'd drifted away.'

'No, I'm sorry for being so harsh. I'm sure it will all even out. I was only being a bitch.'

'I love this bitch.'

'That's because you're a dog.'

I looked up at the ceiling, made an 'O' with my lips and feigned a howl. 'Isn't it mating time?'

'Pia hasn't slept yet.'

'It's Friday night. Let's put her to sleep and then snuggle and watch a movie.'

I lay there after; Urvee had gone to sleep and I stared at her slim and gorgeous rump like some pervert. I couldn't sleep a wink; I felt like someone had injected a double macchiato into my veins. Urvee was spot-on—supposing the case actually went to court and I got an experienced and strong opponent? Any Goliath could crucify me, and then, if Mr Bedi got convicted … I didn't even want to think about that. Instead, I decided to call Dad first thing in the morning.

My conversation with Dad was brief. He was sympathetic and, on his own, asked me to pick up a cheque for five lakh on Monday morning. That would be paid as a settlement for proactively arranging the anticipatory bail. I guess he had either already discussed it with Mr Bedi or the amount was too trivial to need the Mogul's authorisation. Dad also told me that going forward, I could ask for the amount to be replenished as and when the balance dipped below a lakh.

Urvee was exultant at breakfast. A long list of what we wanted to buy started taking shape. Why did an influx of sudden cash make my wife want to buy a new dining table? She also wanted new clothes for Pia and her, which I understood. And Urvee deserved all of this and more, so we went shopping on Saturday, ate out in a fancy Italian restaurant after a very long time and paid with my credit card without a hint of worry. I had earned five lakhs for five hours of work. I normally made ten thousand rupees after wearing away my heels for months. I knew this payment could very well be a one-off, but I didn't want that realism to dampen my family's spirits today.

ACP RANJEET DUTTA

I lived alone in a two-bedroom apartment at Lokhandwala that I once shared with my girlfriend Jasmine, who I had every plan to marry, but cancer had taken her away. She didn't notice the lump in her left breast till much later, and by the time she realised something was very wrong and got to the doctor, it had metastasised and her game was practically over. Jasmine passed away a year ago. My friends tried everything to help me out of my loneliness, but I wanted to be alone for some time. As months passed, they got busy with their own lives and I lost touch with most of them. Now, I revelled in my solitude. I partied with myself, drinking whisky alone, which is never a good idea. And to avoid getting wasted over weekends, I made it a point to work through them. However, this last week had been very hectic and I decided to take a break.

When I arrived at work on Monday morning at nine-thirty, I wished I hadn't taken the weekend off.

DCP Mathur had called in and briefed Advocate Gajpati Apte, a public prosecutor. Apte was a known scoundrel. People like him should be given a psychological test before they are appointed prosecutors for the State. Apte was a mean, bad-mouthed yob. He didn't care if the person was innocent or guilty, he just wanted to prosecute and convict. I had an idea of what might have happened. Manish Desai's alleged girlfriend, Sonia, had probably been as good in bed as promised. My guess was that Desai and DCP Mathur spoke sometime over the weekend or maybe met with or without Sonia, and firmed up the plan. Subsequently, DCP Mathur must have called Apte and set up an early morning appointment at the police station. That was the only possibility because most days DCP Mathur did not arrive in office till eleven, but he was in early today, wearing contact lenses instead of his usual gold-rimmed glasses.

Apte must have latched on to the case the moment he heard the name of Mr Bedi. He would go all out to file a murder case against him. Filing a court case wasn't the most difficult task in this country. It would take a while for the case to come to court for a trial and DCP Mathur—based on his conversations with Manish Desai or on Sonia's curves and curls—had probably convinced Gajpati Apte that the police would gather incontestable evidence by then. I wouldn't have been surprised if Manish Desai had agreed to share some of the booty that might come his way with these louts.

I wanted to explode, but there was only so much I could do when the man in front of me was my commanding officer.

'See what I've done for you, ACP Dutta.' Mathur waived papers at me as I entered.

'We won't be easy on him because he is rich and powerful. Everyone's equal in the eyes of the law,' added a smug Apte. Apte was five-feet-five, with a six-month-pregnant belly, dark, greasy Brylcreemed hair, nicotine-stained fingers and square-framed glasses. He was always attired in a white shirt and a black ill-fitting suit, with a clip-on tie in the inside pocket of his jacket. He was like the slow-burning amber that wanted to spark one last time, and an association with Prem Bedi, even in a case against the Mogul, might grant his career a fresh lease.

'What's the rush to file the case, sir? Why don't we wait till we have some concrete evidence against—'

'I want his bail revoked as soon as possible,' the idiot Apte cut me off. 'DCP Mathur told me he has taken anticipatory bail, which only substantiates his guilt.'

I wanted to snap at Apte for interrupting me, but I didn't want to make him my enemy. Even though I despised his personality and tactics, he had been on my side when I needed a prosecutor. And Apte hadn't come here on his own; he was called here and handed the case, which, bearing in mind *who* the suspect was, any prosecutor would have accepted.

I decided not to share the forensics report I had received Friday evening. The same report had been sent to DCP Mathur. He had been privy to the same information, so if he cared to read and analyse it, he could work out the implications himself.

The two men in front discussed the next steps—who, what, when, where. My mind had already drifted to my next immediate conundrum. Should I call and tell Rohan about the latest development or let him know through the court or his client, who would receive the papers in a short while? I had already helped Rohan before, and this was privileged information, for next thirty minutes—tops. Apte would ensure the media knew about his filing the case before the hour was up. It was best for me to inform Rohan that DCP Mathur was out for Mr Bedi's blood.

It was 10.30 now. I walked out of the police station, pulled out my mobile and called Dr D'Souza regarding the golf club.

'Good morning, Dr D'Souza. How are you?'

'Good you called now and not earlier. I got delayed coming in this morning.'

'Did you manage to check the golf club?'

'Yes, I just finished the tests. I can confirm with ninety-nine per cent confidence that it was a number seven iron.'

'Thanks, but just for the record, what could it be for the other one per cent?'

'A number six or eight iron, but I have another expert coming in to determine that.'

Dr D'Souza knew that even one per cent could create reasonable doubt in a murder trial. However, he didn't know that in this case as long as it wasn't the driver—which was the only missing club in Mr Bedi's set—it didn't matter.

'Thanks, Doctor.'

'Does that help?'

'Certainly. Of course, you'll be called to testify in court.'

'My pleasure. If nothing else, I'll get to meet Prem Bedi.'

I hung up and called Rohan.

GAJPATI APTE

I had been a public prosecutor since the day I began my legal career. I had existed on the margins, subsisted on a meagre salary, minimum benefits and fringe cases. My success rate, while nothing to be proud of, had been moderate. I wasn't one of the bigwig advocates I had aspired to be when I passed out with my law degree.

My grouse was that although I was entirely capable of carrying out legal proceedings in the toughest of battles, I had never got a single opening to get noticed, to demonstrate my talents. I kept myself afloat by prosecuting small fish. But it had to start at some point before the game was over for me. I was close to fifty now, and if I didn't take the opportunity DCP Mathur had just offered me, I'd probably remain a non-entity my entire life. Prem Bedi was one of the biggest fishes in the ocean, and if that wasn't enough, this was a murder trial. As such, based on what DCP Mathur had revealed to me, the evidence was not even circumstantial. Yes, Bedi played golf, and yes, Bedi wore size eight-and-a-half shoes. Was that enough in a murder trial? I'd say hardly, but it appeared that the search and investigation wasn't yet over so there was a chance they might find something to incriminate Bedi. If they did, I was made. The only thing that provided me with a splash of confidence was the bereaved brother's story. I was moved by his interview, and he had proffered a perfect fiscal motive that could work against Bedi. I could tell DCP Mathur that the police did not have enough evidence to take the case to trial yet, and thereby miss the opportunity, and in the bargain also cause friction between him and me. The DCP wasn't going to stop if I had declined the case. He seemed quite convinced and motivated of Bedi's involvement in the murders. He'd call some other struggling prosecutor and pass on the break. Someone would file the case, of that I was certain. The loss wouldn't be DCP Mathur's, it would only be mine. On the contrary, if I took the case, I would be in the headlines. Not sure about national, but local Mumbai coverage was definite.

I would get noticed, whether I won or lost. I could predict that the old fox would hire one of the biggest legal criminal defence advocates in the country to defend him. Why wouldn't he, when money was hardly an issue for him? They would come up with all the experience of big trials and argue me out of the race, but that would come later. Plus, I couldn't overlook the fact that I was being backed by a DCP.

TEJ MALHOTRA

I had never been so happy in my entire life. When Rohan called to tell me that the golf club used to murder Rea and Mahesh Desai was an iron—I honestly couldn't care less if it was number six or seven—and not the driver, the biggest load I had been carrying on my chest vanished. In any murder trial, if the murder weapon was missing and the defendant had lost the same weapon, suspicion began to grow like a wart. Media would have had a field day had they found out. The prosecuting advocate would have laboured the point a thousand times till the judge actually started visualising the defendant holding the murder weapon. It had happened in so many trials. Of course, the police and the court couldn't convict someone if they didn't find the murder weapon, but I wasn't concerned about that anyway. Even a shadow of doubt on his innocence—whether the court convicted him or not—and his reputation would be in tatters. The respect he commanded would be wiped out. It would be difficult to engage with existing business partners, forget adding new ones. People would forever point fingers. It would be a pyrrhic victory—victory that was as good as defeat.

I broke the good news to Prem and Veena over drinks.

'I told you I am innocent,' Prem said joyously.

'I was still worried for you, my friend.'

'I am very impressed with your son, Rohan.' Veena's words filled me with pride. Rohan had done a stellar job so far.

'Have you agreed on his fees?' Prem questioned.

'I was hoping you'd tell me.'

'My name would have been besmirched if Rohan hadn't got the anticipatory bail in time. And now he's given us this excellent news about the golf club ...'

'Can I suggest something?' Veena interrupted.

Both of us turned to her.

'Give him ten per cent of the insurance endowment when you win. Plus expenses, of course.'

'You mean, *if* I win.'

'No, *when* you win.'

'You okay with that, Tej?' Prem looked at me.

'That's a huge sum.'

'It's a huge case.'

The three of us clinked our glasses and smiled.

ROHAN MALHOTRA

Thanks to my new friend ACP Dutta, I had known about public prosecutor Apte preparing to file a double-murder charge against Mr Bedi, and I informed Mr Bedi and Dad on the phone about it before I drove to the Bedi residence. Despite a fresh FIR filed by Manish Desai, we did not have to produce Mr Bedi in front of a Magistrate, as a Sessions Court Judge had already signed off the bail. I was there to represent him. And Gajpati Apte was there to insist and plead that Mr Bedi's bail be revoked.

Magistrate Ramesh Gupta, a timid, soft-spoken gentleman in his fifties, did not find any reasonable grounds for revoking the bail.

'But, Magistrate sahib, Prem Bedi is an extremely powerful man, and if he is enlarged on bail until the case is decided, he might tamper with evidence or buy or coerce witnesses.' Apte argued.

'My client has no criminal history, and the prosecuting advocate has no witnesses yet, so who does my learned friend think Mr Bedi will buy or coerce?' I jumped in.

'At least you should allow the police to detain him for twenty-four hours for questioning, Magistrate sahib.'

'There are no grounds on which I can let you detain a person who has no criminal history. If you bring me any new evidence that has been discovered after the bail was granted, I shall consider your motion, Mr Apte. Unfortunately, until then, I see no reason to revoke the bail.' Magistrate Gupta was firm.

Apte didn't look pleased.

Then the Magistrate turned to me and passed his next diktat. 'And, Mr Malhotra, you are responsible for making Mr Prem Bedi available for any questioning by the police at the Hill Road, Bandra Police Station or at Mr Bedi's residence, whenever asked by DCP Mathur or his delegated representative. Though I believe he has already given a recorded statement to ACP Dutta.'

'Yes, sir.'

'Mr Apte, please inform DCP Mathur that whenever the police wants to question Mr Bedi further for what is not already on tape, they have to give a minimum six-hour notice, and they are legally obliged to have his advocate, Mr Rohan Malhotra, physically present. Is that clear?'

We both nodded.

I was feeling a bit pleased with my performance till the Magistrate threw in the curve ball.

'Mr Malhotra, I want you to submit your client's passport to this court.'

'Sir, Mr Prem Bedi is a businessman. He has to travel to take care of businesses around the world. How is it even possible for a person of his standing to submit—'

'Mr Malhotra, I do not need a synopsis on Mr Bedi's business activities. I want his passport submitted within the next twenty-four hours. Am I clear?'

I had to succumb. I didn't see any merit in arguing further. Magistrate Gupta had made up his mind.

A month had passed since Mr Prem Bedi had appointed me as his defence advocate and my world had changed since that fateful day.

I had returned to my Lower Parel office and offered the exciting bevy of cases I was currently handling to other advocates in my building. Most advocates there, as I mentioned before, were struggling like me, and the distribution was over in thirty minutes. My colleagues appreciated the gesture, and lauded and congratulated me on bagging a case that only came by once in a blue moon.

Accordingly, I informed my clients that I would no longer be their advocate on record, but I had passed on their files to other esteemed advocates and they were in safe hands. Obviously, the clients had a choice to disagree and switch to some other advocate of their liking but, frankly, I didn't expect any to transfer. Most of my clients were like Ramdeen, who went with the cheapest representation. As a last favour—who knew what would be the outcome of Mr Bedi's murder trial—I told them they did not owe me anything for representing them so far, but they could discuss the fees with their new advocates going forward.

Though I hadn't wanted to, I had no choice but to move out of my current office, as the media had been following me around from the time it was announced that I was representing Mr Prem Bedi. The crowd in the small building was making it difficult for clients to approach other advocates in the premises. I did not vacate my office, but on Mr

Bedi's insistence, I started working out of one of his vacant apartments on Turner Road in Bandra. This also meant that I was closer to my new friend Ranjeet Dutta and my new adversary, DCP Mathur.

I had been interviewed multiple times by various local television channels and newspapers, and had become something of a known face. Dad had advised me against making any comments on the case at hand. I had trained myself to say *'no comments'* to any undesirable question to such an extent that I ended up saying 'no comments' to some of Urvee's questions too, which did not go down well. Initially she laughed, but when I used it a few times, she was put off.

I had no one to give me briefs on previous cases and decisions, so I hired an assistant out of the expense account I had been given—Sheila Agarwal. She was young, energetic and sharp. She still had to sit for her final examinations in Pune, but had a few weeks' window for an internship and provided me with a reference from her college.

Moreover, she looked like the girl next door in a pretty sort of a way, but was no siren. She mostly wore shirts and jeans to work and didn't look like someone who would incite any suspicion or envy in Urvee. I knew I would be spending a lot of time locked with her in the new office alone and the last thing I desired was matrimonial discord to add to my growing list of concerns. Despite not being an advocate yet, Sheila was a great help. Someday, if this case went well, I'd have enough money to hire a full staff. However, under strict guidance from Dad, I did not divulge the details of my defence strategy even to Sheila. Neither was she present during my conversations with Mr Bedi.

I had studied the crime scene photos till the details were etched in my mind's eye. It seemed impossible that I would ever be able to erase that gruesomeness from my mind. There was no way that Mr Bedi could have done this.

I dug out myriad past cases, recent rulings and mandates from various High Courts and the Supreme Court. I read numerous law books and journals, and poured over the copious notes that Sheila made for me. I couldn't afford to miss a thing.

Urvee was not happy about me spending so much time at work. We rarely got to spend any time with each other. I asked her to take a few weeks off and go visit her parents in New Delhi with Pia, since we could afford her taking time off without pay now. She liked the idea but was reluctant to leave me alone.

'I can't slip away when you are under such stress.'

'But I'm hardly ever here. Even when I return home I'm mentally engrossed in the case.'

'Can't you come with us to Delhi for some time?'

'You know that if I could, I would …'

'I hope I don't need to worry about Sheila and you?'

'Are you crazy?'

'I had to ask.' She smiled. 'You can come with us for a few days and work from there, can't you?'

'What if the police want to question Mr Bedi the moment I leave from here? How will I get back within six hours?'

'Mr Bedi has become your life.'

'The case is due in court next month. It will be over in a week once it begins. Then we have our lives back and lots of money to take a holiday abroad.'

'Switzerland?'

'If you want.'

'Promise?'

'Promise.'

It took a lot of time but eventually, I managed to convince her. That night before she left for New Delhi, we made love twice.

Judge Amar Singh Chowdhary was appointed as the single judge for our case. No bench. He was known to be bumptious. If you even went a hair against his grain, he would hold you in contempt of court. If there was evidence against you, you were done. If the prosecution couldn't provide untainted evidence, it didn't matter how guilty the accused appeared or was made out to be, you didn't have a chance in Satan's Hell of making the charges stick. The histrionics could only work to a point. The accused's past reputation was in the past. And he ensured that Apte and I knew all this when he called us to his chambers.

'I have been watching the media circus on this case for a fairly long time. However, I want neither of you to speak to any members of the press from this moment on, till I decide on the case. If I find either of you have ignored my instructions, I'll call it a mistrial or hold you in contempt of court. No cameras will be allowed in my court. If journalists want to attend, they should attend the proceedings like a normal member of the public. They can report the case in print if they wish to.'

In plain English, it was a gag order. The advocates, their associates and their clients were prohibited to discuss or comment on anything, directly or indirectly, to any person who wasn't connected to the trial, specifically to members of the media. Of course, there would be leaks. Hadn't we all seen and read news items reported as 'an anonymous source told our reporter'? In summary, if it couldn't be tracked back to you, you were safe, but it was a risk.

He didn't care to ask for our agreements—it was a prerequisite to argue a case in his court. If you cared to complain, you'd better ask your client to hire someone else.

'And do not make the mistake of addressing me as *My Lord*. I abhor it.'

He gave us two weeks to submit all motions, evidence dockets and witness lists.

Then he dropped the bomb. 'Prem Bedi vs. the State of Maharashtra will be argued three weeks from today.'

I had anticipated two weeks after the submission of documents, but I didn't see any point in raising that.

Judge Amar Singh Chowdhary's final words were, 'Do not, I repeat, *do not* even think about requesting for an adjournment unless it is absolutely critical.'

I met Mr Bedi and Dad frequently to discuss the case. Dad was signed on as my co-advocate, so he was party to all discussions. And he had valid points in building a defence strategy. ACP Dutta had confided in me about there being two sets of gloves, highlighting the possibility of there being two suspects, which I knew would be one of the biggest arguments in my arsenal. And then there was that one detail that Mr Bedi professed, and Dad verified, which made me absolutely confident that Mr Bedi couldn't have been present at the murder scene at the time of the crime. No way.

One of the biggest worries was that I did not have a long list of witnesses. Who could I have pulled in? Many people could vouch for Mr Bedi's character, but none could provide an alibi. Not that he needed any. I wasn't planning to put Mr Bedi on the stand unless absolutely necessary. I could only think of two witnesses that I could call on stand—the first being the caretaker of the house, who lived in the quarters behind Mr Bedi's mansion. He would verify that no one left the Altamount Road residence at the time of the murders. If needed, he could explain the alarm system that he had described to ACP Dutta and his investigating team already. The second witness, the name of whom I got from Dad, was Nawab Ismail Ahmed Khan. He, too was from an erstwhile royal family in the Kutch district in Gujarat—a long-term friend of Mr Bedi and a business Mogul of rock-solid social standing. He would principally be called upon, if required, to vouch for Mr Bedi's character. I avoided calling Dad to the stand because it would look too contrived.

I would go after prosecution witnesses instead. In all trials, the burden of proof is carried by prosecutor—prove the guilt beyond reasonable doubt. The defence simply has to quash it by pointing at gaps in the prosecution's case, and hence, my entire strategy was to attack the prosecution witnesses by shooting holes in their testimonies till I tore them apart and provided reasonable doubt.

All documents were sent over to my office before the end of two weeks, as directed by Judge Chowdhury. Gajpati Apte turned out to be more sincere than I had thought. His witness list was exactly as I had estimated. However, it made me suspicious. They weren't dodging me by sending a decoy of a hundred witnesses so that I would be time-starved to go through all. A small list of witnesses usually indicated that the prosecution had something up their sleeve, some core evidence that they would bring in as a surprise, claiming that they only received it last minute. However, the witnesses listed were—

Om Yadav: Rea and Mahesh Desai's driver, who had called Manish Desai—I didn't think he was an important witness. He hadn't even so much as discovered the bodies. If he was called, he'd state the bare facts. There wasn't any merit in cross-examining him.

ACP Ranjeet Dutta: I trusted him to stick to the facts, but he was, nevertheless, a police officer. A State witness. As far as I could grasp, he was straight for the most part, and his bias would only be in favour of Mr Bedi, but I couldn't bank on that.

DCP Dilip Mathur: I very much doubted if he would even take the stand. People like him worked in the background: inciting others, applying pressure on junior officers, taking sides with Manish Desai, who had been organizing girls for him. But if he did, he would be a hundred per cent hostile. I redlined him.

Dr D'Souza: Head of Morbid Pathology, who had done the post-mortem. Challenging Dr D'Souza's résumé would be like pissing in the wind. No chance of success there, hence no point. I couldn't destroy this witness or his evidence. This witness was vital, but—and I had no experience with Dr D'Souza, so couldn't be sure about this—all experts in their fields had a tendency to become monotonous for any judge who had been on a bench for a lot of murder trials.

Dr Anup Kale: Forensics guy. He, too, would be impossible to challenge. I'd be arguing against facts and that was never a profitable strategy. Though, if the prosecutor did not bring up the two sets of gloves cited in the forensic report, I pledged to hammer that point home till Judge Chowdhary went deaf. If there were two sets of gloves, where was the other accused? Was the police sheltering someone?

Mr Manish Desai: He, I was certain, would talk himself into some trap as he rated high on the bullshit metre. Mr Bedi had provided me with enough ammunition to destroy him and his testimony. He was a key player and I promised I will make him look like one greedy loser.

And finally, *Mr Prem Bedi*.

Seeing Mr Bedi's name there was a surprise. Most public prosecutors waited for the defendant to be put on witness stand by the defence advocate, simply because Mr Bedi would understandably be a hostile witness for the prosecution. He wasn't going to admit anything even if he was guilty. Why bother? Maybe this was a ploy to misguide me too. I shared this list with Mr Bedi and Dad and they echoed my line of thinking.

I expected only DCP Mathur and Manish Desai to be hostile to the defence. ACP Dutta had helped me all along, so he would, at worst, be neutral. The other three were likely to be factual. But anything could go wrong anytime.

I practised my opening statement in front of the mirror and polished it as I went along. This was my first real court case and a big one at that. I practised till I had no perceptible tremor or anxiety in my voice, till my tone was naturally levelled.

In the week preceding the start of the trial, Sheila and I were virtually living at the Turner Road apartment-cum-office. We only went home for a few hours in the night to sleep and shower before returning to our headquarters. Logically, I was increasingly becoming a basket of nerves. The shakes had started. I could feel cold sweat running down my back intermittently, while insomnia had become my bed fellow. I had prepared enough, but I could envision that the real performance in the courtroom would be an altogether different animal to tackle.

I couldn't stop thinking about the case even if I tried. Though I missed Urvee and Pia, I had told Urvee not to call too often. Three days before the trial was to begin, Sheila suggested that we go for drinks in the evening to help me relax. I initially declined but then felt a bit guilty about it. Her internship was getting over the next day and there was no harm in going out for a quick drink and dinner. I owed her that much. We walked down to find a restaurant nearby. We decided that we wouldn't talk about the case and have just one drink each. But we didn't stop at one.

In fact, we ended up drinking more than either of us could handle. And when we got back, our office had been broken into. I checked around, but nothing was amiss. Sheila, poor girl, felt guilty for taking me out and leaving the office vacant. I explained to her that a break-in could have happened during the night too, but what worried me was that I could find nothing missing. I tried logging on to my computer and nothing looked suspicious. There wasn't anything valuable in the apartment as such, but there was some cash, and it had not been stolen. Why would someone risk breaking-in but not take the cash? That didn't make sense. But then, nothing was making sense as we were too drunk to focus, so I called a cab to take Sheila home. I told her that we'd carefully check again in the morning to see whether anything was missing.

ROHAN MALHOTRA

Sheila came in the morning—her last day—at ten. I only woke up when she rang the bell. Though she had a spare key, I had bolted the door from the inside. If someone had broken into the apartment once already, there was nothing to say they wouldn't try again. We searched our office once again, this time going over everything, and then it struck me. I had taken a printout of my opening statement that I used to practise in front of the mirror. The three pages were in a file in the bottom drawer of my desk, and they were gone, which meant that whoever had broken-in did not have much time to use a photocopier or camera phone, but had filched the originals with my comments in the margins. I discussed the same with her, and she could understand my dilemma. Whoever had done the this knew that I wouldn't have enough time to prepare another statement.

'Call the police,' she said. 'We know who it could be.'

'No. There would be no way to prove who took three sheets of paper from my office. And besides, if the police go searching, Apte or Manish Desai would know that I have discovered their little theft. Best to leave them thinking I'm unaware of it. Also, if the police get involved at this stage, the Judge would have to postpone the case, which Mr Bedi might not want.'

'I'm so sorry.'

'You don't have to be. If we hadn't gone out for dinner, I wouldn't have stayed the night here. They could have taken the papers then and maybe a lot more, if they had the entire night to snoop around.'

Sheila had to leave by four, so we ordered pizzas.

'I hope they lose this case,' she said.

'They will, don't you worry.'

We exchanged goodbyes. She promised to follow the trial, stay in touch and come back for a job if my practice flourished.

Gajpati Apte's sincerity that had impressed me when he sent me a short witness list now made sense. He wanted to exhibit he was playing fair, when he actually meant to shaft me at the last minute. I hadn't missed the writing on the wall, I had missed the entire damn wall.

Or was it Manish Desai? Even if it was Manish Desai, it only made sense if he delivered my papers to Apte—how else could he benefit from them?

I called up Dad and told him the embarrassing story of burglary at my office and that it took me more than fifteen hours to figure out what had actually gone missing. He took the news calmly. It didn't seem like he blamed me. He asked me to check if any other files were missing, but I confirmed that except for the opening statement, I hadn't printed any other document, and my computer hadn't been hacked.

'Still, check the last opened and modified dates on all documents once again while I speak with Prem. I'll call you back.'

I checked. None of the documents had been printed or opened in the last twenty-four hours.

Dad called back.

'What did Mr Bedi say? If the prosecution uses anything from my opening statement, we have cause to approach the Judge to call it a mistrial.'

'I know that, but Prem doesn't want a mistrial.'

'Why?' I knew, but I still asked.

'A mistrial does not mean Prem's case is dismissed. It will only mean that it will have to be adjourned, which Prem does not wish for. Every additional day that his case drags on, his passport remains with the court and his business suffers. He wants this mess over as soon as possible. He knows he will win, so I suggest you work on a new opening statement tonight. We can discuss it in the morning.'

'But I don't have much time,' I said, knowing it didn't matter.

'Keep it short is all I can say. Then get a good night's sleep. And do not leave the premises alone tomorrow. I'll send Mani in the morning to get the locks changed.'

MANISH DESAI

I didn't want to meet Advocate Gajpati Apte at his office; I wanted to be his friend, not just a witness in the case. Of course, I had met him a few times regarding the case in previous two months, and he coached me on what to say and what not to mention in the court, but this was different. He, too, stayed in Lokhandwala, and that made my task of meeting him at his residence simpler. I carried a bottle of Chivas, as I knew he was fond of whisky.

Ideally, I would have wanted to see him earlier and give him a lot more for his arsenal, but in the end I had decided that a last-minute filching was the best thing. But that meant that Rohan Malhotra's opening statement was the only thing I could lay my hands on.

Mr Apte lived alone in a one-bedroom apartment that resembled a squalid public toilet. The furniture looked like it was procured from a junk dealer, the cushions stank, the curtains were in tatters, the walls were as dirty as any indoor walls could possibly be—greasy black spots from visitors that had sat on the rundown sofas and rested their oily heads against the walls over the years. The paint on the walls had peeled off in most parts and the ceiling paint was cracked in several places too. In the corners of the ceilings, there were enough spiders to start a carnival. The fan—originally painted white but now yellow and grimy—spun with all the strength it had left after working for two decades or more, wobbling and threatening to descend on people who sat below it. Maybe Apte had been ambitious once, but it seemed like he had given up that dream a while back. He was halfway through a bottle of some rancid moonshine when I reached him.

'Welcome, Mr Desai—'

'Please call me Manish.' I handed the bottle to him.

'Don't spoil me, Manish. What's the point of tasting something that I can't afford? Suddenly, my local whisky'—he raised his bottle of hooch—'will not taste so good after I consume this foreign liquor.'

'Please don't embarrass me by not accepting a small gift, Mr Apte.'

He didn't need any further persuasion. He thanked me, opened the bottle and was kind enough to offer me a glass of it.

'What did you want to speak to me about?' he asked.

'It's something important about the case.'

'You don't have to worry, I'll nail Prem Bedi.'

If only it were that simple. If you had nailed anyone even ten times weaker than Bedi, you wouldn't be sitting here in this apartment, drinking cheap alcohol.

As far as I could glean from his interest, his only motivation was the publicity he could get from prosecuting Mr Bedi. If he lost the case, he didn't care; certainly not as much as I did. There was no money in it for him.

'I have some information on what Rohan Malhotra has been working on.'

'How?'

'You don't want to know that.' I pulled out three A4 pages.

He looked at them, and his face paled. 'I need to know how you got that. If they come to know, they can get us in serious trouble. Maybe even call for a mistrial.'

'No, they won't.'

'Why not?'

'I am certain that Rohan Malhotra won't even know this is missing.'

'So whom did you get this from?' he asked as he glanced at the documents.

'Straight from Advocate Malhotra's office. I expected a lot more, but Mr Bedi's camp turned out to be far too meticulous. There were no printouts of anything else and I couldn't break into his computer.'

Apte contemplated for a second. 'Thanks for this. Let me see how I can oppose some of the critical points in his opening statement so that he thinks I've anticipated his challenges without getting hold of his documents.'

'If he does not challenge it then and there, do we get an edge?'

'Of course.'

'Good. I didn't want to miss any trick here. I want to see Mr Prem Bedi get life imprisonment for the murder of my brother and his wife.'

Sonia was in my car when I came out of Apte's building. I had picked her up from another rendezvous with DCP Mathur. I was working overtime to keep both Apte and DCP Mathur happy. I took Sonia home, banged her and paid her. She asked for more, claiming that DCP Mathur was mistreating her, but I wasn't having any of that.

GAJPATI APTE

I rushed down the stairs as soon as Manish Desai left in the elevator, to follow him and check what I had suspected. He had a girl in the car. DCP Mathur had mentioned that Manish had access to some gorgeous women in Mumbai.

I was reasonably impressed with Manish Desai. An abecedarian couldn't have got into an advocate's office to purloin these documents. That took balls. Additionally, his timing was impeccable. There was hardly any chance for Rohan to discover that the papers were missing and alter his strategy. Manish looked resourceful, and the amount of money he was going to inherit indeed made him someone I needed to befriend long-term.

But the best joke in the whole drama was Prem Bedi, if you asked me. Was he a moron to have hired a novice to defend him in a murder trial? Ever since I had come to know that Rohan Malhotra was representing Bedi, my whole outlook had shifted. I no longer felt that it didn't matter whether I won or lost, as there was no way I could lose. If, for instance, I was a rook on the chess board, wouldn't you have got the queen to squash me? Instead, Bedi had hired a pawn. I seriously wondered if the old man had gone senile. That was only his first mistake. My guess was that he was not even aware of our tactics—yes, we would play dirty and yes, we would do anything to win. There was a lot at stake for Manish and I.

I had a ton of work now. I had to go through that amateur's statement and prepare responses. His opening argument wasn't bad, and would have taken me by surprise, but now I had him by the gonads. I had been livid ever since that Magistrate had declined my request to revoke Bedi's bail. How had Rohan managed to get the anticipatory bail? And why? Bedi hadn't been declared a suspect by the police till DCP Mathur and I had met. Why was the application for bail even submitted in the first place? Were there feelers sent to the Bedi faction that it was an imminent possibility? I couldn't think of anyone but a mole in the police department who had informed them. And though I wouldn't bet my apartment on it, I had a reasonable idea that it was ACP Dutta. He had indicated the other day that he did not feel too inclined to file the case yet. I had worked with him in the past and he was too honest for my liking, and I was aware that DCP Mathur and he weren't exactly Jai and Veeru. I made a note of warning DCP Mathur when I met him next.

ROHAN MALHOTRA

Fort Mumbai got its name from Fort George, built by the East India Company to fortify the then Bombay Castle from attacks by the Portuguese and Dutch pirates. The fort was demolished in 1865, and though only crumbling ramparts now remained, the name had stuck. Besides other businesses and embassies, the area also housed the Bombay High Court.

I arrived there minutes after 8 a.m., much before Mr Bedi and Dad, to avoid the media madness outside the court. Even at this hour, I could see the crowd gathering, and I knew these people were there chiefly for my client.

Judge Chowdhary had asked us to meet him in his chambers before the trial began, for any motions that we wanted to file. Gajpati Apte walked in two minutes after me.

'Any preliminary matters to discuss, gentlemen … any submissions, motions?'

'None, Your Honour,' I said.

'Only one, Your Honour. We want the bail for the defendant revoked.' Apte said.

'On what grounds, Mr Apte?'

'The accused is likely to take flight, Your Honour.'

'If I'm not mistaken, Mr Apte, you had filed the same submission to the previous Magistrate, and it was declined. And the accused hasn't fled yet, so why should he flee now?'

'May I please, Your Honour?' I interrupted, but politely.

'What is it, Mr Malhotra?'

'You Honour, my client's passport is already confiscated, so I can't see how he can flee …'

'Good point. What do you have to say about that, Mr Apte?'

'He might have a fake passport, for all we know—'

'It's highly presumptuous of you to think that a person of Prem Bedi's standing in the city has a fake passport, Mr Apte. This isn't some pickpocket we're talking about, are we?' Judge Chowdhary said.

'We cannot enlarge the accused after the evidence we present to the court today, Your Honour.'

'First of all, Mr Apte, it's not you who decides whether we can or cannot *enlarge* him, and secondly, shouldn't I decide on that after you present that evidence to the court? Motion dismissed. Anything else?'

'No, Your Honour.'

It was a small victory over Gajpati Apte but it was a victory nevertheless. I didn't give him any indication that I had discovered the theft in my office, since I didn't want him to know that I had altered my opening statement overnight. As a matter of fact, Dad had asked me to pull forward the golden nugget Mr Bedi had dispensed earlier—which, as per our original plan, we'd have used later—and which we knew would indeed be the one jarring gap in the prosecution's case, even without any of us knowing their case strategy. It was the one fact they couldn't even have imagined because, till I was told, I hadn't either.

Bring on the courtroom action. I was ready.

But, was I?

Courtrooms, with all their grandeur are still dour places, and this one was no different. Like many others in the country, it had wainscoted walls in dark wood, a central isle and benches on either side. This was one of the larger rooms, as a big turnout was expected, and it was fully packed, like an overweight man bulging out of his tight jacket. There was a railing between the viewers and performers—the advocates. There were tables for the prosecution and defence. The Judge's vast bench was directly in front of us, facing the court. The witness box was on the prosecution's side, the court clerk on mine. I had a few files at my desk, but Mr Apte had brought a truckload. He needed two associates to carry them. Keeping lots of documents on your desk showed off how much material you had studied for the case. Maybe Judge Chowdhary would be impressed, maybe he'd think Apte was a jerk. I noticed that Manish Desai was not in the courtroom, since he was listed as a witness. As a rule, witnesses do not get to watch the trial to prevent their own testimony from getting prejudiced. Although I was quite sure that Apte would keep Manish abreast of everything that transpired inside the courtroom, so that he could alter his testimony when he took the witness stand. *The poor grieving brother, the misfortune he's suffered, so pitiful!*

The noise behind me broke my reverie. I turned to see that Mr Bedi had arrived in the courtroom with Dad by his side. He wore a dark-grey suit with white open-neck shirt. Dad, of course, was in a black suit and I had a gown for him to don before the Judge arrived. I was surprised to see several people standing up in deference. I supposed that Mr Bedi and his family, over generations, had helped people in their times of need by giving to various charities. I wanted all this adulation to culminate before the Judge arrived. It might not have gone down well with the Judge, seeing people treating the accused like a Mogul in the courtroom. Both Dad and Mr Bedi came to my desk, and we shook hands before they sat down.

Ram Singh, the court clerk, arrived a little later and gave us all at the front desks a smile before taking his seat.

'All rise …'

Honourable Judge Amar Singh Chowdhary entered the courtroom. Everyone present in the courtroom stood up. He bowed to the public prosecutor and me and took his seat at the bench. We reciprocated the bow before taking our seats again. The Judge gave a cursory glance across the courtroom and his eyes rested on Mr Bedi sitting beside me. A slight smile of recognition passed his lips. From the corner of my eyes, I observed Mr Bedi nod in acknowledgement.

Ram Singh announced the case on the floor: PREM BEDI VS. THE STATE OF MAHARASHTRA, and named Gajpati Apte and I as the lead advocates.

'Are the prosecution and defence ready?' the Judge asked. It was routine question. He had already ordained that there should be no adjournments, so what the heck were we doing here if we weren't ready?

'Yes, Your Honour.'

'Mr Apte, please proceed.'

'Good morning, Your Honour. My name is Gajpati Apte and I am the prosecutor in this case. It is my pleasure to represent the people of the State of Maharashtra and Mr Manish Desai, the bereaved brother of Mr Mahesh Desai.

The defendant in this case,' Apte stopped and pointed at Mr Bedi for effect, 'mercilessly murdered Mrs and Mr Desai at their residence under the cover of darkness and escaped. Your Honour, this case is about the defendant's uncontrolled avarice and unrestrained hatred. Just to recapitulate for my own benefit, I should assert that Mrs Rea Desai was the defendant's ex-wife and had fought a bitter battle for divorce against him to get what was rightfully hers in the first place. Such is the greed of the defendant that when he came to know about the maturity of an old insurance policy, he could not see anything but a windfall coming his way. On the fateful night of June the 7th, he surreptitiously drove to the victims' residence at Pali Hill, Bandra, and butchered them with *his* golf club. Please allow me to draw a complete picture of how the defendant planned and executed the murders and exactly how it happened. He isn't what he appears to be. He isn't what the people think he is. And he isn't what the media says he is. That is all a façade, a charade. He is a powerful, cunning, wealthy man who, for money and old animosity, killed his ex-wife and her husband in cold blood. I will prove to the court that he did it. I will prove how he did it, and I will provide evidence of the same. We haven't yet found the murder weapon, but I've been assured that the investigators are very close to establishing its whereabouts ...'

Really? Close to establishing where the golf club used for the murders was? I made a note to ask ACP Dutta when I saw him during recess.

The problem with all opening statements is that the opposing advocate isn't permitted to object. Nevertheless, I could feel my pulse rising. I turned to look at Mr Bedi and then Dad. Both sat like they had taken a swig from the fountain of tranquility. Not a bead of sweat or worry showed.

Whether Apte and company had dirtied their hands by stealing my opening statement would soon be clear. My original opening statement comprised asking why, if Mr Bedi wanted to kill Rea and her husband, would he use a golf club, since he'd have known that using that would point directly at him?

'My learned friend, Mr Malhotra, will argue why would Mr Bedi use a golf club when that will make him the strongest suspect in the case ...'

I was fuming. The swine had stolen my papers after all!

'But let me enlighten the court, Your Honour. The golf club was primarily used as a double-bluff. And this is all that my learned friend will have to say in defence of their client. They do not have any witnesses; they do not have any alibi for the defendant at the time of the crime, nothing.' He exchanged glances with his associates at the prosecution table, which made me wonder if any of them had been responsible for the theft at my office.

Apte carried on and on. I wondered if the Judge would ask him to hurry it up, but he didn't.

'... this wasn't a crime of passion, Your Honour. The defendant did not meet the victims accidentally and an argument or a fight ensued. The defendant drove to Mrs and Mr Desai's residence with the intention to kill. It was a planned murder, a cold-blooded homicide ...'

Apte was now repeating himself. Judge Chowdhary began looking uninterested.

'Your Honour, I have seven witnesses and I will provide the court with enough evidence and testimonies, and at conclusion of the case, I will strongly recommend for a verdict of guilty and a death penalty for the defendant.' Apte pointed towards Mr Bedi again as if the Judge had forgotten by now who it was he had been incessantly talking about. 'Thank you, Your Honour.' He then bowed, and sat down.

'Well, that was fairly comprehensive, Mr Apte. Mr Malhotra, how long is your opening statement?' the Judge asked.

'Just a short one,' I said, looking towards the prosecution desk. I saw Apte and his associates trading glances. The thieving bastards had obviously expected a rendition of three pages that they had pinched from my office.

'Please proceed then.'

I stood up and walked from behind my desk to the forefront, facing the Judge, and introduced myself for the record. 'Your Honour, my learned friend, Mr Apte, detailed the whole incident so clearly that it sounds like a script from a bad television broadcast. Unfortunately though, I will have to term it as a flop thriller since it has a gap big enough to drive our cars through. I only have one thing to ask the court.' I turned, looked at Apte, gave him a smile and continued. 'On the fateful night of the murders, how did my client, Mr Prem Bedi, get to the Pali Hill residence of Mrs and Mr Desai? Mr Ganesh, Mr Bedi's driver for last twenty years, was not in attendance at the time of murders—estimated to be around midnight between 7 and 8 June. Mr Ganesh's sworn testimony is in the documents we've submitted to the court and also to my learned friend's esteemed office. So how did the defendant get to the murder scene? And back?'

There was an eerie silence in the courtroom. Judge Chowdhary looked at me like he wanted to say: 'He must have driven to and from the scene, wasn't that what anyone would have done? What was all the fuss about?'

'That is the large gap I referred to earlier, Your Honour. My client, Mr Prem Bedi, does not have a driving licence from the State of Maharashtra, or from any state in India for that matter, since he does not *know* how to drive any kind of motor vehicle, which my learned friend, Mr Apte, failed to check before building his entire theory.'

Judge Chowdhary looked at Mr Bedi, who nodded almost imperceptibly. I could feel the tension rising in the prosecution camp. They had certainly not expected to take this big a fall right at my opening gambit. I could see the media people furiously scribbling notes, lapping up this new information. Mr Bedi couldn't drive? Wow! Some would cover the news as *poor Prem Bedi*; others would cram pages with editorials on the *luxurious lives of the rich*.

'My learned friend might want to argue that my client could have easily taken a taxi instead.' I was on a roll now. 'Your Honour, I would like the court to take a look at my client, please. He has been on cover of every magazine in the country for last twenty or so years and on front pages of all dailies in Mumbai since the tragic murders. Is it possible that not even one of the two taxi drivers would have come forward by now to say that they had driven my client on that fateful night, especially if he was travelling with a golf club in the middle of the night? And if my client did take a taxi, where did the taxi driver take him later to hide the murder weapon?

'Your Honour, while we all want to convict the guilty, I urge the court that we must not be in any haste to penalise the wrong party. Convicting an innocent person, I strongly believe, is a bigger crime than the one already committed. That's all from me, Your Honour.' I bowed, walked back to my desk and sat down. Mr Bedi gave me an appreciative smile and a nod. Dad put his hand on mine and I knew I'd done him proud.

'Well, well, well, we have now heard both sides of the story, haven't we?' Justice Chowdhary began. 'Let's break for lunch and get back at 3 p.m.

Ram Singh stood up with a jolt like he had taken a brief nap. 'The court is recessed till 3 p.m. now. All parties must return and be in order latest by 2.55 p.m.'

We took our seats at 2.55 and you could set your clock to Judge Chowdhary's arrival on the dot.

'Had a good lunch, all?' the Judge asked no one in particular. 'Mr Apte, please call your first witness of the day.'

'Your Honour, the State would like to call on Dr Donald D'Souza as the first witness in the case of Prem Bedi vs. The State of Maharashtra.'

I might have been a rookie, but I still knew that the prosecutor would have kept the most damning evidence for the beginning and at the end of the trial. That's an old trick; an ace to start with and an ace to hold on to. Courtroom tactics were no different than any professional negotiation. I wasn't surprised that the Desais' driver, the one who had made the call to Manish Desai had not been called to the witness box first. I wondered if he'd be called at all.

A lanky, bald gentleman walked through the aisle and entered the witness box. He took the oath: *'I swear in the name of God that what I say is the truth and nothing but the truth…'* and sat down.

'State your name, please?'

'Dr Donald D'Souza.'

'What do you do, Dr D'Souza?'

'I am head of the Department for Morbid Pathology in JJ Hospital at Byculla, Mumbai.'

'And how many autopsies have you done in your career, Doctor?'

'Don't know, maybe five hundred …'

Apte pulled out a sheet from his desk and read, 'Seven hundred and twenty-one, including the autopsies of Mrs and Mr Desai.'

'I'm sure you're correct.'

'I certainly am. Your Honour, could we have the slides of the victims up for the court, please?'

'Go ahead.'

There was little point in making an objection to that. It was standard operating procedure. If I were the prosecuting advocate, I'd have done exactly the same: displayed the photographs of the two victims in situ. This was a graphic depiction of the heinous act that no description in words could contest with. The law permitted advocates to flaunt these photographs, as they were considered '*probative*' to the case. Rea and Mahesh Desai's photographs were grisly, as the heads had been smashed open with a golf club.

Apte let the image burn in the mind of the Judge. I glanced at Mr Bedi. He looked shocked at the pictures initially, but then his face relaxed into a calm, attentive expression. He didn't look worried; he didn't react to Apte's obvious theatrics.

'Can you, Dr D'Souza, tell the court what time the death occurred?'

'Given the stage of rigor mortis and the other tests we carried out, I'd say the death occurred between midnight of June 7th and 2 a.m. on June 8th.

'So, looking at the pictures, what do you think the victims were killed with?' Apte pointed towards the carnage still displayed on the screen. The Judge and everyone's eyes followed. There wasn't much by way of testimony that Apte would achieve. The ploy was to keep those damn pictures there for as long as possible.

'The victims' skulls were smashed with something hard like metal; the hit came from something that had a long shaft to provide an extended arc that gives the leverage for force and impact. Both victims were killed with a single blow.'

'Hmm.' Apte's scratched his chin as if this was new information. 'So, in your opinion, what weapon was used?'

'We checked various things, then shortlisted a golf club among other similar tools. We then used a golf set to measure the lacerations and indentations and validated that it was a golf club.'

'Golf club? The same game that the defendant—'

'Objection, Your Honour. The witness is an expert in morbid pathology. He isn't in the know of golf or who all in this courtroom play golf,' I stubbed Apte's meanderings.

'I withdraw my comment, Your Honour,' Apte came back quickly before Judge Chowdhary could intervene. He asked a few more inane questions but did not mention anything about what kind of golf club it was.

'Thank you, Dr D'Souza. That's all, Your Honour.'

'Do you want to cross examine the witness, Mr Malhotra?'

'Yes, Your Honour.' I got up and walked to the witness box. 'Dr D'Souza, your résumé is absolute stellar, so I won't even dare question any of your expert findings. But I have one question. Did you do any further examination of the victims' wounds to find which kind of golf club had been used as the weapon—by kind of golf club I mean, was it an iron or wood or … ?'

'Of course.'

'And what did you find?'

'The marks proved beyond doubt that it was a golfing iron number seven.'

'Your Honour, may I ask the court to record this finding for later use, please, when I cross-examine another prosecution witness?'

The Judge nodded.

'Thank you for your time, Dr D'Souza, I have no further questions for you.'

'You are dismissed, Dr D'Souza. Thank you for your testimony today.' Dr D'Souza descended from the witness stand. 'Gentlemen, it's almost 4 p.m., so I think we should wind up for today. I shall see you all at nine tomorrow morning.' Judge Chowdhary got up, and so did everyone in the court.

Thankfully Apte did not mention the revoking of Mr Bedi's bail again. I guess he understood that he hadn't provided anything today that could persuade the Judge to even consider it. His opening statement, however brilliantly delivered, had been hit out of the boundary for a six by me. I could bet he would ask his guys to confirm if Mr Bedi had a driving licence.

Mr Bedi, Dad and I sat at the desk, discussing Apte's embellished narrative in his opening statement till everyone including the prosecution team had left the courtroom. We all knew that it was someone in the prosecution camp that had broken into my office. I had wanted to catch ACP Dutta to have a little chat, but he had left too. Though police officers, even if they were mentioned as prosecution witnesses, were exempted and could be approached by the defence advocates regarding other matters, it was best that we didn't speak in public. I was conscious that while the courtroom was now nearly empty, the media bodies would certainly be waiting outside for photo opportunities. We waited an hour till the noise outside subsided and then walked out. There were still a few flashes and questions thrown at us but we quickly raced to Dad's car and drove away. I could always collect my car the next day.

'How do you think it went?' I asked once we were on our way.

'Very good work, Rohan. As I told you, this is all a smear campaign at best, but I cannot work out who is behind this.' Mr Bedi said.

'You're right Prem, it looks like Manish Desai, but I can't imagine him killing his own brother …'

'I don't think he has. I think he's capitalising on an opportunity that's been thrown at him.'

'Who can it be then?' I asked.

'My guess is that given Mahesh Desai's penchant for digging dirt on anyone and everyone, he got himself into hot waters with someone powerful. I have a feeling the attack might have been on him, and Rea was collateral damage—they wouldn't leave her if she had witnessed it. If that supposition is correct, that *someone* who made the hit or ordered it, knows me, and knows me well enough personally to know my shoe size. It's public knowledge that I play golf, but my shoe size isn't known by just anyone. They planned well so that I take the hit, which means they don't care if I sink as long as they get away. I'm least worried if that's the case, as it should be a one-time thing and I know I'm innocent. But if someone is out to destroy *me* per se, they will keep on targeting me till something sticks because we simply do not know what they'll come out with next. It is important we figure out who they are. Rohan—would you know any private investigator we could hire to ask around, please? I don't want them to know I'm looking for someone so it's best if you take the initiative, please.'

'I can easily arrange one.'

'Thank you,' he said and then switched the conversation. 'I think we need to prepare for when Manish Desai takes the stand. Who do you think the prosecution will call first tomorrow?'

'The forensics guy?' I was still learning the ropes. I didn't think it would damage my reputation if I could get some real advice from these two. They hadn't been in murder trials before as defendants, but they had seen other courtroom trials. Plus, their combined experience was almost twice my age.

'Nah.' Dad shook his head. 'Unless he has something incriminatory I think he'll either skip the forensics guy or bring him in later so he gets the opportunity to present those morbid photographs from the crime scene again. If I were him, I'd bring in ACP Dutta before Manish Desai, but we can't be sure. Let's prepare for both. What say, Prem?'

'I agree.'

We got to Mr Bedi's residence a little after six. In view of my recent history with alcohol, I decided I'd only have one drink if, and only if they insisted. I had another full day in court tomorrow and I did not want to wake up with a hangover.

Veena ji was waiting for us. I wasn't sure why she hadn't come to court that day. She gave Mr Bedi a bear hug and asked how everything had gone.

'Rohan was excellent.'

'I knew he is a bright kid.'

'Thank you, ma'am.'

We sat and discussed the questions I had prepared for Manish Desai and ACP Dutta. They agreed with my line of questioning in general, but we polished some bits. I had used the one thing Mr Bedi had told me earlier—that he couldn't drive—very effectively. He now laid the second golden egg, and this one, I envisioned, could be as monumental as the first one. I then had dinner and was driven home in my own car by Ganesh, who was asked to stay over with me. If the prosecution could play dirty to get my opening statement, they could stoop to any level. Why take a chance?

MANISH DESAI

From all accounts that I heard today, I think Mr Apte had been an awesome find by DCP Mathur. I couldn't have asked for a better prosecuting advocate. His opening statement captured the entire gist of Mr Bedi's avarice and deceit, painted him like the Devil's son. I had done my part by stealthily procuring valuable documents from that amateur. He really thought he'd make an argument by talking about death by golf club as a double-bluff? He was a rookie; Apte would chew him up in the coming days.

But what was all that crap about Mr Bedi not being able to drive? How much of a sissy was that old fool? No wonder Rea had let other men drive her. But was it even true? I made a mental note to ask Apte to check.

Besides Sonia, I had also promised a good sum to DCP Mathur from my imminent inheritance. I wondered if it would be a good idea to offer something to Apte. I didn't know how much Apte earned; probably not much from his salary or commission, bearing in mind what his apartment looked like. Would that be enough to fight hard? Wouldn't a financial bonus be an extra incentive? I had to nail Bedi, and this could well be my only break. I couldn't be penny-pinching on this.

I decided to get the DCP and Apte together for a merry-making party. I'd pay for the expensive Scotch and the girls. In the long run, it could all be written off as an investment. However, I was too drunk now and it was slightly late to run my idea past DCP Mathur or Apte.

Tomorrow was another day. I wouldn't be on the witness stand, as I knew my turn was on the day after. Tomorrow, I knew Apte would be quizzing that ACP. That twat looked suspicious to me. I could sense he didn't like me. But why? Was it because of the rivalry between the DCP and him? Did I care? I would rather be holding on to his boss, which looked like the better option to me.

I switched off my bedside lamp and faded into sleep.

ROHAN MALHOTRA

It was the second day of the trial and I felt like I already needed a break. I wanted to drive to the airport, buy a ticket to New Delhi and take a few days off with Urvee and Pia. Much as I had wanted the attention and the money, I hadn't foreseen the stress. The pressure of being in a murder trial, in a case this monumental and this precarious, was getting to me. Many a times I didn't even realise I'd been holding my breath till I let it out. From what all I knew now, as his advocate, I was confident that Mr Bedi was undeniably innocent, but what if, on some flimsy ground or some missing evidence, I lost the first and the biggest case I had ever got and let Mr Bedi go to the gallows? What if the chips fell on the other side? I'd be kissing my career goodbye even before it began and might not get another case or a job anywhere. And then there'd be the guilt of living with the defeat and its consequences. Mr Bedi was right—someone seemed out to get him; scavengers like Manish Desai were only seizing the opportunity to pull him into a ditch. I had a passing thought of going to Mr Bedi and saying: I give up. Please get a bigger, better, more experienced firm.

I made myself a coffee and called ACP Dutta in the morning to tell him about the little sleight of hand that had been carried out at my office. He was certain Manish Desai was behind it. He reminded me that the guy was unscrupulous—used hookers, paid bribes. ACP Dutta also told me he was testifying today. So Dad had been right. The forensics guy had been delayed. Maybe they had uncovered nothing damaging. Anyway, with the ACP on stand, I wasn't going to break him or his testimony. He had been a help all along. And he could be a help to me in future too. We just had to get through this.

I arrived at the court at 8.30 and the media circus was already in place. I ran up the stairs before they could thrust a microphone into my face.

Dad and Mr Bedi arrived a few minutes later. Apte and his entourage were also seated before the doors opened to let the crowd let in. Judge Chowdhury arrived, greeted the court and asked Ram Singh to recommence the proceedings.

'Thank you, Your Honour.' Apte stood up and walked in front. 'The State calls ACP Ranjeet Dutta as a witness …'

ACP Dutta was in gear—Khaki uniform with tan polished shoes. He walked into the witness stand and took the oath.

'State your name for the records, officer.'

'Ranjeet Dutta.'

'What do you do, Mr Ranjeet Dutta?'

'I'm Assistant Commissioner of Police, attached to the Bandra precinct.'

'How long have you been in the Police?'

'Eight years.'

'Is it correct that you have the record of solving maximum number of homicide cases in Mumbai in the last few years?'

'Yes.'

'And am I right in understanding that you are the chief investigating officer in the murders of Mrs Rea Desai and Mr Mahesh Desai?'

'Yes.'

'Could you tell the court what happened, from the beginning?'

ACP Dutta detailed the call from Manish Desai as the first contact, who had already been inside the house before he and his team arrived, and within minutes, secured the scene. The bedroom resembled a slaughterhouse with blood all over the place and some on the walls. The scene was photographed, all evidence was collected and then the bodies were tagged and transported to JJ Hospital in Byculla.

'What did you do next?'

'We started our investigation—'

'And that persuaded you to contact the defendant—' Apte pointed towards Mr Bedi.

'Objection, Your Honour, my learned friend is leading the witness.' I stood up and interrupted the moment Apte interjected ACP Dutta.

'Sustained. Mr Apte, please ask, don't lead the witness.'

'My sincere apologies, Your Honour. Let me rephrase the question, ACP Dutta. What pointed you to the defendant so quickly after the murders?' Apte turned and dared me to object.

'My first contact with Mr Bedi's office wasn't for any reason other than to inform him of his ex-wife's death, but he was out of the country at the time so I left a message.'

'Is that true? I mean if someone's been divorced for twelve years, why would you want to inform them about their ex's murder?'

'I didn't know if Mrs Rea Desai had any other relatives.'

'Mr Manish Desai was already at the scene, so there was a relative present, don't you think?'

'Yes, but he is Mr Mahesh Desai's relative, so to speak.'

'Well, let's not get entangled in semantics, ACP Dutta. Isn't it true that when you came across the murders, and you knew Rea Desai was the defendant's ex-wife, your first suspect was the defendant?'

'You could construe that.'

'No, ACP Dutta, I want you to acknowledge that.'

'Yes, it's natural. In any murder, the spouse or ex-spouse is always a suspect.'

'And you went there the second time. What led you to Mr Bedi's house after the second visit?'

'I wanted to check where he was on the night of the murders.'

'And what did you find out?'

'He was at his home at Altamount Road.'

'Did someone in the house corroborate that?'

'No. He is normally alone at nights. The guards at the gate leave in the evening and the house is secured by electronic alarms; the housekeeper returns to his family that stays in the outhouse behind the main house, within the premises that Mr Bedi resides in.'

'So, no one corroborated the alibi?'

'Not any human being, if you mean. But we checked the alarm system. If the gates open any time after the guards leave, the alarm sounds in both the main building and the outhouse, so no one can enter or leave without the caretaker in the building knowing about it. He confirmed that no alarm had gone off, we checked the computer to confirm his narrative, and so it is safe to deduce that Mr Bedi had been there the whole time.'

'Where can this alarm be switched on and off from?'

'From the caretaker's quarters only.'

'So if the defendant wanted to go out of his own house he needs the caretaker to let him out?'

'Yes.'

'Don't you think that's strange, ACP Dutta?'

'I'm not here to pass judgement on how the defendant's household is run.'

That was a fantastic response to a purposeless question. I wanted to get up and shake ACP Dutta's hand.

Apte wasted another twenty minutes before he asked about the golf club, asking if the missing one was the murder weapon.

'The golf club missing from one of Mr Bedi's sets is the driver, which he accidently broke on his recent trip to South Korea. The murder weapon was actually an iron number seven. They are two different things, entirely,' ACP Dutta said firmly.

'How many golf sets does Mr Bedi have at his residence?'

'Seven.'

'How do you know there wasn't an eighth one—'

'Objection, Your Honour. My learned friend is asking a police officer to speculate. How can anyone prove a non-existence of anything … ?'

Judge Chowdhary contemplated on my theory for a minute. 'I am inclined to agree with you, Mr Malhotra, but I want to know what the witness, being a police officer, has to say. You can answer that one, ACP Dutta.'

What nonsense, I wanted to shout. *If you agree with me then sustain my objection, Judge.*

'No, I wouldn't know,' ACP Dutta responded.

'Your Honour, I want the court to record that there could well have been an eighth golf set that was not found. So instead of just throwing away the golf club, maybe the defendant got rid of the entire set.'

'Objection,' I stood up again.

Thankfully the Judge saw it too. 'That's highly speculative, Mr Apte. But we shall put it on record.'

'Let's talk about the shoe print now, ACP Dutta.' Apte, freshly invigorated, segued into the only other physical evidence he had. He put the magnified print of the shoe up on the screen. It was a Nike Lunar Control golf shoe. 'Please tell the court about the shoe print your team found at the murder site and what did you do?'

ACP Dutta summarised that he had found the print, searched Mr Bedi's various properties and found nothing. Apte kept up his theatrics of amazement that the ACP hadn't found the shoe yet.

'So it is possible that the shoe was disposed of never to be found, like the golf set?'

'Objection, Your Honour, my learned friend is stretching the speculative theory to its limits now.'

'Sustained. Mr Apte, I think I've heard enough of the possibilities. Do you have any evidence or are we here to listen to these conjectures all through the trial?' Judge Chowdhury evidently sounded peeved.

Good.

'Apologies, Your Honour, but that's all I wanted to ask this witness.'

'Mr Malhotra.' The Judge looked at his watch. 'How much time do you need with this witness?'

'Not much, Your Honour, maybe a couple of hours, maximum.'

'Let's break for lunch then.'

During the break, Dad coached me again, with Mr Bedi sitting silently on the side. He looked stately, serene; but I knew it was a façade. He had admitted to the tension and turmoil he was going through. He just wasn't letting it show on his face. We agreed that during my questioning, I would try to find out what the forensic evidence the prosecution was holding back was, and how long might that take to be presented in court.

'ACP Dutta, was there any forensic evidence found on the scene of crime that links to my client?' I asked after the formalities were done post lunch.

'Not yet,' he said in a measured voice. He was a police officer; decidedly he'd been a witness in several trials. He wasn't going to blabber or lose control, but he had successfully hinted that there might be some evidence there.

'It's been over three months since the murders, so shouldn't it be on the evidence list now?'

'They're analysing it again one last time and so, I cannot talk about it yet.'

'What is it?'

'Objection, Your Honour.' Apte cried out. 'The witness is bound by police ethics and laws here.'

'Sustained. Mr Malhotra, please move on to what we already have on record. And, Mr Apte, I want the forensic department to divulge the evidence as soon as possible.'

'Yes, Your Honour.'

'ACP Dutta, is it true that forensics discovered two sets of glove prints at the murder site and reported them both?' I asked.

'Yes.'

'And my learned friend here did not mention them. Why do you think he didn't?'

'Objection, Your Honour. Speculation.'

'Sustained.'

Even so, my point had been made.

'So in your opinion, how did those two sets of glove prints appear on the scene, and what is your conclusion?'

'Objection, Your Honour,' Apte was on his feet again.

'Your Honour, the witness is a police officer who works on such forensic reports to construct theories that help him in investigations. My learned friend just told the court that ACP Dutta has a record in closing murder cases, so I've only asked him something about what he does on a daily basis. It's not a mere opinion, it is an expert opinion.'

'Overruled, Mr Apte. ACP Dutta, could you answer the question?'

'Thank you, Your Honour.' I said.

'I think there were two people involved,' the ACP said.

'What makes you form that premise?' I pressed.

ACP Dutta explained his hypothesis. One set was used for entry and exit, the other one for the safe. The entry and exit prints told him that the same person broke in, the other set of prints pointed out that the person who broke into the house did not touch the safe.

'What if the perpetrator changed gloves after the murder, broke the safe and then slipped the first set of gloves back on before leaving the house?' I asked.

'In my entire experience in the police service I haven't seen such a cool-headed murderer who would do that. It sounds implausible to me.'

'Thank you, ACP Dutta,' I said and spoke directly to the Judge. 'Your Honour, if there were two people involved, I am at a loss to understand why my learned friend, the public prosecutor, Mr Apte, is holding back any information on the other person?'

The Judge didn't say anything. He looked at Apte.

'Your Honour, as I mentioned, the forensics are still comparing some specimen found at the scene of crime. We shall definitely get them to court to explicate the findings soon.'

'Make that very soon, Mr Apte. Who is your next witness?'

'Mr Manish Desai, Your Honour.'

'That will take long, won't it?'

'Yes, Your Honour.'

'Let's adjourn till tomorrow then.'

Mr Bedi, Dad and I were contented at the end of the day's proceedings as we drove out. Exactly as we'd hoped he would, the Judge had asked Apte to take the curtains off the forensic evidence.

'Do you really think they are still analysing anything?' I asked to no one in particular.

'You mean do they actually have whatever they say they have and are taking their time bringing it to court?' Dad asked.

'Yes.'

'It's a possibility. You cannot prepare for something if you don't know what it'll be. And so, you won't be armed to challenge it.'

'What could it possibly be?' Mr Bedi finally spoke. 'When I haven't been into that house in the last decade, how can forensics find anything that can even remotely link to me?'

'Prem, you know these guys can stoop to anything. What if someone planted something?'

'Like what? My hair, my skin, my blood?'

'Print can definitely be taken of something you touched ...'

'Can we find out what it is in advance?' Mr Bedi asked.

Both men looked at me expectantly. They knew I had a direct line to ACP Dutta. But I doubted if this time, this line would work.

ACP RANJEET DUTTA

It had been a long day in the witness stand and I just wanted to go home and crash, but I had a message waiting as I got out of court. It was from Dr Kale, the lead forensic expert who was handling the Desais' murder case. I heard the voicemail before I sat in the vehicle.

'ACP Ranjeet Dutta, hi, this is Anup Kale. I think I might have come across something, but I wouldn't like to say anything on the phone, particularly not on a machine. Please give me a call when you get this message.'

To be honest, I didn't have a clue what this could be about. I had only echoed what Apte had relayed in his statements and arguments—that something, other than what was already in the evidence docket, was coming. I couldn't imagine what it could be, since everything that had been taken from the scene of crime had already been checked, rechecked, examined and discarded. There had been no alien DNA found.

I called Kale but got his voicemail now, so I left a message that I was on my way.

I asked my driver to take me to the forensics unit, and then closed my eyes and took a power nap. He woke me up only after we parked.

The nap had rejuvenated me. I ran up the steps to meet Dr Kale. I wanted this to be over and go home for the day.

Dr Kale sat in his office, still wearing the white coat most doctors wore. I had only dealt with him once before and I found him to be an amicable and decent sort of guy. He wasn't bad-looking either, with a full head of hair and longish sideburns like an MTV VJ.

'Good evening, ACP Dutta.' He stood up and extended his hand from across the medium-sized desk he sat behind. 'I'm glad you could come.'

'Good evening, Doc, it's my duty. What have you got for me now?' My mobile rang. I pulled it out to see the caller—Rohan Malhotra. I ended the call and put the phone on silent. 'I'm sorry.'

'It's okay. In your line of work you can hardly know when the next customer is going to call. Or worse still, maybe your customer's next of kin …' He smiled at his own joke.

I let out a polite grin too. He wasn't wrong.

'You were saying …' I prompted him when he didn't say anything for a few nanoseconds.

'Yes, it is something strange and I have never seen it before so I thought I would speak to you first, before I am called upon by the public prosecutor. As you know, we tried to recover any DNA from the room we found Mrs and Mr Desai's bodies in and found nothing. No alien blood, which isn't a surprise if the murderer didn't get hurt. But as Mr Edmond Locard, the eminent French forensic pioneer said, *every contact leaves behind some trace*, and it was challenging for me to believe that this murderer didn't. You see, it's different when we find some trace evidence and cannot attribute it to an individual because of lack of suspects, but not finding anything at all …'

In plain English, what Dr Anup Kale was saying was that the fuck-ups only happened because of the police, because we couldn't find the suspect. I could easily have turned it around and asked him that if the forensics took three months to find trace evidence within a single bedroom, how did he expect us to find a suspect that easily, but I saved the sermon for another day.

'Well, we finally found foreign trace evidence on the bed along with the corpses; on the bed sheet, as a matter of fact. More than a few clear drops. They had dried without leaving any marks and hence, were missed in the initial tests.' He stopped and looked at me.

'Semen?' I asked. It was common to find semen near the murder scene. But seminal fluid detection was very simple. Taking into consideration the presence of various proteins in semen, it fluoresced in specialised lighting. If the experts did not find any incandesces but they still suspected its presence due to change of the texture of the fabric, they had other techniques like Acid-Phosphate. It shouldn't have taken three months to come up with that.

'No.'

'Sweat?'

'No, it was lacrimal secretion.'

'What?' I was nonplussed.

'Teardrops. We had a thorough analysis of the entire sheet and on the side that had Mrs Rea Desai's corpse, there were a few teardrops that had soaked into the sheet, and dried without leaving any stain as the composition of tears is much like water, only salty. Once we discovered these on the sheets, we checked the mattress too. We found the same marks exactly where we had expected, right under the sheet … though not as blatant.'

My mind was a Ferrari now, my foot on the pedal. 'Couldn't they have been there from before?'

'No. In that case the density—if they had at all remained on the sheet after a wash—would have been far less. And the fact that they were right on top of the marks on the mattress signifies that the sheet hadn't been changed.'

'So can you tell me their age?'

'Recent, but I cannot tell you if they were from before or after the murders.'

'Do tears have DNA?'

'In theory, yes. The probability of extraction of DNA from tears isn't high, but we'll try our best. We just need a sample from the suspect for comparison.'

'What do you think about the whole thing?'

'I have no idea. Why a killer would shed tears is a mystery to me.'

'Who have you told this to already?'

'No one as yet, but I cannot suppress this information, and you know that.'

'I am not asking you to either. But I want you to contain this info for at least twelve to fourteen hours, till I find out more. Could you do that, please?'

'Absolutely.'

I took a copy of the detail report, thanked him and left.

'Take me home,' I told my driver.

Tears? I couldn't get over it. It could be a sign of regret post murder or grief as the killer smashed the heads of his victims. Suddenly the *burglary-gone-wrong* premise started to crumble.

Why would a stranger, a burglar—someone unrelated to the victims, cry? The suspect pool was reduced to two people that I could think of. Manish Desai and Prem Bedi—however bitter the divorce might have been, there could always be an element of regret or grief in killing someone you've once shared your life with.

But then, Manish Bedi could have shed tears in the morning when he discovered the bodies.

The shoe size matched Mr Bedi's, not Manish Desai's.

Mr Bedi had enough resources to buy a gun. But he could easily hire an assassin and accomplish the repugnant task. Why would he get his own hands dirty instead? And he didn't have a driving license, though that did not in any way prove that he could not drive a car. The city was full of unlicensed drivers confidently driving around. The problem was I couldn't prove a negative. If someone said they could drive when they actually couldn't, it would be simple to prove them wrong. But if someone said they could *not* drive, how could you prove that they could, unless someone had seen them actually driving a car? I decided to ask some informers I'd worked with in the past to snoop around and find out if someone had ever seen Mr Bedi drive.

I was on my third drink when I recalled that Rohan Malhotra had called me. I looked at the time: 8:40 p.m. It wasn't to late to call him back but I wasn't sure yet if I wanted to share the discovery of the tears with him. In my opinion, both Manish Desai and Mr Bedi would be asked for their DNA samples. No doubt about that. And there was nothing either of them could do about it. So what was the point of keeping it from Rohan?

But I didn't call him.

I wanted this process to be impartial. I would authorise Kale to submit the report in the usual manner. And I would let him explain his discovery when he got to the witness stand the day after tomorrow. And then, the Judge could decide what he thought was appropriate.

MANISH DESAI

The simplicity and virtuousness with which some people operate in this world makes me chuckle. They are naïve and unworldly. I had expected ACP Dutta to be smarter than that. I was disappointed that he thought he could throw a curve ball at Mr Apte or me and get away with it? Mr Apte was an experienced public prosecutor with connections, not an amateur like the defence advocate, and I was anything but stupid.

Dr Anup Kale might have promised ACP Dutta that he would not reveal the report to anyone. But who the fuck was Anup Kale? He had no standing in this investigation; he had no right to hold back any information if DCP Dilip Mathur demanded it. And that was precisely what happened.

Everyone with an IQ in three figures could comprehend that the investigators would now zero in on just two suspects. Consequently, unless there was a twisted psychopath in town and this was his first outing, those two suspects were Mr Bedi and yours truly.

Tears. Ha!

I was sure they weren't my tears. They were welcome to my DNA. I wasn't a fool to cry when I was about to come into money. Yes, Mahesh was my brother and I was sorry he had died. But one had to be a bit objective. Everyone has to die. I would miss my brother, of course, but the truth was that he was dead now and tears wouldn't have brought him back. No, I wasn't the kind to cry for my brother. If anything, my only regret was that I hadn't fucked that slut, but again, it wasn't something I'd be crying about. With the money she had left me, I could find better, younger women.

I had no doubts they were Mr Bedi's tears. But then, from the very beginning I had said it had to be him. The rich, old fool. What kind of a dimwit wept over an ex-wife who had cheated on him and then dragged him through such a public and shameful divorce?

Anyway, it wasn't my problem.

For the record, DCP Mathur told Mr Apte about the tears, and he told me. To make sure they weren't my tears, DCP Mathur sent me for a test to a centre close to Lokhandwala. It was private, and the results might not be admitted in court, but at least my friends would be satisfied. So if the court ordered me to go for a test, they wouldn't be in for any nasty surprises. I was happy to play by their rules.

Tomorrow Mr Apte would be putting me in the witness box, the now orphaned younger brother whose only remaining family member was killed mercilessly by the defendant. And then the amateur defence advocate would ask me some random stupid questions. Mr Apte had promised me he'd intervene should something detrimental to the case pop up, and I believed him. No sweat.

To be honest, I had been shocked for a minute when I first saw the two corpses, but the shock turned to disbelief, and then my brain finally clocked that this was an opportunity.

At times I'd contemplated whether I should have told the DCP that I had opened the locker? But I decided that confessing that was not a noble idea. I was only overreacting because I was guilty. How could they ever find out? I had used gloves and then dumped them in the sea. I put a lid on the morass of such paranoid ideas and tried to look at the bright side. In a few days this would all be over. The old fool would be finally nailed, and forever. I would inherit fifty crore rupees. I could almost smell the money now. I pulled out a five-hundred-rupee note, brought it close to my nose and took a whiff. The sweetest smell known to mankind.

ROHAN MALHOTRA

I couldn't sleep. I hadn't had a restful night's sleep for a few weeks now. Even when I'd catch a few hours, I'd wake up in cold sweat. The case, and the very thought of its result, had been driving me mental now. Judge Chowdhary had a real poker face; I had no idea how to read what he was thinking.

So far, I had shot down Apte's highly embellished opening statement that Mr Bedi drove to the Pali Hill residence and cold-bloodedly offed Rea and Mahesh Desai. In my mind I was winning 1:0. But maybe the two glove prints had turned this into a plus for Apte, if the Judge found it plausible that whoever drove Mr Bedi to the crime scene might also have been the accomplice.

Apte had himself highlighted that the murder weapon—a golf club—was used by Mr Bedi as a double bluff. I had seen the Judge assiduously listening to that yarn. Even if for a second he was with Apte, I had sufficiently quashed that theory when I cross-examined Dr D'Souza and made him clarify that the club used to commit the murders wasn't the same type as the one missing from Mr Bedi's set. Was that a 2:0 lead? I couldn't tell.

My biggest worry was Mr Bedi's alibi at the time of the crime. I was certain he was home—no doubt about that—but it was ultimately up to the Judge to admit the alibi provided by the electronic monitoring system.

Tomorrow, we all knew, Apte would have Manish Desai in the witness stand. Besides trying to win everyone's sympathy, I knew that the moron would want to cry hoarse about Mr Bedi's motive for the murders. I knew how to counter that.

People might have thought that I did not labour hard enough on Apte's speculation that Mr Bedi could have a seventh or eighth set of golf clubs, or another set of size eight-and-a-half shoes. But I hadn't forgotten that Apte had insisted that both these points be put on record. I would come to it. Actually, Apte had dug the pit that I would be pushing *his* prized witness into. Unless Apte knew something I didn't, he had a blizzard coming his way tomorrow.

I had also spoken to a private investigator. It was difficult to find one in the city who didn't know Mr Bedi or hadn't heard about the current case. I had however called one to meet me in office the next day to outline what I wanted. Above all, I would make him sign a contract to ensure that he'd be discreet.

Mr Bedi and Dad had shown, I profess, more confidence in me than I'd ever had in myself. Perhaps I had, in some way, steered them to believe in me and now it had become the bane of my life.

TEJ MALHOTRA

The daily calls from board members of Bedi & Sons were coming twice a day now. Their trepidations were now about their own survival.

'*What if Prem loses the trial?*'

'If the stock price tanks, what will happen to all the shareholders who hold stocks? They'll become junk overnight.'

The board members themselves held stocks that were worth millions.

Then sell the damned stocks now and exit while you can, I felt like shouting. But they wouldn't do that just yet. What if the Mogul came back? If they uncashed the stocks, they'd lose the seat on the board. And if they wanted to return later, there was no chance they'd be reinstated, considering they had deserted Prem in his bad hour.

They decided to sit on the fence.

I had been in my apartment all evening, nursing my drink for quite some time now. The ice had long melted and I could feel the blues.

The truth was everyone wanted to, and made money off Prem, including me.

Rea. All she ever wanted Prem for was money. And then she had blown it with her malevolent ways. I had never met Rea Desai but my several tête-à-têtes with Veena over the past few days only made me conjure an image of a femme fatale, a woman who used her beauty to ensnare men and steered them into precarious, and often compromising situations.

Mahesh Desai, Rea's husband, had certainly been influenced by her. He had no business to harbour any rancour against Prem. If anything, it should have been Prem lashing out at him. Mahesh had been the one who had been caught having an affair with Prem's then wife. How did Mahesh become the wounded party? It was all about money. The entire smear campaign that the media keenly broadcast was about nothing but money. If Prem had stepped in and offered to pay the Desais, it would all have been over before it even began.

And now it was Manish Desai, that evil son of a bitch, who was after Prem. To be honest, I didn't think he was grief-struck at all. It was more about the greed that had mushroomed in his convoluted little brain. And though Prem couldn't believe that anyone, including someone like Manish, could be evil enough to kill his own brother, I wasn't convinced anymore. History was awash with stories of sons killing fathers and brother killing brother.

Rohan, my own son, despite all his noble intentions, would also net a colossal, life-changing sum of five-plus crores at the end of it all. He could have never imagined making or saving that kind of money in his entire life, even if he ran his solo practice till he was eighty years old. And the whole thing was all one-sided. If Rohan failed in defending my friend, all he would lose is the *marginal* reputation he had as an advocate; more a notional loss. He would still get to pocket the money, whereas Prem would lose his freedom, reputation and money. Not at all bad a deal for Rohan, was it?

What about me? I was Prem's friend and colleague. But would I have worked for eight years for someone if it hadn't been for the money? What if he had stopped paying me four years ago? Would I have still remained a close friend?

Mr Lee had called to let us know that he planned to come to Mumbai next week Wednesday. I was certain he'd been following the news, waiting to see if Prem was guilty or innocent. If this case lingered on, I didn't need a clairvoyant to tell me that our deal would be off the table. Mr Lee might even cancel his trip.

Two generations of good work and heritage could be tarnished in one day, one judgement from Judge Chowdhary. I hoped Rohan had engaged a sharp private investigator to sniff out whoever had done this.

All said, Prem had one thing going against him. He was headstrong. Almost pig-headed. Maybe it was his upbringing, maybe it was his royal genes, but he just never budged once he made up his mind. Even in this very incident—he could easily have bought off that scum Manish Desai and the rest of them and walked out of this mess, but he wouldn't. He was like some holy crusader who wanted to prove that truth always triumphed!

That brought me to what Prem had said a while back. It wasn't easy being under the spotlights your entire life; people saw your glitter, but they also saw you crap, didn't they?

I decided to chuck the drink and retire.

I could feel the blues.

First thing I checked with Maya the next morning was if there were some last-minute secret meetings being held between some board members in the office. She said no. So, unlike my reservations, the calls to me from several directors weren't conspiratorial. They were just being propagated by fear. Either that, or they were scheming outside office, which somehow didn't seem likely. They had been a loyal bunch for years, I had to give them that.

ROHAN MALHOTRA

Manish Desai was the prosecution's chief witness on the third day of the trial. Clad in jeans and a white full-sleeve cotton shirt, he sported a few days' growth on his jowls and red eyes, playing the part of a brother in mourning.

Pathetic, but I guessed some people were born that way.

'And how are you related to the deceased Mr Mahesh Desai and Mrs Rea Desai?'

'Mahesh was my elder brother and only living blood relative, and Rea was his wife, my sister-in-law.'

Apte took his time in questioning and letting Manish explicitly describe the macabre scene that he had witnessed first-hand on the morning after the murders. The acting was so good that even I'd have shed tears if I could bring myself to believe him. I could sense some people in the courtroom lapping up the story. Judge Chowdhary stayed stoic. I reckoned he'd seen a lot of such theatrics in his courtroom before. I could gather that this was stage-setting before Apte steered Manish towards pointing fingers at Mr Bedi.

'So why did you register a police complaint against the defendant, Mr Prem Bedi?'

'It was obvious ...'

'Would you mind telling the court why you think it was obvious that the defendant had been the one who attacked your brother and his wife?'

'Rea Desai was once married to Mr Prem Bedi,' Manish craftily turned and looked at Mr Bedi.

'Objection, Your Honour.' I stood up. 'The divorce is irrelevant to this case.'

'But, Your Honour, that *is* the starting point of everything,' Apte shot back.

The Judge looked at me, then at Apte. 'I'll allow,' he finally said, 'but I'll strike it out if the prosecuting advocate does not tie it up with the case.'

Manish Desai took this as a licence to throw as much shit at Mr Bedi as he could. I could have objected a few more times but didn't. I quietly made notes for my cross-examination.

The divorce saga was followed by mention of the sparkling editorials that Mahesh Desai had written on Mr Bedi to expose his alleged manipulative business practices.

'Mr Desai, in your opinion—'

'Objection, Your Honour,' I interposed.

The law is clear on this. Doctors or other experts in their scientific and professional fields are permitted to draw broad conclusions based on hypotheticals that befit their qualifications and experience. Their 'qualified opinion' is allowed. But Manish Desai, not being an expert on anything in this case, had no right to give an opinion. He was here to state the facts as they were.

'Sustained,' Judge Chowdhary, thankfully, didn't overrule me on this.

Apte was careful in phrasing his questions from then on. Desai went on to highlight that the op-eds his brother wrote further fuelled the already existing ill-feeling. I objected wherever I could. Some of the objections were tactical, purely to break Apte's performance or break the Judge's concentration when I thought he was getting too attentive. But I did all by the book; I didn't want Judge Chowdhary to think I was causing a nuisance.

At one point, I wanted to stand up and shout—that was fuckin' twelve years ago, but I sat quietly. I glanced at Mr Bedi, who sat in his own oasis of calm despite Desai slandering him in an open court. He wasn't going to get into the mud to fight with a pig.

After what felt like decades, Apte finally arrived at the topic of the motive: the insurance policy. But either because he didn't know the whole story or was consciously avoiding the key parts, he left Manish Desai sufficiently exposed before he concluded his testimony.

'Your Honour, I am confident the State has established the defendant's motive. No more questions for the witness.'

Thank the Lord for small mercies. Apte had taken the whole of the morning session to establish, well, nothing … nothing that I could not break when I got Desai on the stand after lunch.

As we started exiting the court for recess, I could sense a furtive exchange taking place at the prosecution between Apte, his two stooges and Manish Desai. As Mr Bedi, Dad and I passed them they paused their conversation abruptly. I tried my best to listen in, but they were far too cautious. I could guess they were up to something devious.

'What do you think?' Dad asked.

We were locked in a room now. I had sent one of the attendents for coffees and some bites since I hadn't eaten anything for breakfast.

'Well, he said everything that we suspected and nothing we didn't,' Mr Bedi responded.

'Yes,' Dad continued, 'and you made good objections wherever possible.'

'Thanks, Dad.'

'I didn't think Manish Desai's testimony covered any new grounds.'

'Did you see Apte and team conspiring as we walked out?' I asked.

'Yes, what was that about?'

'Don't know, but you can never trust these guys.'

'Of course not, not after we know they broke into your office.'

'Not sure if I told you two,' I said, 'ACP Dutta thinks it was Manish Desai who might have carried out the theft.'

'Why am I not surprised?' Dad sniggered. 'Do you want some time alone, Rohan—to prepare for your cross examination?'

'That would be good.'

I opened my briefcase, took out the notes and immersed myself in the papers. I had worked conscientiously and remembered all the questions, but it was always different when it came to the actual act. So many things could go wrong. Apte wouldn't just sit there either, letting me shred his star witness.

'All set?' I heard Dad from the other side of the room. I had lost track of time when his voice broke my concentration.

'Yes.' I looked at my watch. 1.53 p.m. 'Let's go.'

Back in the courtroom, the crowd had already settled down. I noticed Apte and his minions still furtively discussing something at the prosecution desk, but didn't let that disturb me. For all I knew, it could be a tactic to break my attention.

'All rise …' Rama Singh's voice boomed. Judge Chowdhary arrived and took his place.

Manish Desai sauntered into the witness box.

'The court reminds the witness, Mr Manish Desai, that he is still under oath,' the Judge served the cautionary.

'Yes, Your Honour.'

It was time for me to take on Manish Desai and I couldn't wait. 'Mr Desai, I am Rohan Malhotra'—*the guy whose office you broke into*—'and I am the advocate representing Mr Prem Bedi. First of all, please accept my deepest condolences for your loss—there is nothing like losing a close family member.'

He nodded.

'Mr Manish Desai, do you play golf?'

'No.'

'Have you ever played golf?'

'No.'

'Are you sure?'

'Of course, I would have known if I—'

'How many golf sets do you have?' I cut him off mid-sentence.

'I said I don't play golf.' Manish Desai raised his palms as if to convey what kind of a nutcase I was.

'I heard you when you said you don't *play* golf, Mr Desai.' I had practised the inflection. 'Nevertheless, playing golf is not a prerequisite to owning a golf set, is it?'

'It is not, but I don't have any.'

'You don't have any what?' I wanted to buttonhole him.

'No, I don't have any golf sets.'

'You don't have any golf set now or you've never had one?'

Manish Desai looked at Apte, but I knew Apte couldn't object to my questions.

'Mr Desai, I didn't hear your response. Do you not have any golf set now or did you never own one?'

'I've never owned any golf sets.'

'Can you prove that you've never owned a golf set, Mr Desai?'

'Can *you* prove you don't or didn't have any golf sets?' Manish barked at me.

My technique to harass him had finally worked. I had, from the beginning, wanted to push him hard against the wall and I had succeeded.

'Let me help you here, Mr Desai,' I said it as calmly as I could. I knew the Judge would not intervene if I stayed courteous. 'I will explain this in simple language. *I'm* the advocate. *You* are in the witness box. *I* ask the questions. *You* answer them. *I* don't have to answer any of *your* questions and *you* cannot decline to answer any of mine. Is that clear?'

'Yes.'

'I'm at your service to explain this again if you so desire ... ?'

'I understand.' He looked deflated.

'Good. So we can start again. Can you prove that you never owned any golf set, Mr Desai?'

'Objection, Your Honour, I am not sure what my learned friend is trying to achieve by this line of questioning?' Apte was talking to the Judge, but his glare was drilling holes into me.

I soldiered on without losing my composure. 'Your Honour, I'm only advancing the theory my esteemed friend propagated yesterday. How do we know that Mr Desai here,'—I pointed at the witness stand—'did not have a golf set, and after killing his brother and sister-in-law, simply got rid of it? The fact that he does not own a golf set now does not in any way mean that he never owned one or had access to one.'

'This is preposterous, Your Honour …' Apte cried.

Courtroom etiquettes forbid the prosecuting and defence advocates conversing with each other. Advocates have to communicate through the Judge on the bench.

I waited for Judge Chowdhary to intervene, but he mutely watched us play it out amongst ourselves.

'Your Honour, all I want to impress upon the court is that if my client, Mr Bedi, could possess a seventh or eighth golf set and that he disposed off, it isn't a quantum leap to reason why this witness,' I again tersely pointed at Manish Desai to irk him, '… couldn't have done the same thing.'

Judge Chowdhary nodded. 'Point noted, Mr Malhotra. I can appreciate that it was essential for you to make that point to the court, and it is now on record. May I request you to please spare us a similar line of circuitous questioning to arrive at the same logic for the missing shoe? I am sure this witness could have thrown that size eight-and-a-half shoe away exactly like your client. The court records both as deficits; moreover, the missing golf set and shoe are redundant arguments till the investigating team recovers either of them and presents them to the court.'

Fat chance.

Every Judge in every court in every part of the world had the sole discretion to disallow evidence or to veto questioning a witness about something that they deem redundant or repetitive to save the court's time. If an advocate strongly felt that the particular evidence or questioning had impeded their chances of altering the outcome of the case, they could be taken up on appeal if and when the case was tried in a higher court. But it wasn't unfair of Judge Chowdhary to stymie me at this point, particularly as, on this occasion, he had pre-empted me. And my point had been made.

'Mr Malhotra, could you advance the case, please?'

'Yes, Your Honour.' I smiled pleasantly.

Apte, who had been standing for the last few minutes of the skirmish, finally sat down. I noticed him and his underlings still whispering at the prosecution desk, but I ignored them. I did not let my mind stray for more than a moment. I walked to our desk, exchanged a barely noticeable, ephemeral smile with Mr Bedi and Dad and shuffled the papers to review my next point.

'Mr Desai, you had mentioned the old deep-rooted bitterness that the defendant has carried against your kin for over a decade …'

'Yes, he is—'

'Mr Desai, I request you not to interrupt me when I'm talking,' I said sternly.

'Mr Desai, please only answer when Mr Malhotra asks you a question,' the Judge reinforced, before Apte could even register what happened.

'Yes, Your Honour,' Desai meekly acknowledged.

Finding him on back foot once again, I fired, 'Mr Desai, besides the historic and, at best, tenuous references to the hostility between your family and my client, do you have any evidence of the same?'

'I'm not sure what you mean.'

'Let me rephrase it for you then. Did my client ever threaten your brother or his wife?'

'Maybe. I don't know.'

'Did your brother or his wife ever mention to you that Mr Bedi had threatened them in any fashion?'

'Not exactly, but being a brother I could sense his fear.'

'So… it's not even hearsay, it's hypothetical—an imaginary fear that your brother *might* have fostered for an unidentified reason, right?'

'But the whole city knows that my deceased brother tried to expose the defendant.'

'That's not the answer to my question, Mr Desai. And the whole city, unfortunately, isn't on the stand to confirm this threat that your brother felt from my client, Mr Desai. Do you agree that the whole fear that your brother ferried for years may well have been imaginary?'

'Objection, Your Honour.'

'State your objection, Mr Apte.'

Okay, here's the thing. Normally when an advocate objected, the judge would have already anticipated it, albeit he'd wait for the opposing advocate to raise the point before he took any action. But if you raised an objection and the judge had to ask you *why*, it generally meant the judge did not see or hear anything untoward.

'Your Honour, my learned friend is making the whole situation sound hypothetical, as if there was no animosity between Mr Mahesh Desai, his wife and the defendant.'

'I don't think so, Mr Apte. I think the defence advocate is only trying to establish if the witness thought his brother was actually threatened or merely paranoid. Objection overruled.'

'Thank you, Your Honour,' I said and turned to my witness. 'Mr Desai, was my client the only businessman your brother attempted to malign or expose?'

'Objection, Your Honour.'

'On what grounds now, Mr Apte?'

I was gloating. This was the second time in a row that Apte was digging himself the proverbial grave by challenging me on something that the Judge did not perceive as disagreeable.

'Relevance, Your Honour. There is no relevance to this … this hollow line of questioning …'

'Mr Malhotra?' The Judge's eyebrows went up, questioning me.

'Your Honour, I am merely trying to establish if the deceased Mr Mahesh Desai wrote provocative, near inflammatory articles and opinions about people other than my client. That will help me to be au fait with the much talked about hostility, and if this hostility was something exclusive between Mr Mahesh Desai and my client, or did it exist between Mr Mahesh Desai and other parties that he slandered, that's all.'

'Objection overruled, Mr Apte.'

I could have walked up to Judge Chowdhary and kissed his hand.

'But, Your Honour—'

Apte was seething. I could feel smoke coming out of his ears and nose, and maybe his other orifices. Seeing that the Judge had declined his objection, he should have stopped carping if he wanted to avoid the Judge's ire, but now he was inviting trouble.

'Your objection is noted and overruled, Mr Apte. You may answer the question, Mr Desai.'

'Sorry, what's the question?' asked Manish Desai.

'Do you know if your deceased brother, Mr Mahesh Desai, wrote *inspiring* articles expressing his strong opinions about anyone other than my client, Mr Bedi?'

'You don't have to be sarcastic, Mr Malhotra.' The Judge had noticed my nuance and my wrist got slapped. No real harm done, but I decided to be careful.

'Apologies, Your Honour.'

'You may answer the question, Mr Desai.'

'I wouldn't know. My brother was a well-regarded investigative journalist and he published numerous articles. I'm sorry but I didn't keep a record of everything that my brother wrote.'

'Fair enough,' I uttered and walked to my desk, pretending like I was reading a document in the file when I knew the whole story backwards. 'It was nine businessmen and two businesswomen.'

'Like I said, I don't know, but if you say so, it must be true.'

'It *is* true. And you seem to believe Mr Bedi was the only one who had sufficient motive to kill your brother. Sounds like a theory propagated by convenience, doesn't it?'

'But none of those he wrote about had their ex-wives married to my brother.'

'So the animosity didn't originate from the articles, like you just mentioned?'

'Of course not. It was a lot more deep-rooted than that. The articles just added the fuel.'

Mr Bedi had stipulated that I would not bring up Rea's character up for debate in the courtroom. I could have easily highlighted that Rea was still rolling between sheets with other men while she was married to Mahesh Desai , but I was restrained by my own client's wishes.

The Judge saved me. 'Mr Malhotra, we have already dwelled on the divorce in the prosecuting advocate's session this morning. Could we move on with the case now, please?'

'Yes, Your Honour.'

But before I could begin, Judge Chowdhary changed his mind. He glanced at his watch and decided to call it a day. He was right in a way. It was almost getting to 3.30 p.m. and everyone's kidneys needed a break.

'How much longer do you think you need with this witness?'

'I would need a few hours, Your Honour.'

'In that case I think we should adjourn the court for now and meet tomorrow morning at nine. Do you have any objection, Mr Apte?'

'None whatsoever, Your Honour.'

I could see the delight on Apte's face. Considering how the afternoon session had gone with his foremost witness, it didn't need Sherlock to figure out that he'd coach Manish Desai to dodge the next round of bullets from me when he returned to the witness box.

'Mr Desai, please make yourself available again tomorrow for the cross examination.'

TEJ MALHOTRA

Rohan had done me proud, very proud. I had never expected him to give such a brilliant performance. The flame of the State's case was dwindling, and after what Prem and I had discussed with Rohan, the evidence we had for the one final line of questioning, it would be extinguished totally. But I also knew that the nightmare wasn't over till it was.

For starters, we still hadn't been notified of what, if any, evidence was being analysed by forensics. Eleventh-hour witnesses and evidence submissions weren't looked upon very positively by judges, but everyone knew undertows like that existed, and they were entertained. What was it that the prosecution had been hiding? And how damaging could it be? I believed Prem. If he said he hadn't been near that Pali Hill property in over a decade, I didn't doubt him. But there were instances in the annals where evidence had been fabricated.

For someone to use a golf club to commit the double murder and leave a size eight-and-a-half shoe outsole print behind, it was evident that the person or persons knew Prem or, at the very least, knew *about* Prem. How difficult was it to procure a hair from Prem's head or body from his office or places he visited regularly? Or skin residue from a bathroom at some club?

It was a disquieting thought.

I called Rohan. 'You left straight from the court so we didn't get to talk today. Mr Bedi was extremely pleased with the manner in which you cross-examined Manish Desai.'

'Thank you, Dad.'

'I think that, unless the forensic team springs some nasty surprise on us, Apte won't be able to provide anything to the Judge that we should be worried about, don't you think?'

'I think so too.'

'Did you manage to speak to ACP Dutta?'

'He's not taking my calls. I've left messages for him, but he hasn't yet called back.'

'That's very unlike him. I mean, he initially went out of the way to help you and provided you with classified information, something that could have jeopardised his career.'

'You're right, Dad. I don't know what's happened to him. Perhaps he's just busy elsewhere. I didn't see him anywhere around the court today either. I'll try him again.'

'Thanks, Rohan. Let me know if you get through to him. Otherwise we'll see you at the court around eight-thirty tomorrow.'

'Sure, Dad.'

'Good night.'

I was still uneasy. Something gnawed at me. Maybe I had ensconced myself in some invisible fountain of pessimism in these last few weeks. I checked the time: 07.39 p.m. Seoul was five-and-half hours ahead of us; it was too late now to call Mr Lee. I made myself a drink to relax.

ROHAN MALHOTRA

The doorbell rang the moment I disconnected Dad's call. I was exhausted, struggling to keep my eyes open, but this was important. And urgent. I pulled myself together by convincing myself that it was the last appointment of the day. I had called the private investigator and told him to come to my residence instead of our earlier agreement to meet at my Bandra office.

I had found Freddy Vakil through my contacts from the not-so-distant previous life. I hadn't used his services personally, but the law firm I worked for—Dadawala & Partners—had recommended him. That made me chuckle. When I had split from the firm, no one bothered to return my calls. Now, with the spotlight on me for being Mr Bedi's defence advocate in a murder trial, I could sense deference in their voices when I called, and an eagerness to extend any help I needed. I had a feeling that if I walked into their offices tomorrow morning even some of the partners might genuflect. Or maybe offer me partnership. It wouldn't be such a bad idea though. I could think about it once this was over, but I wasn't giving them a piece of action in my existing gold-crusted case.

'Good evening, Mr Malhotra.'

Freddy Vakil was an unassuming Parsi gentleman. Five-feet-eight, curly brown hair, in his early thirties. Nothing in his face was noticeable enough to stand out. Unless you saw him or met him at least four or five times, there was no way you could describe him. Except his glasses, which I assumed he changed often enough to keep himself even more camouflaged. I imagined that his unremarkable face was a good measure of his résumé.

'Good evening, Mr Vakil.' I shook his extended hand and moved sideways to let him into my apartment.

'Nice place,' he complimented as he walked into the living room. I wanted to say it was all Urvee's doing, and as I was out most of the time since she had been away, I hadn't got the chance to disturb or mess up anything.

'Thanks. Can I get you anything to drink?'

'Thanks, I'm okay for now.' He took out is pad and pen. 'How may I help you, Mr Malhotra?'

'Call me Rohan.'

'I'm Freddy. How may I help you, Rohan?'

'As I told you on the phone, I need total discretion for this job—'

'Trust me, Rohan, my right hand does not know what my left hand does. That is the main dictum of my business. I wouldn't have survived a day in this line of work if I ever spilled the beans.'

'I'd still need some contractual obligations out of the way before we got into the details.'

'Sure, why not …'

He took a few minutes to read the paperwork I had prepared. It was simple contract about non-disclosure with a heavy financial penalty if he jumped it. It obviously outlined that if he discovered any criminal activity for which he was called upon by court to testify, this contract wouldn't stand in the way. It seemed reasonable to him; without questioning anything, he signed it.

'Tell me now, Rohan.'

'You've heard of Mr Prem Bedi.'

'Who hasn't?' He smiled. 'He's been all over the news for quite some time now, implicated in the murder of his ex-wife and her spouse.'

Just as I had known—it was impossible to find anyone who hadn't heard of my client or his case.

'He couldn't have done it,' he added.

It made me curious. 'How can you say that?'

'For any crime to happen, there are two important requirements: motive and opportunity. Of whatever little I know, there is some motive—some insurance money, which to some extent is plausible, irrespective of however rich an individual already is.' He stopped and looked at me. I nodded.

'What's the second?'

'Opportunity, obviously. If Mr Bedi does not drive—as you said in the court—there was never an opportunity for him to get to the crime scene and back. No court in any country can even establish a circumstantial case if the opportunity is non-existent.'

I had known both the points, but Freddy's confident recital gave me the right words to nail my closing statement.

'He's what they call a circumstantial victim; circumstances, as you would know, can make us all victims,' he added.

Freddy Vakil seemed like an intelligent guy. If nothing, he had provided me with the right words. I had never thought of threading together the two words to refer to someone as 'circumstantial victim'.

'He has been badly blindsided.' I said.

Nod.

'So is he the client?' he asked.

'Freddy, I am retaining your services; I'm your client. You take the brief from me and you furnish the report to me. Does that work for you?' Politely, but in as many words, I made it amply clear that Mr Bedi wasn't hiring him.

'Of course. What do you want to know?'

'Freddy, you might have been jaundiced by the media and Manish Desai shouting himself hoarse. But you have to start with a brand new slate here. The brief here is simple. This murder trial, as I just mentioned, will go away but someone definitely fosters an ill feeling for Mr Bedi, deep enough to have attempted so hard to incriminate him. It could be some business rival, some acquaintance or a personal contact, someone in the distant family … we don't know.'

'So you think this problem isn't going away even if you win the case?'

This guy was sharp.

'That is the assumption. Whoever has started the war isn't going to sit still if Mr Bedi comes out defeating them, would they?'

'Got you.'

'I want a thorough search done on who these people could be? I guess if we know who they are, it will be relatively simple to work out what their motivation was or still is.'

'Correct. How long back in the past do you want me to look?'

'As long into the past as it takes you, Freddy.'

He nodded.

'This isn't a time-bound job; this is more a do-what-it-takes to accomplish the mission kind of assignment. Fee is not a problem at all, though I'd like to know how much, and when can you start?'

'Well, I can work on it alongside other cases, which is cheaper but, if money is not a problem as you say, I can devote my services full time on this.'

'I'd want to retain your services full time.'

'All yours, but I can only start after two days. I am investigating something presently that I shall need to hand over to some colleague, which I'm sure you'll appreciate.'

'Sure, that's fine by me.'

We discussed the fees and per diem expenses; they weren't cheap, but they wouldn't bankrupt Mr Bedi either.

'And, Freddy, I know I don't need to reiterate, but please be discreet.'

'Don't worry, Rohan.'

Zeno's Paradox of Achilles and the Tortoise made a lot of sense in situations like these. Interestingly, if Achilles gave the tortoise a head start in a race, then Achilles would never catch up with the tortoise if everything else remained constant. When Achilles would run the distance to the tortoise's starting point, the tortoise would have inched further. Then Achilles would take more time to cover that distance, but the tortoise would have advanced still further. In simple terms, whenever Achilles would reach somewhere the tortoise had already been, he still had to run further. If Mr Bedi only played a catch-up game—

running after whatever distances his rivals had already covered, he would never outrun them. It was therefore mandatory to change the speed or the game or the route. Freddy Vakil needed to find that *difference*. And he needed to find that before the tortoise got to its next point of destruction.

It was close to nine-thirty and I decided I should scramble some eggs for dinner as I was too weary to order and wait for the food to be delivered. It was then that I saw the blinking icon on my mobile phone. There was a message waiting. I called my voicemail and listened.

'Hi, Rohan, ACP Dutta here … Listen, I need to see you tonight. Give me a call as soon as you get my message.'

What was so important that he wanted to see me? It indeed sounded ominous.

A thin train of icy-cold sweat travelled down my spine as I picked up my phone and dialled him. He didn't want to divulge whatever he had on the phone so we decided to catch up for dinner.

The extreme fatigue I had been fighting for a few hours simply vanished.

ACP RANJEET DUTTA

I had been upset since the morning, from the time Dr Kale had called me. I had woken up to my radio-alarm clock just like any other day, then brewed and savoured a strong black coffee, taken a shower and was looking forward to another day at the court when Kale called to let me know that, despite my advising him not to divulge the discovery and the ensuing analysis to anyone, he had had to break the news to my own boss. I bellowed, gave him a verbal walloping, but eventually realised he hadn't had much of a choice. DCP Mathur had called him last evening for an update and he had been caught off guard. He had no reason to conceal the breakthrough anyway. I could also give him the benefit of doubt that he didn't know that DCP Mathur was a bent cop, and I didn't consider it appropriate to highlight it. After all, he was an outsider. It didn't feel right to be washing our internal dirty political linen in his presence. He said he had tried calling me last night itself—right after his call with DCP Mathur—but my phone had been switched off. I remembered I had switched it off to avoid Rohan's calls.

I apologised for losing my temper for a moment, but he sounded okay.

Then guilt took over. I had evaded Rohan's calls to abstain from telling him about the latest discovery. And the scoundrel Mathur had taken the same piece of information and—I didn't have to stretch my imagination—would have gladly passed it on to Manish Desai for a poontang with another so-called girlfriend of that vermin. I knew I had helped the defence advocate too, but that was in the beginning of the investigation, when I had no idea if this whole thing could ever go to court. To correct my past indiscretion I had decided to stay away from being prejudiced yesterday. And by doing so, I had, in fact, unwillingly let the opposite camp take undue benefit of the situation.

Quite frankly, Rohan did not worry me. He looked like a man in control and not a scared cat that had lost its way. He had performed the task that Mr Bedi had trusted him with, and with each passing day, his confidence had only grown. But could he keep Mr Bedi safe from the coterie of those three evil men? Or did he need me holding his hand because I knew what he couldn't possibly be aware of?

I felt wretched. I decided I'd take a day off. I wasn't per se required at the court. And even if I was required, one could always fall sick.

Any feeling of however microscopic a loss always made me miserable since the time I had lost Jasmine to cancer. It always had a snowballing effect on me. Once I was miserable, every other misery in my life somehow came to the forefront. And I turned to the only remedy I had in my cabinet: the whisky elixir. I pulled out a bottle and took a generous sip, then another. I called up my driver to let him know I wouldn't be travelling to the court today.

I remember having ordered some more whisky to be home-delivered after I had polished the half bottle I had by lunchtime. Then I had ordered pizza. I had contemplated calling Rohan but realised he would be in court. Then I was so under the influence that I forgot everything else and crashed out.

Later, as I sat watching television after having ruined an entire day in my life, I looked at the missed calls on my phone; there were five from Rohan Malhotra. Before I had heard from Kale, I couldn't decide if I should let Rohan know about the newest discovery or not. But now, it was different; I was only levelling the playing field.

I called Rohan back late in the evening. His phone was engaged and I left a message that I wanted to see him tonight, whatever time he was free. I didn't wish to divulge the forensics' discovery of the new evidence on voicemail.

Rohan called around nine-thirty. He got hyper when I told him I wanted to see him to tell him about something that I couldn't disclose on the phone. And it was comprehensible. He was in the middle of a murder trial. I was the lead investigator, calling him to tell him I had something that could impact the proceedings. He agreed to pick me up from my place after ten and take me for dinner. I was sure he had a big expense account from Mr Bedi, so why not? Besides, my apartment was in a state of appalling disarray and I was in no disposition or shape to clean it. I looked like a mess too, but that only needed a shower and cologne. I was ready by ten and took the elevator down.

Rohan was already downstairs. He updated me about the events at the court earlier in the day as we drove to Trikaya, a restaurant at Seven Bungalows in Andheri West.

'How are you feeling?' he asked after we had ordered. Maybe I still looked like shit or maybe he asked because I had been absent from court.

'I had a terrible headache, like someone was hitting me between my temples with a hammer intermittently since last night, that lasted till this afternoon.'

'Oh, I'm sorry to hear that.'

'Sorry I missed your calls.'

'That's okay. What do you have? You mentioned you had something significant on the phone.' He sounded anxious.

'Same terms like last time—I never told you this …'

'Of course, without a doubt.' He kept his right hand on his heart to make it appear more solemn than required. It made me smile. He wasn't a conniving advocate representing some mafia don; he was an everyday guy who had been tangentially connected to Mr Bedi and hence got handed the opportunity of representing him. If Mr Bedi was at all guilty, wouldn't he have found a devious advocate who would mete out a thrashing to Apte and Co.?

'First, what I'm about to tell you, Apte and party might have known for over twenty-four hours, I think. Don't ask me why, but some police official'—I had no desire to mention the name of my own boss to Rohan either—'must have disclosed it to them.'

The waitress came to serve the soups so I paused for a few seconds.

'The forensic team have found teardrops at the crime scene that do not belong to either Rea or Mahesh Desai. They could belong to Manish Desai as he was first at the crime scene, and the macabre tableau could have disturbed him enough to shed a few, albeit crocodile ones. So if it comes out that the DNA from the tears matches his, he would use the grieving brother strategy. However, if the teardrops match Mr Bedi's DNA, you have a problem … you see what I mean?'

Rohan Malhotra looked like a ghost. He swallowed a few times, coughed, finished the glass of cold water kept at the table and ordered some more.

'Don't fret too much. It could turn out that they can't find DNA in the tears—it's not that simple—or the tears might not belong to either Mr Bedi or Manish Desai, they might belong to the third party … the murderer.'

'I am not worried.' After the initial distress, Rohan appeared to be returning to his element. 'I know for certain Mr Bedi couldn't have been at the scene of the crime.'

'Yeah, I meant to ask you that for some time now. Does he actually not know how to drive?'

'No. I know it sounds very pretentious, but he's never needed to. He's been chauffeur-driven his entire life.'

ROHAN MALHOTRA

It was close to midnight when I dropped ACP Dutta and drove home. Should I call Dad and tell him about Kale's discovery? Deciding that this was significant, and this had a shelf life, I called him and narrated the evening's meeting with ACP Dutta. He was equally aghast. I told him to use his own judgement if he wanted to speak to Mr Bedi right then or pass on the message in the morning.

After I got home, I went straight to my little work desk to put together some papers I required for the next day. It was 12.15 a.m. I knew it was late but I called Urvee. She was still awake. 'How're you, honey?' I asked her.

'Could be better. Pia asks me about you all the time, Rohan.'

'How's my munchkin?'

'Your daughter misses you a lot.'

'That's good to hear. At least she hasn't forgotten me.'

'She might very soon, if we don't return.' Urvee let out a chuckle. 'When do you think we should come back to Mumbai?'

'I think the hardest part is over. Why don't you check if you could get tickets for sometime early next week, maybe Tuesday or Wednesday?'

'Yes, I'll check. How is it going?'

'It's not been bad so far. I bet you're reading about it all in papers.'

'I'm following the news but I'm sure there are nuances that don't get reported, the inside story ...'

'And you know me. I cannot disclose any information about that.'

'What's your feeling, though?'

'I think we are almost through,' I lied—stray teardrops floating in the air and diffusing all around me.

'I'm so happy for you. It's your first big case and you seem to have done really well. The media has really been generous, they've been positive about you all the way. I'm very proud of you, Rohan.'

It was awkward—getting congratulated for something you've just lied about.

'Thank you, though there's nothing to be proud of yet. I mean, you know how a million things can go wrong between now and the Judge's verdict.'

'Be optimistic.'

'I'd rather be a realist.'

'Whatever. Are we still going to Switzerland for our next holiday?'

'Yes honey, in December.' I kept my voice steady. We would surely be wealthier by the end of the trial. However, if Mr Bedi lost the case, a holiday funded by him wouldn't feel so right. Moreover, Mr Bedi losing might also mean that the case would continue. He wouldn't just accept defeat and go to prison for a life term or death penalty. He wouldn't rely on his innocence proving itself by fair means, he'd most likely start calling in all his chits, which he hadn't this time around, then appeal the judgement and expedite the hearing through his connections. It could mean a lot more work or completely no work for me. If I lost this initial case, this could well be my final payment. He would surely—and Dad would agree with him—move to a more experienced advocate. I might myself suggest taking the appeal to Dadawala & Partners and running along with them rather than getting fired and going back to squat in my previous office, handling petitions for Ramdeens of Mumbai. It was a scary line of thought.

'You there, Rohan?'

'Yes, just got side-tracked by something regarding the cross-examination tomorrow. I think it's quite late, so I'll let you go now. Let me know when you can fly back, please.'

'I wish I was with you now.'

'It's been a long time.' I meant it.

'Think about me, good night.'

'Good night.'

TEJ MALHOTRA

I had died a trillion deaths, the blood in my veins had frozen enough to be wrapped on a stick and sold as iced lolly to some blood-devouring cannibal, since the time Rohan had called me to let me know that the latest and final discovery by forensics was drops of saline water, analysed and proven to be lacrimation. It was close to midnight, but I thought this was important enough to call Prem about.

Prem's phone rang a few times before it went into voicemail. I didn't think it appropriate to leave a message, so I hung up.

He called back.

'Sorry, by the time I got to my phone, it had stopped ringing.'

'I'm the one who should be sorry about bothering you at this hour …'

'I'm sure it must be …'—I heard him yawn—'… imperative or you wouldn't have.'

'Rohan found out the latest evidence at the crime scene.' I told him about the discovery of tears, their location and that Apte and Manish Desai were aware of the same.

At first I heard a chuckle, and then a roaring laugh.

'Are you okay, Prem?'

'Okay? I'm relieved.'

Relieved? Was he being frivolous? Or had he finally lost it after brilliantly putting up a brave front for so long?

'Relieved, how?'

'Tej, is that the only evidence they've found?'

'Yes, and I'm told they've now closed the file and sent the final report to the police, and the prosecutor. But, I'm afraid I don't follow you … why are you relieved?'

'Tej, the only worry I had was that someone might have easily taken a strand of hair from my hairbrush or picked up some body hair and planted it at the scene of crime to incriminate me. But no one could have possibly collected my *tears* and dropped them at the crime scene; so if that is all they have, I see no problem.'

I didn't say anything.

'I know you've had your moments of doubt, my friend, and I know even I would have had the same suspicions if our roles were reversed, but the truth is, I haven't been near that Pali Hill property for over a decade. And if, as you said, the tears were found on the bed sheet, there is no chance on God's earth that those tears are mine.'

I let myself breathe finally, and the relief I felt was a liberating feeling.

'What does Rohan think?' he asked, as I mutely hung on to the phone.

'He was concerned too.'

'I think we're closer to celebration than ever.'

'Yeah, that is right. I'll see you tomorrow. Good night, Prem.'

'Thanks for letting me know, I can sleep better now. Good night, Tej.'

As I cut the call, I could feel the blood thawing in my veins, a touch of triumph seeping into my pores. Were we finally over the line?

Bad news always found equally vile partners. The morning call from one of the board of directors made me wake up to another harsh blow. I dressed and rushed to Prem's residence. There was no way to avoid this conversation with Prem, and I wanted to have it before we left for the court.

Stock trading was a vicious circle. If bad news brought a stock's price down, panic selling started, which led to the price dropping further. With the ongoing murder trial against Prem Bedi, the stock of Bedi & Sons was trading at its all time low, a whopping 35 per cent drop from the closing price on the day we had returned from Seoul. It was seriously bad news.

'Any predictions on stock prices, Tej?' he asked, gesturing towards the newspaper which was open at the stock pages and kept on the table across him.

'I didn't expect this.'

'Neither did I, but then neither did I expect Rea and her husband to be murdered. Nor did I anticipate being accused, so I guess I'm not the best fortuneteller in town,' he smiled mirthlessly.

'We'll recover, Prem.'

'How?'

'I can't think of anything right away, but I'll work out something, trust me.'

'Buy the stock. As far as I know, there is no legal clause against buying my own stock up to, I think, eighty per cent. However, I do not want to be seen doing that, as it might lead to further panic. People might think I'm scared and that will scare them even more.'

I looked at him but didn't say a word. How confident was he? He was being tried for double murder, the verdict of which wasn't known. He could be incarcerated for fourteen years or worse …

'What?' he asked. Maybe he saw the apprehension on my face.'I thought you predicted that the stock price will go north and fetch in more profits when we win the case. So, either you were mollycoddling me then or you still have doubts about my innocence … which one is it, my friend?' He smiled.

'I know you're innocent, Prem. But who knows what the outcome of this trial will be?'

'Exactly. When I win the trial I win fiscally too—we'll put the money back into business, declare a generous dividend to reward those who stayed with us or give bonus shares. You might think I don't care about money if I lose, but I cannot lose. I cannot let so many people down.'

I just nodded again.

'Speak to our brokers. Spread the buying; you know how to keep the identity of the buyer under wraps better than I do.'

MANISH DESAI

It was well past midnight and the party was finally winding down now. We had been celebrating our impending victory—DCP Mathur, Apte and I. Sonia had brought a friend, Aarti, with her, who was equally hot, deferential and yielding. Of course, Sonia was no girlfriend of mine, and Aarti was no friend of hers. Sonia and Aarti were barely in their twenties, good-looking girls who had moved to Mumbai from separate small towns somewhere in the north, with ambitions of making it in Bollywood. They were still hopeful, but like many others, they were cash-strapped, and with Bollywood slamming doors in their face, there had turned to the numerous patrons of their bodies.

The celebration was prompted by the news DCP Mathur had communicated to us earlier in the evening. He had called up the Versova clinic to expedite the results of the DNA profiling they had run on the blood sample I had provided yesterday and it had turned up negative. The teardrops found on the scene of my brother's murder weren't mine, which I had known because I was positive I hadn't cried when I had seen the corpses or since. Nevertheless, Apte wanted to be definite. Once the results were confirmed, DCP Mathur asked Apte to ask me to bring the '*booze and babes*'—Apte communicated it to me verbatim—to have a good time. Apte offered his apartment and we decided that his dirty as sin apartment wasn't so blemished a place that it couldn't host the depraved party we were gathered there for.

I had bought two bottles of Chivas Regal and accompanying mixers, as well as some beers. And then I'd called Sonia to and asked her to bring a friend along. I could have run a University course on how to burn money in milliseconds. But it was all for the greater good—spend today, inherit tomorrow.

'It has got to be … the Bedi guy. He must have … felt a pang of … of pain … or guilt after, after killing his hot ex-wife …' The DCP was drunk. He was slurring and his movements had become clumsy. He had all but torn off Aarti's top and his hands fondled and squeezed the girl unashamedly. He ignored Sonia, his entire focus on the new girl in the room. 'I think … we should go now.'

Apte and I looked at each other. I sensed that even Apte was grateful that the DCP had decided to leave.

'Come, Aarti … you come with me,' the DCP lunged at the girl.

Aarti's expression articulated that she was scared. Of course, she was an escort who had been paid for the all-night party, but she hadn't expected to go home with the drunk cop. I gestured Sonia to take Aarti aside and convince her to go with the DCP. I knew he was violent, but Sonia knew that I would take care of everything later—financially.

Once the DCP and Aarti had left, Apte took Sonia to his bedroom. He didn't want her staying back at his apartment; he didn't want his neighbours seeing her leave in the morning. Moreover, he wanted to sleep soon so he would be fresh for tomorrow. I sat outside, listening to the rock 'n' roll of his bed springs for twenty minutes before Sonia appeared, straightening her skimpy dress. I left Apte's apartment with her around one. I had no intentions of taking Sonia to my place either as I, too, needed to be fresh for the last bit of my cross-examination in the morning.

ROHAN MALHOTRA

I had been restive and distressed all night. I had been exhausted since the start of the evening and then crashed at my desk. So while I had caught good six or seven hours of shuteye, I didn't feel revitalized. Nevertheless, the phone call at seven-thirty in the morning from Dad reinvigorated me. He was convinced the tears could not belong to Mr Bedi, and that was enough to assure me.

I was in court a half hour before the trial was to resume for the little conference I had insisted upon with Mr Bedi and Dad. Mr Bedi repeated what Dad had narrated. I felt even more respect for Mr Bedi when he offered to provide a sample for DNA profiling, so that he could be ruled out as a suspect, once and forever. Game, set, and no DNA match.

Forty minutes later, all court formalities and protocols out of the way, I recommenced my final tirade against Manish Desai.

'Mr Desai, you mentioned in your testimony that the foremost motive for my client defendant to "*cold-bloodedly murder*",'—I gesticulated the quote marks for everyone to see, '... your brother and sister-in-law was greed, the money he would gain from the insurance payout, correct?'

Manish nodded.

'Mr Desai, the court cannot record nods, so you will have to vocally respond to my questions, if that's okay?'

'Yes, you are correct. Mr Bedi is—'

I cut in his meandering with enthusiasm. 'Mr Desai, may I remind you that the rules of this court haven't changed since yesterday. You must respond to my questions, and keep them brief enough to just answer them. Please refrain from adding your enthusiastic embellishments.'

'Okay, I was only—'

'Mr Desai, I second the defence advocate's words. Please refrain from lengthy explanations that are not requested for by the questioning advocate,' Judge Chowdhary said.

Manish Desai grimaced. He was visibly discomfited, which is what I wanted. He looked askance at Apte, but I was shrewd enough to walk a few steps to my right to block Apte from his sight. Apte could always stand up and object if he thought I was crossing the line. Fact was, I was correct.

'So, Mr Desai, did your brother and his wife—the deceased Mrs and Mr Mahesh Desai, have any children?'

'No.'

'How many other brothers and sisters do you have?'

'None.'

'Do you have no other living siblings then, Mr Desai?'

'No.'

'Oh.' I made a sorry face, like I was just as indignant that the only sibling this poor man had had been taken away by the cruel hands of kismet. 'Do you know if Mrs Rea Desai has any family—parents, siblings … anyone?'

'No one at all.'

'So they wouldn't take me to a mental hospital if I assumed that you are now the sole beneficiary of Mrs and Mr Mahesh Desai's entire estate?'

'I think so.'

'You think so? You're not sure then?'

'I mean there is no one except me that I know of.'

Advocate rule 101: never ever ask a question in the courtroom you don't already know the answer to. You didn't argue a case in a court to discover things. You discovered things and then took them to the courtroom. My search so far had predicted that the Desai couple had died without any registered will. People like Manish Desai didn't wait for the will to turn up. This eager beaver standing in the witness box would have dug up graves if he had to, and found out if there was any other beneficiary.

I paused for effect. I let the Judge take it in so that he would realise, without my having to point out later, that Manish Desai wasn't an ignorant, innocent brother like he wanted everyone to believe, but a shrewd, calculating man.

'Is there no registered will then?'

'Not that I know about.'

'So how do you know my client would benefit financially from the death of your deceased brother's wife?'

'She told my brother and me.'

I smiled and looked at Judge Chowdhary. It was hearsay, pure and simple. Any out of court statement was hearsay. For it to be taken up as evidence, it needed to be provided under oath at the court so that I—the defending advocate in this case—could cross-examine the witness. In dire circumstances, it could be accepted if the person, whose statement was being provided, was deceased like Rea, but that was a Judge's prerogative. My imploring look at the Judge was to plead before I uttered: 'Hearsay, Your Honour.'

He nodded. There was no way to confirm if the deceased had ever mentioned anything to Manish Desai or if he had got hold of a copy of the insurance policy.

But I decided to carry on with his play. 'Did she, I mean, did Mrs Rea Desai or your brother ever mention to you that if the insurance money was not paid to the defendant, who might be the sole beneficiary of the fifty crore rupees in question?'

'No.'

'She didn't mention that part ever?'

'No.'

'Would it be a substantial leap to assume it would be you?'

'I wouldn't think so.'

'I'm suggesting you would be.'

'Objection, Your Honour, my learned friend is speculating. Mr Bedi is present here.'

'While it is an interesting deduction, where is this heading, Mr Malhotra?' The Judge wanted to know.

'Your Honour, if you will please indulge me for a few minutes …'

'Granted, but please advance the case.'

Apte looked dejected. First objection of the day overruled. He sat simmering.

'Thank you, Your Honour. So, Mr Desai, if Mr Bedi were to vanish from this planet tomorrow, I am sure you understand you will be a *hundred*-crores richer, am I right?'

I heard a rustle of papers, scratching of pens in the audience. The stakes in the game had just been doubled and the media was taking notes. They should have done the math themselves but they hadn't. If, for any reason, Mr Bedi was disqualified from inheriting from Rea's insurance policy, the fifty crores from her share would go to Manish Desai—that was simple math. And lest anyone had overlooked this, the insurance policies in question were to mature in any event; Rea's death only made it an insurance claim and expedited it by a few months. Legalese on an off-the-shelf insurance policy wasn't everyone's forte. This one was bespoke for Mrs and Mr Prem Bedi; it was hardly in everyone's remit to grasp it completely. One of the clauses added had outlined the inheritance tree—Mr Bedi had shown this golden egg to me and then explained it to ensure that I had followed the intent of the words in the contract. It unmistakably stated that the first claim on Mr Bedi's policy was Rea Desai's. If Rea Desai wasn't around or declined it for any reason, the second claim was Mr Bedi's; however, if Mr Bedi couldn't claim it for any reason, the third claimant of the money was Rea's successor before Mr Bedi's heir. With Rea dead, and if Mr Bedi got convicted and lost the right to claim the insurance payment, the immediate beneficiary was, yes, Mr Manish Desai!

I walked back to my desk and Dad handed me copies of the insurance policies. 'Your Honour, the defence submits copies of Clause 7-B, page nine on the addendum, added to the standard insurance covenant.' I handed Ram Singh a copy, who passed it on to the Judge, then I quickly walked back to hand a copy to Apte. I waited a few minutes, gazing at the Judge as he turned pages to get to page nine on the addendum. He read it intently, then nodded and passed it on for record to Ram Singh. 'Continue, Mr Malhotra.'

'Mr Desai, do you know that if the defendant is alive, compos mentis and present, what is one of the only reasons he can be disbarred to receive that sum from insurance?'

'I wouldn't know.' Manish Desai's swagger had evaporated.

'Your Honour, I want the court to record that if the defendant, for any reason, is convicted in a capital crime, particularly committed on the other beneficiary, he would be excluded from any insurance claim. Please note Clause 7-B-iii on page ten of the addendum I submitted to the court only minutes ago.'

Ram Singh sifted through the sheets, read it and nodded to Judge Chowdhary, who didn't look as if he could be bothered to scrutinise it personally this time.

'Mr Desai, let me explain it in simple words. If Mr Bedi got convicted for the murder of Mrs Rea Desai, he loses the right to the money that was presented by the State as his motive to murder. In that instance you—and only you—would be entitled to Mrs Rea Desai's insurance money and Mr Prem Bedi's insurance payout too. So while you are bereaved, and I'm really sorry for the awful act committed by whoever it was that did it, you have a very good motive to get Mr Bedi convicted in these murders, don't you think?' I turned and glared at him.

'Objection, Your Honour, my learned friend is speculating without any facts,' Apte barked from behind.

'I can't comprehend what you're objecting to, Mr Apte. The defence advocate has just stated a fact, and backed it with documentary evidence. Did you not read it?' Judge Chowdhary looked irritated.

The knavish grin on Apte's face all but disappeared and fear crept into the eyes.

I turned to look at Manish Desai. Though Mr Bedi and Dad didn't agree, I still had this terrible hunch that Manish Desai was in some way—directly or indirectly—involved in the murders. In any case, he was left looking like a bare-faced opportunist now.

'As a matter of fact, wouldn't you agree, Mr Manish Desai, that considering the present financial status of my client vis-à-vis yours, you would relatively benefit more than—'

'Objection, Your Honour, this is unnecessary.'

'I withdraw my statement, Your Honour.' I knew I had punched it in, withdrawing it did not mean that Judge Chowdhary hadn't heard it. As I said, the whole courtroom drama was for the audience of one, the Judge.

'Strike it,' the Judge told Ram Singh. He looked at his watch. I knew it was time for me to wrap up. I had covered all my points and Judge Chowdhary had surely gotten a precise vignette of Manish Desai. I didn't want to carry on until he got jaded or thought I was being unnecessarily repetitive.

'I have no more questions for this witness, Your Honour.'

'Thank you, Mr Malhotra.' He looked at Apte. 'Do you have any questions for this witness on rebuttal?'

'No, Your Honour.'

Apte's expression suggested that he wanted Manish Desai out of the court's sight forever. Whatever damage could be done to his earlier testimony for the prosecution had already been done. There seemed little point in the Judge getting reminded of Manish Desai's dishonest mourning any longer.

'Before we recess for lunch, what other witnesses do you have for the day, Mr Apte?'

'We have the forensic expert Mr Anup Kale as a witness but, unfortunately, he cannot be here on the stand today. I request

Your Honour to grant time to the prosecution to rethink and return tomorrow, as Mr Kale would be our last witness.'

'Why is he not here? What urgent work does he have today?' The Judge sounded irritated. 'Has there been a homicide that he has been called at the crime scene?'

'I wouldn't know that, Your Honour.'

'Then I don't care. The court will be in session at 3 p.m.—please note that I have delayed the afternoon start—so ask your witness to turn up. Unless he is occupied elsewhere and you can convince me that his presence elsewhere is more urgent than his appearance in my court at three today afternoon, I will hold him in contempt of court, along with you. Do you understand?'

'But, Your Honour—'

'Overruled.'

'You nailed it,' Dad beamed at me when we got to the chambers.

'Yes, Rohan, I have to say you were fantastic today.' Mr Bedi added.

'Thank you.'

'Why do you think the prosecutor wants to delay bringing in the forensic expert?' Mr Bedi asked.

'My guess would be that it's to keep us hanging. He doesn't know that we already know about the latest find, so he's just playing us, I think.' I had asked ACP Dutta the same question and he didn't have a suitable answer either. 'My guess is that Apte will have to pretend that the prosecution also found out about the new evidence at the last minute, unless he wants to face the Judge's wrath for concealing evidence.'

My mobile vibrated. ACP Dutta was calling me.

'Good afternoon, ACP Dutta.'

'Are you alone?'

'No, I'm with my client and my associate.' Well, Dad was also my associate, technically.

'Okay, look. Anup Kale is not available this afternoon. I got a call from my boss to stand in for Kale, so I do not want any embarrassment. You know our little understanding.'

'You don't even have to mention it, my friend. Thanks for letting me know.'

Disconnecting the call, I told them what ACP Dutta had said. If he took the stand, I lost the right to put up a fight or appeal to the Judge that the State had concealed vital evidence, which I would have certainly screamed, had Kale been in the witness stand. I couldn't point fingers with the ACP on the stand when I actually knew about the damned evidence. It would put ACP Dutta in jeopardy if I said that he had informed me about the said evidence. Whereas, if he lied that he hadn't told me, and I pointed fingers at the prosecution, I would suborn him into committing perjury. Mr Bedi and Dad agreed we couldn't push ACP Dutta under the train. The best way to handle that would be to look disturbed by the events, and let the Judge read my expressions without me having to opening my gob.

'All rise…'

'Mr Apte, have you ensured that your next witness is here now?' Judge Chowdhary didn't seem to be in any disposition to waste time on pleasantries.

'Your Honour, due to reasons I cannot explain, we could not locate Mr Anup Kale at this last minute, but I have recalled an earlier witness, ACP Ranjeet Dutta, to provide us the forensic evidence that Mr Kale would have presented to the court. I apologise—'

'You're a very sharp man, Mr Apte. I give you full marks for making the effort and I also appreciate you bringing in ACP Dutta.'

I was very disappointment that the Judge wasn't one bit chagrined.

'Thank you, Your Honour.'

'The State calls ACP Dutta once again to the witness stand.'

ACP RANJEET DUTTA

I walked into the courtroom once more and took the oath again, since this wasn't a continuation of my previous testimony. I wasn't scared, but I was a tad apprehensive. Lying under oath was a crime in itself, irrespective of however noble the intentions. I was solely responsible for the precarious position I had put myself in and, albeit for a brief moment, I repented having passed on classified info to Rohan. If I hadn't told Rohan Malhotra about the newest forensic discovery, I would have been in the clear. But I had, and at the time I had no indication that I would be filling in for Anup Kale. It wasn't that Kale wasn't available, like Apte had falsified to the court. Apte was shrewd; he suspected that Rohan would create a fuss if Anup Kale took the stand, whereas with me he wouldn't. The evil genius had somehow convinced DCP Mathur to send me to the slaughter, and here I was. I was hoping and praying that Rohan had fully comprehended what I had alluded to in the brief phone call I had made to him during the recess.

'Welcome back, ACP Dutta,' Judge Chowdhary addressed me before Apte could begin. 'I believe …' he looked at some paper he had in front, 'Dr Anup Kale couldn't make it so you have volunteered to progress the case.'

'Yes, Your Honour.'

'Thank you.' He turned to the advocates: 'As ACP Dutta is here to provide us with evidence on behalf of his colleague, I would not permit unnecessary questioning directed to him by either of you. ACP Dutta will state the facts and nothing more. Is that acceptable to both advocates?'

Apte nodded. I was too tense to glance at Rohan, but I was sure he nodded his acquiescence too. This was turning out to be an even bigger problem; not that I could have easily dodged questions from either advocates in the court, but if the Judge asked me point blank questions, I was screwed.

'So tell the court what new evidence have you got for us to consider, ACP Dutta,' asked Justice Chowdhary.

This was straightforward. I explained the whole discovery of lacrimal secretions found at the scene of crime, and although the probability of DNA extraction from tears found on any surface was barely ten to fifteen per cent, in this particular case, the forensic team had been lucky; the forensics had the DNA profile of whoever had shed those tears. I didn't elaborate on the discovery or the analysis or the theory preponderated by DCP Mathur and Apte that they should or could belong to the murderer, and I didn't obviate anything. I merely reported the facts.

I gazed at Mr Bedi, directly into his eyes, when the recovered teardrops were mentioned. I knew he'd have known this before through Rohan but I still wanted to see, to appraise his reaction when it got mentioned in a courtroom, because he had, on tape, told me that he hadn't been near the crime scene for over a decade, at least. All I got was a near imperceptible shake of the head and a smile, as if he wanted to stand up and say: *stop this nonsense, guys, it's enough*. My assessment, still, was that either he was downright innocent, repulsed at being dragged into the smut pointlessly, or that he was an actor of phenomenal calibre. The Judge's voice broke into my thoughts.

'And the prosecution's conjecture is that they could either belong to the murderer or someone who was in the vicinity during the crime, or immediately before or after it, as the analysis disclosed the recency of the sample. Is that correct, Mr Apte?'

'Yes, Your Honour.'

The Judge looked back at me. 'ACP Dutta, when were these, these… lacrimal secretions discovered?'

'Your Honour, we were told that forensics had recovered something a while back and hence, they had only submitted the interim report, which we couldn't disclose earlier. However, they only came to know that these were teardrops two days ago.'

The Judge didn't look pleased and justifiably so. This was crucial evidence, and two days was a long time.

'When did the State and the prosecuting advocate know about this?'

'I have no knowledge of that, Your Honour. I did not communicate with Mr Apte or his team. My immediate superior DCP Dilip Mathur did that.' That was the truth.

'Has the defending advocate or anyone on the defence team known about this?'

'No, Your Honour.' Rohan said aloud, saving me from perjury.

'Mr Apte, when did DCP Mathur convey this information to you or to anyone in your team?'

Apte stood up, opened his mouth but words, it seemed, dried up in his throat.

'And if you even as much as think of being ambiguous or attempt to mislead me, I promise you that you'll be sorry.'

Apte's mouth was still agape. His brain didn't seem to work out how to respond.

'Mr Apte, please answer my question. And remember, no glossing please.' Judge Chowdhary was getting testy now.

'Your Honour, I … came to know about them late at night the … day before yesterday.'

'I see. And you chose to sit on it, come here and feign that the forensics had recovered something but you had no idea what?'

'Your Honour, I wanted the expert to tell the court.'

'And you could not get the so-called expert to come to the court.'

'I apologise, Your Honour.'

'I want to see you in my chamber as soon as we leave the court today. I do not tolerate deliberate concealing of evidence.'

'Yes, Your Honour. The State profusely apologises for this occurance.'

I was pleased the Judge did not confirm with me if Rohan's camp had been aware of this discovery.

'And you think this discovery is pertinent to this trial, why?'

'Your Honour, the State resolutely believes that these tears belong to the murderer. And as the defendant was once married to one of the victims, it is logical to deduce that he was remorseful after the barbaric act he had just committed …

'Another logical deduction by the State?' the Judge let out a mocking smile. 'Of whatever you've presented so far, Mr Apte, I'm aghast that you even strived to bring up this case against the defendant. It's so facile. The whole thing reminds me of Birbal's khichdi.' He shook his head in disgust.

Soft laughter passed through the court at the reference.

'Order …'

'Mr Apte, listen to me carefully now. If this is another one of State's knee-jerk theory, and the defendant's DNA does not match the DNA found in the teardrop samples, I will dismiss this case with prejudice. You will not be able to make an appeal or retry this case. This is plain mockery and waste of the court's time.'

Apte stood and nodded.

'The court orders the defendant to appear for DNA fingerprinting at the centre that is recognised by the court. Ram Singh will inform you of the name and location after the session.'

'Your Honour …' I saw Rohan stand up to address the Judge.

'Do you have something to add, Mr Malhotra?'

'Yes, Your Honour, the defence team would like to request DNA profiling of Mr Manish Desai too.'

'I agree. The court orders DNA profiling for Mr Prem Bedi and Mr Manish Desai. Both parties will attend the clinic that Ram Singh will advise, at 10 a.m. tomorrow morning and provide a blood sample. The court orders both advocates and ACP Dutta to be in attendance at the time. Furthermore, I do not want anyone from the prosecution or defence teams to have any contact with the clinic whatsoever, after the said samples have been provided. ACP Dutta, you will bring in the result of the tests to the court, in a signed and sealed envelope. If I hear that any of these directions have been violated, I will be compelled to punish the guilty party to the full extent of the law. Is that understood by all the parties concerned?'

'Yes, Your Honour,' I said confidently. I guessed the difficult part for me was over now. I could breathe. I heard acquiescence from both advocates in the background.

'To be certain, the court orders blood samples, not saliva or buccal swabs.'

'Thank you, Your Honour.'

I looked at Mr Bedi. He looked unaffected by the request. I guessed he was confident they weren't his tears after all. Anyway, it was only a matter of days now.

'The court will resume at 9 a.m. on Monday. I want all the parties present with their advocates, no excuses whatsoever. Any further motions?'

'The defence would like to request the court to dismiss the case for lack of evidence, Your Honour,' Rohan spoke first, his eyes brimming with confidence.

'Noted, but I will take that call on Monday. Anything else?'

Apte stood up again.

'Your Honour, the State would like to request that the defendant's bail be revoked with immediate effect.'

'On what grounds?'

'The defendant is a flight risk now, Your Honour.'

Rohan stood up, 'Object—'

'Sit down, Mr Malhotra. The prosecution advocate is talking to me.'

Shit. I had no reason to sympathise with Mr Bedi, except for the fact that Apte, Desai and DCP Mathur had played dirty the entire time, but I was cocksure Judge Chowdhary wouldn't revoke the bail.

'Be serious, Mr Apte,' the Judge said derisively. 'The motion is denied. The court is adjourned. Meet me in my chamber now, Mr Apte.'

ROHAN MALHOTRA

By now the media had recognised and conceded to the fact that neither the prosecution nor the defence team would talk to them regarding the proceedings or offer any views. The journalists had left for their offices to write up the day's story, but sure enough the cameramen had hung back to snap pictures of Mr Bedi, me and Apte; Manish Desai hadn't been in attendance since the morning. A fresh story warranted fresh pictures, as if the public cared that Mr Bedi's worsted suit was a different shade of grey today. We decided to convene at Altamount Road, then walked out, the camera flashes going off in our faces. Dad and Mr Bedi went separately and I drove my car.

Veena ji was happy to see us all. Mr Bedi summarised the days' events for her and told her about the DNA sample he had to provide the next day.

'What happens next?'

'Judge Chowdhary was adequately clear,' I explained. 'If the DNA sample does not match, he's not even awarding this case a decision; he's going to dismiss the case with prejudice for lack of sufficient evidence.'

'And … ?'

'It means no case, and Mr Bedi cannot be tried in any court of law unless the investigation reveals some fresh and concrete evidence incriminating him somehow. And it will be a fresh trial, not an appeal. I'm certain the police and any prosecutor will think numerous times before taking it to court the second time around.'

'That's great news then.'

'Yes, ma'am,' I responded happily, but there might have been a touch of nerves in my voice, because Dad looked at me with furrowed brows.

'Are you still worried, Rohan?' Mr Bedi asked.

'Not at all.'

'Good. Because as I explained to Tej last night that if the discovery had been of hair or skin residue or something, it could have been planted there without my knowledge and we should have been worried sick. But I cannot think of any possible way someone could have stolen my tears.'

He sounded confident and the *what-ifs* in my mind finally retreated to the back seat. This might finally be the start of new life for me, Urvee and Pia.

'Let's plan logistics for tomorrow. Rohan, would you like to meet Prem and me at the clinic in Byculla or come here first?'

The court had ordained that we were to provide the sample to Dr D'Souza next day morning. Where Dr D'Souza would get the sample tested was something none of us were supposed to know. The test results would be picked up by ACP Dutta on Monday morning before he came to the court.

'I'll see you there at eight-thirty?'

'Fine. And thank you, Rohan,' Mr Bedi said. 'Tej, I think we should get Rohan's pay check ready now.'

'You're welcome, sir, and there's no rush.' *Please give it to me ASAP*, I said under my breath.

Urvee told me that she had booked tickets for the Tuesday morning's flight, a day after the trial got over.

Everything seemed to be coming together in the end. Mr Bedi's confidence was infectious. I, too, gloated now; victory was imminent. What could possibly go wrong? After a very long time, I slept early, and deeply.

I met Mr Bedi and Dad outside the Byculla clinic. Apte and Manish Desai were already in attendance and we exchanged forced but polite smiles as we waited for ACP Dutta, who had called to inform us that he was running late. Once he arrived, a junior doctor took blood samples from both Mr Bedi and Manish in everyone's presence. As per the Judge's edict, we did not ask any questions about *how, what, when*. We were let go after twenty minutes. As there was nothing to do for the next few days, I first played with the idea of flying to New Delhi to surprise Urvee and Pia, and then called Dad. He said that if the Judge wanted to see the advocates about anything, he'd attend as an associate. I drove to the airport, parked my car and bought a ticket for a Jet Airways flight that was leaving for Delhi in two hours. I also booked a return ticked to Mumbai for Sunday afternoon.

MANISH DESAI

Apte was understandably upset after the dressing-down by the Judge yesterday, but he had no one to blame. He was leading the prosecution; he was the one in charge. It had been his strategy to keep the Bedi camp in the dark for as long as he possibly could. The original suggestion might have come from DCP Mathur but, ultimately, it had been his call. If he had even as much as tried to point a finger at DCP Mathur, he knew he'd lose a limb in the bargain later; DCP Mathur could be vicious. As I drove back from Byculla after giving my blood sample, I fantasised about the money. I regretted the commitments I had made in anticipation of the money. I was fine with paying DCP Mathur; having a dishonest guy like him on your side couldn't hurt in the long run. I had to ensure that I somehow captured or recorded when I paid him the money after the win. Who knew when one might need evidence? My grouse was the promise I had made to Apte. He didn't deserve the money. I mean, the main evidence would be the DNA, not Apte's meaningless arguments. If anything, the guy had been sloppy; he had even irked the Judge. If the DNA evidence hadn't been presented when it was, we'd have lost the case and the money, all thanks to that moron, Apte. Moreover, I couldn't think of ever needing to engage him for anything else. If I needed an advocate, I'd hire a respectable one.

I kept thinking about how to renege on the money as I drove to my apartment. And then a terrific idea surfaced. What if I sweet-talked the DCP into the plan? If I paid him more than we had previously agreed—maybe a ten per cent more, now that the overall basket had inflated—wouldn't he help me? I would still be better off than paying Apte. To my mind, it was a win-win situation for the DCP and me. In any event, what could I lose by asking DCP Mathur? I called him on his personal mobile as soon as I got in.

'Good afternoon, sir.'

'Is that Desai? Is everything okay?'

'Yes, sir. I provided the blood sample today.'

'We already know the DNA found in the tears doesn't match yours. It must belong to Prem Bedi. Who else could it be?'

'I know, sir. And getting me profiled ahead of time was a brilliant idea. I'm a fan of yours.'

'Experience, Desai, experience.'

'Talking of being your fan, I'm not the only one it seems.'

'Who else is my fan?'

'Both Sonia and Aarti, sir. They told me they could barely walk after the nights with you. You must do something other men can't.'

I could hear him chuckle.

'Did they complain?'

'Oh no, not at all, sir. I think they were awestruck by your sheer physical strength.' Of course it was a lie. The girls had told me they wouldn't go near this brute even if I paid them twice the amount.

'Do you have anyone else?'

'Yes, sir, I'll find someone else for tonight.'

'So let's have another party at Apte's place then.'

'It will be better if you came over to my place. I don't think we need to include Apte in every party.'

'Hmm, okay. What time?'

'Should we say seven-thirty?'

'Sure. Get a good one.'

'Don't worry, DCP sahib.'

Apte thus eliminated, I'd get some time to talk to DCP Mathur, explain the situation, and make him a fresh proposal.

One step closer.

ACP RANJEET DUTTA

I had sneaked in to see Judge Chowdhary immediately after Apte left his chamber with a sullen face.

'You wanted to see me, ACP Dutta?'

'Yes, Your Honour.'

'What is it about?' He took off his glasses and placed them at his desk, but still kept standing like he wanted me to finish quickly and leave.

'I do not trust certain people in our own police department, and I can't rule out some sabotage of the samples that might occur despite your warning.'

'Sit down and explain.' He gestured me to the chair across his desk.

Without mentioning names, I expressed that I suspected someone in our department was breaking protocols to supply information to the prosecution. The Judge asked if I knew that this had happened in exchange for money, and though I wanted to mention Sonia, I didn't. I had broken the protocol too, by talking to Rohan, but I had enough morals that I wouldn't contaminate samples or coerce any doctor to give a wrong report.

'So what do you propose we do?'

'The samples should not be processed where you've said they would be. The pathologists there work with the police all the time, and someone can influence the results.'

The Judge nodded. 'Okay.'

Okay? Was he going to take some action or not?

'While I appreciate your honesty, ACP Dutta, you have given me no names to take action against. So while I am inclined to believe what you've told me is true, what gives me the assurance that it isn't you who, in fact, colours that test?'

He was right. He had no way of knowing my intentions.

'Here's what I'll do. I will issue a separate order that the samples taken at the centre are packed and taken elsewhere for testing. A court-deputed person would be in attendance to preserve the chain of evidence. Even you won't be privy to where they go. And please don't attempt to follow my person to figure that out. That's only fair.'

'Yes, Your Honour.'

'Leave your mobile number with Ram Singh. You'll be asked to accompany the court clerk to collect the sealed results and return to the court on Monday.'

'Thank you, Your Honour.'

'Anything else, ACP Dutta?'

'No, Your Honour. Thank you.'

When we all turned up for the blood sample collection the next morning, I got there late, but it wasn't because I'd been stuck in the traffic. I had been driving around to make sure that none of DCP's boys were sneaking around to eye where the samples were headed for DNA profiling. All marks to the Judge—the court clerk who was to attend the session did not make an appearance in front of the advocates or their clients. He stayed in the other room and met me only after the donors and their advocates had left. We waited two hours, and in the meantime, the man from the court went out several times to check if anyone was snooping around. Before he left with the samples, he politely reminded me that I was not to leave the premises for another hour after his departure.

TEJ MALHOTRA

Surprisingly, I had never suffered from insomnia before this nightmare began. And until the DNA profiling was complete, I could imagine that the stress level wouldn't drop.

I researched a bit about DNA. Teardrops contained DNA, like many other bodily fluids. I liked the fact that the Judge had kept it straightforward: since in a buccal swab the cells weren't apparent, it wasn't visually verifiable if the DNA had been taken, whereas a blood sample consisted of biomarkers like proteins, antibodies, and metabolites; there were no doubts that blood contained DNA.

All things considered, there was nothing anyone could do now. The samples had been provided, the results would convict or exonerate Prem. I had faith in ACP Dutta that he would not let Apte play foul at this juncture.

Mr Lee had confirmed he was flying in Monday evening. The cars had been booked to pick up him and his associates. This was his third visit to Mumbai since our negotiations had commenced, and this was the first one where he had requested us to book rooms for him. And I could see why. If the verdict wasn't in Prem's favour, he'd simply cancel the trip, no hassles. The thought sent tremors through my already traumatised brain. Prem realized this too, but he asked that we booked them at the Taj.

Freddy Vakil called me. He explained he had been hired by Rohan and he wanted to 'pick my brains' about Prem. He wanted to know who Prem interacted with personally—social, golfing partners, other interactions—to check if any of those relations had felt hurt or offended enough about something to carry out a nasty revenge. Having dealt with ample sleuths before for background checks on new business partners, I appreciated his approach. He wished to establish if Prem had 'screwed someone real bad'. He was keen to explore Prem's business connections too. I joked if all his research would be via me. He clarified that I was to give him the first point of contacts and then he would stem out wherever he thought there could be leads. He specifically wanted to know if Prem had made any hostile business takeovers or some last-minute withdrawals from some deals that could have hurt someone financially or personally. He needed a start. It had to be someone close to Prem.

Honestly, the undercurrent of the looming Monday morning's court decision dominated my life and my brain. I told him I was busy so I'd meet him next weekend for a longish session. It also gave me time to reflect and collect my thoughts rather than provide him with piecemeal mentions of people and situations.

Rohan called to say he was with Urvee and Pia. Prem had been right; it was time to pay Rohan. He had been brilliant throughout, though the final outcome now hung on the DNA profiling. But if it hadn't been for that discovery, the Judge had indeed looked pro-defence.

ROHAN MALHOTRA

I had a lovely weekend with Urvee and Pia. We first went shopping, and then I had taken both my girls out to India Gate and Red Fort. I was now onboard my flight to Mumbai. Everything seemed to be going my way. I was confident that the teardrops recovered from the crime scene could not have come from Mr Bedi and the DNA profiling would absolve him conclusively. The only aspect that was still unsettling was the malevolent nexus of Apte, Manish Desai, and as I now knew, DCP Mathur: first-rate conniving bastards. What if they sprung another last-minute surprise? What if they had found a way to eliminate ACP Dutta from the loop and we were caught off guard yet again? But Apte would be reluctant to risk Judge Chowdhary's indignation one more time. The Judge had the powers to suspend him, even start the procedure to disbar him. That said, who could tell how much cash Apte was promised by his devious partner Desai? Maybe enough to ensure that he never needed to set foot in a courtroom again. That could change everything. A hundred crore rupees was a lot of money. Even a fraction of that would be enough for Apte to quit his non-existent career.

I landed at 4.15 p.m., picked up my car from the parking and called Dad to check if everything was in order. His attempt to sound casual was as flat as a glass of champagne kept on the kitchen table for a week, but he was on the same plane as me.

'We can't do anything more, can we? The evidence will speak for itself.' His voice trailed off towards the end of the sentence.

'How is Mr Bedi feeling?'

'He is in top form. He sounds and appears more confident than me.'

'That's good. If he feels confident about victory, then he has to be innocent, Dad. We should relax. Maybe we're overanalysing things.'

'As you say, Mr Defence Advocate par excellence.'

I could finally sense a cheer in his voice.

'Ha-ha, have a good day. I'll see you tomorrow at court.'

'No, I think we should all travel together tomorrow. Why don't you come over early to Prem's house tomorrow? We can have breakfast together and go to the court.'

I called ACP Dutta later in the evening. I didn't know what I'd say because I was certain I would not mention anything about the DNA fingerprinting results. Perhaps, deep down somewhere, I wanted him to drop some hint that might bring us a bit of relief. He, of course, didn't. The Judge had ordained that the DNA test results would only be opened in the court so maybe he didn't know anything either. Then he nonchalantly mentioned that the blood samples collected from Mr Bedi and Manish Desai weren't being profiled where they were taken in Byculla, but by order of the court they had been sent to an undisclosed location, and it was best that way.

ACP RANJEET DUTTA

My mobile was on silent but the sound of it vibrating on the bedside table was loud enough to wake me up. It was 6.02 in the morning and the display said: *Unknown Caller.*

'Is that ACP Ranjeet Dutta?'

'Yes, speaking. Who is this?'

'Good morning, we met at the Byculla Hospital last Saturday, remember? I was the one who carried the blood samples to be profiled.'

I guessed that was the only introduction the man could provide, considering the fact that he hadn't, at any point in the hours we had spent together, told me his name. All I could picture was a thin man, in his mid-thirties, black wiry hair and glasses so thick they would shame a bottle of street-side lime soda—they even had that green hue.

'Good morning, Mr—' No, I didn't think he would accidently give me his name, it was just that I couldn't come up with any other way of addressing him on the telephone.

'What time could you come to the Hospital at Byculla, ACP Dutta? Could you make it by eight, please?'

Shit! Had I been taken for a royal ride? Maybe, the soda-water-glasses guy hadn't gone anywhere after he left me in

Byculla the other day. Possibly, all he did was to walk a few steps from the room we were into the diagnostic centre, dropped the samples and left, while I waited an hour. If the DNA profiling had been done at JJ Hospital, then there was every chance DCP Mathur had the opportunity to get to the samples, and the results, before anyone else. I had been sincere to the point of being stupid. I wondered if I should call Dr D'Souza. I trusted him, but he was a morbid pathologist. The DNA comparisons would have been done by some other expert, and if Dr D'Souza went around exploring, there was a possibility that our little informal conversation might leak out and come back to bite me in the ass. Whatever the result, there was little I could do to influence now.

'Byculla? I thought you were taking the samples elsewhere,' I mentioned casually.

'I cannot say anything about that, ACP Dutta. It will get us both in trouble.'

His phone was possibly tapped. I didn't want to take a chance.

'Oh no, that wasn't what I meant. I'm sorry I just blurted it out without thinking. Eight, did you say?'

'Yes.'

'I'll be there. Where should I meet you?'

'In exactly the same room as last time, ACP Dutta.'

'Okay.'

I rubbed my eyes, got out of bed and put the kettle on for a strong coffee. As I sipped my coffee, shaved, showered and got dressed, I wondered what I could do if certain facts had been deliberately manipulated to change the outcome of what the media had now termed as 'THE HUNDRED CRORE WAR' or 'THE TRIAL OF THE DECADE'. I wasn't inclined to protect anyone, as I always maintained, but if DCP Mathur had somehow laid his hands on the reports, I could wager anything that Mr Bedi wouldn't be returning to his residence after court today. And that would be wrong. The Judge couldn't compare the analysed samples himself; the ruling would depend on the sanctity of the report. Apparently Rohan could ask for a retest, but that would take days, perhaps weeks, and it might require a formal appeal to today's judgement. Mr Bedi's bail, in the meantime, would be revoked.

Should I call Rohan? Yes or no? I decided I wouldn't. I had done enough, and I had no basis to support what I had been speculating. It could all be my imagination. And it would only cause anguish. Besides, it might lead to some dire or unwarranted action that everyone might regret later.

TEJ MALHOTRA

On the day of the verdict, Bedi & Sons' stock opened at 61 per cent lower than its price on the day of our return from Seoul. It was at the new lowest point in 52-weeks, probably lower than its trading price four years ago. My phone had started ringing at six in the morning and hadn't stopped till I switched it off. The tyre was about to hit the tarmac, but none of the occupants had yet jumped off the bus. All directors had held on to their positions. None had sold their stocks; none had resigned.

Were they scared about their future? Yes.

Were they impatient to know the verdict? Of course they were.

Nevertheless, they had stuck to their Mogul.

ROHAN MALHOTRA

There was a bigger throng outside the court today than on any of the previous days. The media had vociferously broadcast that the murder trial, Prem Bedi vs. the State of Maharashtra, concluded today.

This was the first time since this trial had begun that we drove in Mr Bedi's car, the shimmering black Mercedes S500 with privacy glass. I speculated it was his way of demonstrating to the media and everyone that he was so confident he was in the clear that he didn't care what they wrote about him after this, that he was no longer prepared to play the part of someone under the haze of suspicion.

'Is it true that if you are not guilty you inherit the hundred crores and not Mr Manish Desai?'

'How wealthy are you that even a hundred crores don't motivate you?'

The barrage of questions continued as we walked up the steps. The media, for some unknown reason, thought that Mr Bedi or any of us were permitted to respond to them today. As we got to the door of the court with cameras following us, Mr Bedi stopped. He had worn a steel-grey worsted suit—must be custom made to fit him so well—and he turned around to give the cameras what they had been wanting for weeks: a half-smile, like he had just granted every newspaper their front page photograph for the evening news. The flashes blinded us.

The courtroom was packed. Not a single empty space. Apte was the first known face I spotted as we walked to our desks. As the trial was now over, and witnesses could not contaminate or corroborate each other's testimonies, I saw Manish Desai sitting right behind Apte. All smiles too. Just a few minutes before the hour, ACP Dutta walked in the courtroom with Ram Singh. Something in his countenance wasn't right. His demeanour had *alarm* written all over it, a kind of hopelessness that outlined a defeat. Something had happened since the time I had spoken to him last night. But what? Surely, he couldn't have opened the sealed envelope and seen the result—God—had he? And was his expression displaying that? I had never known what really being frightened meant before this moment. I could feel the earth shaking, spinning, people blurring into the background, noises ebbing and dying …

'*All rise.*'

The moment of truth was here. I missed the arrival of Judge Chowdhary. From the corner of my right eye, I saw someone rising.

'Sit down, Mr Apte, I am in no mood to indulge either of you advocates today. I'm not even extending the courtesy to either of you for closing arguments. The court has heard both sides of the arguments and witness testimonies and I'm sorry to say that to even bring this trial here was a waste of court's time. However, what we have here today is science talking. By all accounts, from what the court has heard, the defendant *never* visited the scene of crime in the last ten years, leastways'—the inflection on 'never' was unmistakable—'so if the DNA profiling proves his presence at the crime scene, this court will give a judgement. If not, I believe I had already clarified the court's position last week. And so, without any further ado, could the two suspects please rise?'

The word suspect wasn't used in the strictest sense of the term here. It referred more to the suspected DNA match.

Mr Bedi, Dad and I stood up. Manish Desai walked out from behind the barrier and stood alongside Apte.

'ACP Dutta, could you tell the court the results of the DNA profiling, and if any of the samples provided match the lacrimal secretions discovered at the scene of crime?'

'Yes, Your Honour.' ACP Dutta's hands shook. He opened the envelope, pulled out the first A4 sheet and read: 'Mr Manish Desai, male, age 32. On analysis we found that the sample provided by the known contributor does not match the unknown sample from the crime scene.'

There wasn't any cheering at the prosecution table. But my heartbeat became irregular. If it weren't Manish's tears—who could possibly be the only soul to cry at the dead bodies—I didn't want to think … I heard Dad let out a cold sigh. I guessed he was also depending on a DNA profile match with Manish Desai's.

Mr Bedi didn't lose his composure. None whatsoever. He stood tall like a lighthouse watching the storm at the sea.

ACP Dutta pulled out the second A4 sheet from the envelope and read: 'Mr Prem Bedi, male, age 53. On analysis we found that the sample provided by the known contributor does not match the unknown sample from the crime scene.'

I heard a loud thump; Dad had slumped into the chair with relief.

ACP Dutta walked to Ram Singh and handed him the two documents that were then passed on to the Judge, who only glanced at them for a minute.

'It is the judgement of this court that there is insufficient evidence to believe that the defendant had any opportunity to carry out the crime he had been charged with. The financial motive presented by the prosecution happens to be the same for the plaintiff here. Based on what was presented to the court in the past week, this court rules that the case did not have any merit to be tried. The case of Prem Bedi vs. the State of Maharashtra is hereby *dismissed with prejudice*.

'Mr Bedi, I apologise on behalf of the State and the Court to have imposed this trial on you, and, Mr Apte, I'd like to see you in the chamber in ten minutes.'

That was it. The torment was over.

'All rise …'

Even before Judge Chowdhary left his bench, I heard people rushing out of the court—the media guys—to get their cameras and microphones ready for when the Mogul walked out.

We exchanged hugs: Mr Bedi, Dad and I. We looked at the long faces of Manish Desai and Apte. Then I saw ACP Dutta walk towards us. He congratulated Mr Bedi first, then Dad and me. He then walked to Apte's desk and all we could see was they shook hands. Understandably, there were no congratulations, nothing to celebrate. Then ACP Dutta walked out of the court.

'Should we?' Mr Bedi was the first to speak.

If I said I expected him to wait until the crowd outside becalmed I would sound imprudent. The fashion in which we had arrived at the court today said everything one needed to know about him. He had kept his emotions in check at all times, never displayed any disgust or distress or delight, never indicated anything that could lead the crowd to believe he even contemplated defeat. And he had been shut quiet by the court. All bets were off now, all shackles taken off.

'Come on, Prem.'

Mr Bedi did not even as much as looked at the prosecution desk when he turned to leave.

The crowd couldn't stop shouting:

'Congratulations, sir.'

'Mubarak, Janaab.'

'How does it feel to be found not-guilty?' Someone held out a microphone for Prem Bedi. He took it.

'Firstly, thank you all. I appreciate the support. To answer your question *"how does it feel to be found not-guilty"*, I think it's best to interpret the court's adjudication appropriately: Honourable Judge Chowdhary quite clearly stated that the court did not find any evidence that could even remotely link me to the murders and he didn't pronounce me not-guilty, he has dismissed the case; they are two altogether different decisions. I am innocent.'

'Have you actually never been to their house at Pali Hill in the last ten years ... ?'

'You mean the Pali Hill bungalow that once belonged to my family, and which now, with the sad demise of Mrs Desai, belongs to me again? No, I haven't been there, but I will go there shortly to pay my respects to Rea, who was once my wife, and the only woman I ever loved. Now if you could excuse us, please?'

Wow! I hadn't known that. Maybe Dad did. But I was happy that Manish Desai did not get the Pali Hill bungalow.

'How about interviews, sir?'

'Call up my office and arrange them. Once again, I thank you all.'

Then, like the water splits to let the ship through, the crowd parted to let the Mogul walk to his car.

Veena ji was waiting eagerly. Obviously, the jubilance announced that she had already seen the result on local channel.

'Thank you, Rohan.' Her voice was understandably choked. 'Drinks on me, no one goes home.'

Damodar brought Rémy Martin XO and the snifters. It was a lifestyle I could easily get used to.

'Congratulations, Rohan,' Dad said. 'And you too, Prem.' He raised a toast with the Cognac. 'Bedi & Sons's stock price has gone up 17 per cent today, already.'

MANISH DESAI

I wanted to slap Apte, kick him, wring his neck and kill him or take him and dump him into the same sea that I had dumped Rea's jewellery in. I had had it all planned, I had done all the hard work, but he had let me down. He had been an incompetent asshole, a wrong choice. He had it all laid out for him, but he just couldn't bat. He was such a fuckin' waste of space. And it was all that fuckin' DCP's fault. He was the one who had got Apte involved when he could have got the best advocate in Mumbai for the case. What was the fuckin' rush? I could have waited till we had enough evidence or arguments to take that rich bastard to court and grill him like a *tandoori* chicken. Talk about a wasted opportunity!

I had mentally started spending the money on renovating my new bungalow at Pali Hill.

But that wasn't meant to be.

I found out the same evening that the bitch who fucked my brother hadn't written a will and hence, some earlier ancient testified will was still fuckin' valid. How could that be? But I did not have the wherewithal to fight another battle with Bedi.

I regretted throwing away the jewellery I had recovered from Pali Hill bungalow's safe locker. I had acted in haste. It could have fetched me a few lacs, at least. Fuck, this was the biggest proverbial fall for grace if there ever was one. One minute I was fantasising about inheriting a hundred crores and the next I was scavenging for a few lacs.

I raided Mahesh and Rea's bank locker and netted six lacs in cash. They had three bank accounts that bestowed me another eight lacs and change.

I was hounded by the media; wherever I went, they followed me—papping me, questioning me. I couldn't imagine what they wanted to write about me, though if the first local telecasts were any indication, the coverage didn't look positive for me. Not in any narrative. The same people who couldn't shower enough sympathy for me a few months earlier, suddenly believed I was the villain. It was not funny how soon the fuckin' world changed sides. The only solace I had was, like everything else, this news would get old and boring in a few days too. But until then I would have to fly under the radar, maybe disappear from Mumbai.

I wish I had a gun; I would shoot Apte and DCP Mathur.

This incident, this colossal loss would continue to plague me till the end of time, I knew.

GAJPATI APTE

I had gotten a call from DCP Mathur the morning of the final day at court. Curt and threatening, he said, 'If you as much as *think* about dragging me into this trial or shame me in front of the Judge, I will make your life hell, Gajpati Apte.'

Duplicitous bastard!

Truth was, I had fucked up big time. Period. Nobody's fault but mine. If I had stuck single-mindedly to my ambition, I would have been just fine. But greed took a free ride. Greed biased my judgement and perhaps, all went down from there. Perhaps I deserved it. My biggest grudge was losing to a rookie. I had it all within my grasp and then the sand had begun to slip through my fingers. My throat went dry every time I remembered that cold conversation with Judge Chowdhary, which was actually a monologue, a warning:

'*What were you thinking, Mr Apte?*'

'*Your Honour, I—*'

'*Let me tell you how it appeared to me: you guys just wanted to persecute an honourable gentleman for sheer kicks or some kickbacks, and I don't want to disgrace you any further by asking which one.*'

'*Sorry…*'

'*You had no evidence to begin with. The whole case reeked of prejudice, of some vendetta that Manish Desai seemed to be carrying. I'm not sure how you even bought his unrealistic theory. I mean you are a man of the world, with so much experience.*'

'*I promise I will never again let emotions and irrationalities affect my judgement, Your Honour.*' The Judge could ruin my career in a minute.

'*You'd better not try. Not in my court, not in any other judge's court, because I will be watching you.*'

I nodded in acquiesce, what was there to say?

'*Put all this behind you. I will not put this on record, I give you my word. You have wronged Prem Bedi … if I were you, I'd think about making amends. I can't tell you how.*'

'*I will, Your Honour, and I promise nothing of this sort will happen ever again.*'

'*Good, Mr Apte. And do not think I don't know who else was involved in this.*'

As I sat sipping my cheap whisky, I cursed myself. Why had I taken advice from that asshole DCP in the first place? What the fuck did he know about practicing law?

All dreams lay shattered around me, piercing my entire body and soul like little shards. Manish Desai wouldn't be coming around with pots of gold or Sonia now. He hadn't answered my phone or returned my calls, and I had called seven times. That's how thankless some people were.

And Mr Bedi, the innocent gentleman, I wondered how I could send my congratulations on his victory and my apologies for prosecuting him. I thought about calling him to let him know that I had been pushed into it. Maybe he would understand, maybe not. But I decided to wait.

I did the next best thing instead. I called Rohan Malhotra. He was polite and courteous. He understood my dilemma. I assumed that the sweet taste of victory in such an epic case had wiped off his slate of any ill-will. Success frequently did that. You easily pardoned the losers, notwithstanding all the dirty tactics they tried during the fight. He offered to pass on my compliments to Mr Bedi, and promised to be in touch. We both knew that wasn't going to happen.

I called ACP Dutta too. He was less friendly than Rohan in the beginning, but finally came around. He wanted to probe me on DCP Mathur's involvement but I insisted he let that go, and forgive me since we would have to work together in future. I didn't want this sordid episode to blemish any of the cases I filed in the future. Eventually ACP Dutta realigned with me on the condition that our relationship would stay strictly professional till he could trust me again.

I gulped a few more shots of local whisky, closed my eyes and tried sleeping.

As I said earlier, I had fucked up big time.

ACP RANJEET DUTTA

The file on the murders of Rea and Mahesh Desai was reopened. I was happy that the innocent Mr Bedi hadn't been convicted despite the underhand tactics of DCP Mathur and Manish Desai. I didn't hold much against Apte. As a matter of fact, I could sympathise with him after he called and apologised. DCP Mathur had misguided him, and false confidence made an ass of the best of people. If Apte hadn't been padded up with the deception, and if he had been given sufficient time to study the case, maybe he wouldn't have let DCP Mathur use his clout to push for a quick trial. Maybe he would not have even taken the case when the evidence was so sketchy, but it was all spilt milk now.

I briefed my team to carry on the investigation, to look for fresh leads, contact new set of snitches and to focus on other similar robberies where two people had been involved. The murders, I had always believed, were collateral damage. Had the Desais not been home or hadn't woken up at the wrong time, they wouldn't have experienced the fate they did. Terribly unlucky, but what I now knew about Rea and Mahesh Desai, I wasn't going to weep over them.

I called Rohan later in the evening but he was at Mr Bedi's residence and sounded slightly inebriated. Mr Bedi took the phone to thank me and invited me to his residence for a little celebration they were having. I politely declined twice but he insisted. He told me he was sending his driver to pick me up, so I didn't need to travel in the police jeep. I couldn't blame him. After weeks of the media seeing the police vehicles coming in and out of his residence, the last thing he wanted was to give the cameras another chance.

I met Mr Bedi's cousin, a Ms Veena Singh, who was both royal and graceful.

Cognac was served to me the moment I sat down.

'It wasn't a fair fight,' I mentioned frivolously after two quick drinks. 'You were three brilliant legal brains against the poor Apte.'

'Wrong,' Ms Veena Singh said. 'You forgot to add me. I have a law degree too. That makes four against one.'

I came to know that the Pali Hill bungalow was Mr Prem Bedi's now and not Manish Desai's. 'That must be worth ...' I didn't even want to guess.

'It's no longer mine,' Mr Bedi spoke. 'As token of my appreciation, I'd like to give that to Rohan, if he is willing to accept.'

'What?' Rohan came alive. 'You can't be serious.'

'I don't need any more properties, Rohan. I would have gladly given it to Manish Desai if he had come to me as a bereaved relative of Rea. But all he did was to carry on the smear campaign his brother had started years ago.'

I looked at Mr Bedi in awe. I could believe him. I had an urge to call up Manish Desai and tell him what he had actually lost, but what would be the point?

We had dinner together, and then Rohan and I left after midnight, all of us promising to stay in touch. Mr Bedi told me that he would really appreciate if I'd keep him abreast about any progress finding the murderer.

Mr Bedi's driver took us home. We tucked Rohan in first—he was in no state to walk or crawl—then the car dropped me home.

ROHAN MALHOTRA

When I got up in the morning, it felt like someone had put my head in a whirlpool; it was still spinning. Then I remembered the little victory celebration at Mr Bedi's place. I had fragmented memories of the evening, as I had been in and out of senses in my smashed state. One thing was certain: I couldn't handle alcohol. But then, yesterday had been an epic victory for me as an advocate, as a son, as a husband, as a father. I had earned a salary that could shame the best partners in my old firm. All of it on my own. I vaguely remembered something about Mr Bedi offering the Pali Hill bungalow to me. Had I heard that correctly or had I been hallucinating? And what did I say? Did I accept it? I wanted to call Dad to check but I still had a massive hangover to make any coherent conversation. And what would I say that wouldn't sound materialistic? Mr Bedi was, after all, Dad's friend and not just a colleague.

However, if Mr Bedi had promised that bungalow to me, would Urvee be willing to live in a property that had just been a crime scene? Anyway, Urvee and Pia were flying back this evening. Maybe I would ask about her feelings about the property before breaking the news that we might be getting it.

We could always pull down the bedroom where the murders had occurred. The Pali Hill property, if I were to guesstimate, was worth a lot more than the five-crore fee I had earned for the murder trial.

There was still one task left, although I didn't think my payment would be stopped for that. I still had to liaise with Freddy Vakil to get to the bottom of the entire issue. Until then, we carried the risk of it re-occurring, and we couldn't afford that.

The phones—both my mobile and residence—started ringing by eight. The reporters wanted to talk to me. I had become a minor celebrity of some sort. They wanted my impression of Mr Prem Bedi, my opinion on Manish Desai, on Gajpati Apte. What were my plans for future, what had been my fees? I told most of them that I would not be available till the end of the week. My family was returning home after months and I wanted to spend some quality time with them first.

Everything else could wait.

TEJ MALHOTRA

It was scheduled to be a busy day with Mr Lee arriving from Seoul in the evening. But first, I had an early morning appointment with Freddy Vakil at my residence. In light of Prem's recent victory, this was significant; those yearning to debilitate him must indeed be upset at their miscarried attempt, particularly when they had come so close. A defeated opponent should never be taken lightly: an aggrieved animal is always twice as dangerous.

Rohan called around nine the morning. Poor boy had overdone it again the previous night, but I deduced it would be one of his last big evenings with Prem and me. Without him asking, I told Rohan that Prem had awarded him the Pali Hill bungalow as a token of appreciation for what he had accomplished.

'Really, Dad?' he sounded ecstatic.

'Yes, it was a surprise, even for me. I know Prem well. He said it last evening in presence of Veena and ACP Dutta. And Prem has always believed that a man is nothing if he doesn't keep his word, so he's not going to renege on that. It wasn't something he offered because he was drunk. Moreover, the new residence will go well with your enhanced status.'

'I've been wondering what to do next …'

'What do you mean by what to do next? You're still an advocate. If anything, you're a better-known advocate now.'

'I mean I don't want to go back to my earlier practice, and I don't see myself getting big cases like Mr Bedi's every day or even every year. This was a once-in-a-lifetime thing. I guess, with all this status and money, I would be … some kind of a misfit?'

'What is on your mind then?'

'Well, I don't know, I thought you might have some good advice.'

In that moment I could see a son coming home to his father. I had done the same eons ago: gone back to my father. Life had done a full three-sixty. Rohan was mature enough to take any decision, and in the manner he had managed Prem's case, he had more than evidenced it. But I wasn't going to walk away from my son, who was in a quandary: *misfit*, did he say?

'Rohan, I see your point. Would a corporate role be more desirable? A steady income, a suitable environment, perhaps … back to your old firm, Dadawala & Partners.'

'You think I will fit in after being on my own for some time now?'

'You definitely will, but obviously you cannot go back to the post you left.'

'Of course not. I was thinking, perhaps at a partner level. They should be more than willing to offer me that now.'

'Go for it, I'd say. Try that for a year or two, learn the ropes, and maybe I'll retire and we can set up our own firm together. What say?'

'Malhotra & Sons.'

'*Sons*?' I sallied humorously. 'I'm not planning to have any more children, so maybe we'll call it Malhotra & Dad?'

Rohan told me Urvee and Pia were returning to Mumbai later today. We planned to get together over the weekend, said our byes and hung up.

Freddy Vakil was probing yet polite. He spent over three hours asking me everything I knew about Prem. Whatever I remembered from the day I first met Prem to how the official relationship became a close friendship. For a while it appeared that I was his number one suspect. Scary, yes, but he made a wonderful point.

'Mr Malhotra, don't misunderstand me, but my brief is to look at friends who could have undertaken something like this.'

It was a shocking eye-opener but the young man—and he was Rohan's age, give or take—wasn't incorrect. I sat and looked at him mutely.

'You'd be surprised, sir, but I've heard so many of my clients tell me that they were deceived by their friends. I find it funny. I want to tell them, obviously, only your friends could deceive you; your enemies would declare an open war.'

His clarification made me smile and open up, I admit.

He left after 1 p.m.

Mr Lee had decided to hire a jet and fly-in with this entourage. Evidently, he avoided all kinds of public transport if he could. He was arriving with his legal and retail teams plus Hyun, the interpreter. The retail team would fly around India to check out our stores that he was planning to invest in; the legal team would obviously stay with him. Prem, Mr Lee, Peter—his legal guy—and I would first go to Bombay Presidency for golf tomorrow morning, then meet at our office in Cuffe Parade to discuss matters, before we took the guests out for dinner.

Despite having been given a timeslot, a private carrier was, at all times, the first one to be dislodged from its landing slot, should there be any delay on account of a queue at air traffic control. With circa seven hundred flight take-offs and landings per day in Mumbai, today wasn't an exception. I had come to the airport alone—Prem wanted to spend time with Veena as he, too, would be busy the next few days, but Mr Lee's flight was now showing an arrival time of 9.15 p.m. I had no inclination to go back home and return later, so I bought a coffee and walked into a books and magazine store. Most newspapers carried pictures of Prem on the front page, but I picked a copy of *In-Business* magazine, which had Prem on the cover with the mot juste tagline: THE MOGUL WINS AGAIN. It made my day to see that the media's narrative was positive towards Prem. The four-page article carried an apt epigraph too; lines from a yesteryear hit from Abba: *The Winner Takes It All* …

> Prem Bedi, the scion of the noteworthy Bedi family, who had been vilified in the past few months by being dragged into court for superfluous charges of double homicide, had the last laugh. Judge Amar Singh Chowdhary, who presided on the case, found the whole purpose of trial pointless. He was aghast that the State even brought up the case against Bedi when there was no evidence. Judge Chowdhary dismissed the case with prejudice. Our correspondent, who attended the entire

trial from its commencement a week ago, added that Prem Bedi stayed dignified throughout the trial, never losing his cool.

The rest of the article was filled with back-stories. Prem's marriage, his divorce, the double homicides, an inset picture of him at a golf course with a caption: *Prem Bedi's Only Drive*, which made me chuckle—the sheer irony of it.

Mr Lee's flight was finally cleared for landing at 9.45 p.m. I quickly bought three more copies of *In-Business* with a mind to distribute them to our guests.

It was midnight by the time Mr Lee and his retainers cleared immigration and customs and appeared in the arrival lobby. Dinner was out of question now, so after pleasantries, I took them through the plan for the following day and excused myself.

The Bombay Presidency Golf Club, BPGC, is eighty-five acres of heaven on earth—probably the best golf course in the country. What made it a tough course was the untamed sea breeze, which could outflank the best of the best. On this course, no two games could ever be alike.

Prem had been a regular here for over three decades, and he was regarded like royalty.

Before we teed off, Mr Lee presented a new Taylormade Superquad driver to Prem, just as he had promised at Nine Bridges.

'Start with this,' Hyun translated for Mr Lee.

'Thanks. Is it some flimflam plan to make me lose?' Prem razzed. Hyun translated and Mr Lee laughed.

We finished at 3 p.m. and travelled back to the office.

It was Prem's first day back at work after the involuntary sojourn, and everyone at work was keen to have him back. After a brief welcome party for Prem and Mr Lee, we sat down in the conference room to discuss business.

'We're pleased to be here, and we cannot express how thrilled we were when we got the news of your victory,' Hyun told us without a prompt from Mr Lee. Perhaps the preface had been discussed on the flight itself.

'What can I say,' Prem responded, 'it was muck-raking from the beginning to the end. I'm sure you have such people in your country too who, for the best part of their lives, have no other purpose but to bring down those who want to move ahead. It was a sad chapter in my life, and I'm glad it's over.'

Mr Lee spoke to Hyun, who asked: 'Have the police now found out who the real culprit was?'

'I don't think so.' Prem looked at me in case I had some new news.

'Nothing yet.'

'Do you think it was business rivalry or personal?' Hyun questioned.

In that moment, it struck me like a bolt of lightning—like some electrical discharge had hit me, my concentration on the conversation was torn asunder. Who could have benefitted the most and in the shortest time frame, if Prem had succumbed to the charges? Who could have known that Prem played golf? Who could have known Prem's shoe size? Who had the wherewithal to carry out a task of this magnitude without stepping out of his house? Without leaving his country even?

Who waited until the case was decided before coming for the next round of discussions—there was nothing stopping him to carry on with the negotiations while the case was in court, his people could have come to scout the markets and the stores in the meanwhile, but they didn't. It wasn't one single thing that pointed towards Lee now; it was a basket of them. My head spun. Sung-min Lee, sitting in front of me smiling, had a motive, he had the means and, allowing for his resources, he could create an opportunity for anything he wanted. Plus the fact that he didn't know either Rea or Mahesh would have made it a lot easier to order the brutal hits. And though it made sense, it was pure conjecture. I had no way of connecting the crime to our guest. Also, it would be near impossible for anyone to connect Mr Lee to the murders. He didn't look imprudent to have gone out shopping for a hired gun himself. There would be six degrees of separation between him and the guy who would have ordered the hit and another six degrees of separation to the actual assassin. And the added complexity of geographies would be a nightmare unless the Interpol got involved. I made a mental note to speak to Rohan to get the word into ACP Dutta's ears, although I wasn't clear what was within the ACP's area of influence. Very limited, I would imagine. Not to mention that the entire theory was cooked by me based on one single fact: that Mr Lee could make millions out of this deal. It sounded like a bad plan, a lose-lose situation. There had to be a way. Freddy Vakil? Could he snoop around? How many ever degrees of separation, the killer had to be on the ground to make the final hit. Someone had physically walked into the Pali Hill bungalow and killed the couple, so there should be something that the police missed because they only focussed on Prem, got tunnel-visioned and botched up. Could Freddy work back to find some pointers? Even if the ultimate discovery turned out that the hit was ordered from abroad, it would be adequately clear that my theory had some legs. So I changed the mental note I had only made a few minutes back. The best and only way that I could plumb at this moment was to somehow ask Rohan to curry favour with ACP Dutta to let Freddy Vakil look at the material the investigators had already collected: glove prints, crime scene photos, etcetera. Only the raw material and initial notes and not the analysis; Freddy's own enquiry would become prejudiced if he read the earlier reports. It was still a semi-formed plan, but it could work.

Somewhere in the background, the clinking of China abruptly brought me back to the present; the teas and coffees had arrived in the room. I suddenly felt sickened by this meeting. Possibly I was overreacting, but from childhood I had been coached that it was a great deal better to err on the side of caution. Suddenly, Mr Lee's words, albeit not coming from his own mouth, sounded hollow. Conniving, flattering, bastard, carrying a gift for Prem all the way from Seoul. In my mind, I had pronounced Mr Lee guilty. I wanted to take Prem aside and run him through my surmise and hence, I announced a twenty-minute break for people to use the facilities or if some of them wanted to stroll out for a smoke.

'What are you saying, Tej?' Prem was as sceptical as I had expected him or anyone else to be when I narrated my deduction. We had moved away from the guests and sat in Prem's corner office. It was soundproof, plush yet minimalistic with straight lines being the dominant theme, like the whole room had been carved out of a single block of ice.

'It all adds up, Prem.'

'But he doesn't need that chicken feed, you know that.'

'It might not be about the cost of 25 per cent stake, the aim might have been to destabilise Bedi & Sons.' I could see his eyes squint in amazement. 'Prem, just humour me for minute, and if you don't think I make any sense, we'll forget we even had this conversation, but please think. There has been no succession planning, so if you are suddenly gone from the scene tomorrow, Bedi & Sons becomes an orphan conglomerate, a prime takeover target …'

Prem raised both his palms to stop me. 'Even if that happened, why would it be Mr Lee's exclusive gain, why wouldn't anyone else buy it?'

'We don't know if he's in bed with one or two of our board members.'

I could see Prem stiffen. Rage. 'You seriously think we have a traitor?'

'I'm not saying that, but the possibility cannot be out-ruled. It won't be the first instance, even emperors have had traitors.'

He didn't say anything.

'Maybe I'm totally off the beam here and there's no one involved at our end. But even if there is someone who turned in our camp, I can't believe even for a second, that whoever defected had anything to do with the murders … and now that person would be in a more precarious position than before, because if anyone colluded with Lee to strike at you, they know Lee's committed a capital crime to accomplish that, which puts them at risk. They either go on cooperating or get destroyed.'

'So what do you suggest we do?' Prem looked at his wrist. The twenty-minute break was almost over.

'Okay … how about this. I make an excuse and leave. I'll go and see Freddy and re-brief him. I'm sure he can hire some legs to do a quick check on all our directors, not an upright thing to do I know, but I can't see any alternative here. Anything dubious about anyone and we dig till we get to the bottom.'

I could see the disgust in Prem's eyes. He didn't seem to want this, but he hardly had an option. Whoever it was, they had come terribly close at destroying him. He understood that to get to those who were partners in the ghastly move against him, he'd have to allow me to proceed.

'Okay, but tell this private investigator that we do not want to know what's happening in our colleagues' private lives, please. No dirt on their relationships, their spouses, their kids, whatsoever. If the search does not reveal any liaison with Mr Lee, we don't want to know. And tell him that in the course of this search if anything turns up, and I find out that any of his contracted people use that against my people I, Prem Bedi, will personally destroy any such rogue individual. And I mean it, Tej.'

I knew he meant it. His eyes were red. The testiness was palpable in his voice. For the first time since this sordid episode had begun, he seemed rattled.

I asked Mani to wait while I called Rohan the moment I sat in the car.

'Hi, Rohan, I need a favour.'

'Of course, Dad, what is it?'

'Where are you?'

'Driving to the airport to pick up Urvee and Pia. They're arriving today since their flight got canceled yesterday.'

'Sorry, what time are they arriving?'

'Oh, at six-thirty, but I was bored so I thought I'd grab a bite and hang around there rather than sitting at home. What is it?'

'I need to see Freddy Vakil urgently, like *now*.'

'Is everything okay, Dad?'

'When and where can I see him?' Freddy had handed me his visiting card at home but I hadn't cared to look or store his number.

'Dad, are you okay?' he asked again. 'Tell me what's going on.'

'Rohan, I don't want to talk on the phone.' Call me paranoid, but when I narrated the possibility of infiltration to Prem, it had struck me even harder. If someone from our office had been influenced, it was always possible that our phones were wired.

'I want to meet Freddy, Rohan. Please call him and ask him to call me back.'

'You'll get a call in ten minutes, Dad. Do you want me to be present?'

'No, you carry on.'

ROHAN MALHOTRA

When Dad's call came, I was on phone with Sheila. She had called to congratulate me on our victory. I told her I had decided to join Dadawala & Partners as a partner and I'd like her to join my team when she passed the bar exam.

Dad's brief call panicked me. Something was wrong, I could tell. I called Freddy immediately. Fortunately, he was in Bandra and, as he was now retained full-time on our case, he agreed to meet Dad and me at the airport. I calculated that even if Dad and Freddy took half an hour to get there, I still had ninety minutes before the flight from New Delhi landed, so I could join them for some time. I wouldn't deny that I had every intention to participate in the furtive discussion, if only to feed my curiosity. I called Dad and asked him to join me outside Terminal 1 at the airport.

The three of us coordinated to meet in the Maharajah Lounge located at the mezzanine floor.

Dad explained how some of the circumstances had indicated that someone from Mr Bedi's own organisation could be part of the conspiracy. He added that Mr Bedi agreed with the theory.

Of course, all this was based on pure assumptions, but corporate espionage wasn't news to me, and I am sure Freddy, too, had come across it previously.

'We have no way to probe Mr Lee directly, but we have to run checks on all our directors on board, that's the first task.'

Freddy nodded.

'We have ten directors besides me, so you need to farm this enquiry out to the most reliable investigators you know, to run all checks in the next twenty-four hours.' Dad handed a sheet to Freddy with the ten names. 'Anything suspicious—unusually high or irregular deposits in bank, any exceptional purchases, *benami* property possessions, or unfamiliar visitors at home or meetings anywhere need to be reported. And any possible connection with men or women from South Korea should raise a flag. And, as Mr Lee is in town with his team, if any of our people meet with Mr Lee's associates outside of work, we should know immediately.'

Freddy took the sheet from Dad's hand.

'And, Freddy, I have to say this as Prem wants it to be made clear to anyone whom you employ for this task—if anyone of these men that you engage for this assignment even as much as contemplate misusing the info gathered in the process for any purpose other than providing it to us, they would be extremely sorry.'

Freddy nodded again.

'Rohan, you need to speak to ACP Dutta to see if he could provide copies of all material that came up in search of the crime scene to Freddy,' Dad told me, then: 'Freddy, if we get that, I want you to see if anything leads you to anyone that could point us further up the chain. You can have unrestricted access to the Pali Hill property to run your own investigation, if required. Pick up the keys from Rohan anytime you want, as he owns it now.'

Freddy looked at me, amazed. I nodded.

'We can defer the signing of the deal with Mr Lee until tomorrow evening. After that, he walks away and we don't get a chance to get to him. If we sign, we've anyway played to his tune and if we don't, we have no clue what he will do next when he returns to his country. So, in short, it's now or never.' Dad said.

Freddy didn't appear daunted by the urgency of the task he had been handed out. I think he had the ability to mobilise resources. However, he wasn't vastly different from where I was when I took Mr Bedi's case. I could feel that he needed cash upfront, for expenses to hire heads.

'Freddy, why don't you go home, run some calculations and let me know how much money you need and I'll transfer it right away,' I told him.

Urvee and Pia arrived on time, ten minutes after my meeting with Dad and Freddy concluded. Although I had only seen them last weekend, seeing them walk out of the airport made my eyes well up. I couldn't wait to break the news about our soon-to-be new residence, but thought against it and saved it for later.

TEJ MALHOTRA

I was going mental, the concerns primarily engendering from the let-down. In my mind, if one of our own had turned Judas, it was the first sign of failure. What could have caused it? More money, control, greed? Or was there something fundamentally wrong that made people on our own board of companies disgruntled? If it was greed, this could be a lone incident. However, if there was one displeased individual today—and dissatisfied to the extent that he or she was partaking in attacking Prem to destroy the company—it was only a matter of time before there would be another one. We couldn't go around snooping for the rest of our lives. In any event, what would be the point if the problem was with us?

Was it time for Prem to step down? He was a brilliant leader, but sometimes it just happened that others weren't happy about existing in the shadows of someone.

Rohan called late in the evening to say that he had advanced cash to Freddy and that his men were on the job already. But I wasn't sure that if someone was a part of the conspiracy, it would be simple for Freddy's agents to ferret out in less than twenty-four hours. Whoever they were, they might have taken precautions.

The reports from Mr Lee's retail team's interactions at our stores around the country had started coming in. Our stores communicated that the guests were quite pleased with our network, the common summary being that Mr Lee's people were positive about the deal. But my worry now was Mr Lee and not the deal. We had eight hours left to uncover anything before Prem signed or declined the deal. Cliché, as it might sound, time *was* running out for us.

On my insistence again, Prem relented that I personally be allowed to pry around a bit. Under guise of a thorough cleaning, I got in an agency to sweep for any bugs. Result: zilch. I had contacts in banks who I called to find out if any of the directors' bank accounts had swelled for no apparent reason in the past one year or money having been transferred from anywhere abroad. Net outcome: zilch again. With no other recourse left, I waited to get some reports back from Freddy.

By 3 p.m. the reports came in. All negatives, nothing found. The whole operation had been futile, a waste of time.

I sat in Prem's office at five, waiting for Mr Lee to return from golf. The deal was verbally supposed to be agreed at dinner today; the papers to be signed tomorrow and Mr Lee to fly out the very next day.

'Nothing?' Prem asked.

'I'm sorry, Prem.'

'Nothing for you to be sorry about. I guess when you told me your theory even I thought it was possible.' He stopped to think. 'But all this has put me in a predicament, Tej.'

'How?'

'I am guilty of invading my own people's private life, don't you think?'

'There is nothing to be guilty of, Prem. No one needs to know. The guys that did the legwork have been categorically warned to destroy if they stumbled upon anything that did not pertain to our query. I'll double-check the same with Freddy, ask Rohan to get indemnity signed, if you wish …'

'Tej, if you aren't caught stealing, it does not mean you never stole. I ordered an immoral thing, I need to apologise.'

'To whom?'

'To our own people; they trust me and I broke their confidence.'

'But you're forgetting something, Prem. We did this to protect you, and the company from any further attacks. If anything, *I* got the searches carried out so *I* should be the one who should be—'

'I agreed to those searches and, as such, *I* owe my people an explanation and an apology.' He softly clouted his hand on the table, which he sometimes did to indicate that the debate was over.

That was Prem.

Mr Lee called at six from the hotel to tell us what we had already known: his guys liked our stores. Our team had already been to Seoul to scrutinise the microchip plant and research facilities that we wanted a stake in, and given us a nod from a technical perspective. Hyun the translator, who spoke on Mr Lee's behalf, had informed us that their team had a surprise waiting for us when we met for dinner for the final handshake this evening.

Couldn't wait.

The Gateway Room at Taj Palace was reserved for the occasion. We had all our board members joining Prem and me for dinner, and Mr Lee had an almost equal number of people who were back in Mumbai after their visits and inspections.

Mr Lee and his team only had to take the elevator down, but we were all there when he arrived, and in his typical fashion, stood straight and bent his upper body to greet. Prem, I noted, was back in his usual element that gave away nothing about the deliberations and furtive activities of the past twenty-four hours. Champagne did the rounds as we all stood talking to one another, communicating in morsels of broken English. After meeting some of his team members and apologising for missing the meeting last evening, I gravitated towards the two Moguls.

'I heard you have a surprise for us, Mr Lee,' I politely prodded.

I think he caught the word *surprise* and understood what I meant without the need for a full language translation by Hyun. That, or the crafty Mr Lee understood English but used an interpreter like a host of other people who employed them merely to take time to think through their responses while the translation was in progress. Some even feigned ignorance of language to make you comfortable so that you made the mistake of saying something sensitive in their presence—a known business tactic.

'In a minute,' Hyun responded.

As we sat down around the table, Hyun stood up to make the surprise announcement for which he had already been briefed. He read from a piece of paper.

'Mr Lee wants to thank all of you for the generous hospitality extended to all of us. He's travelled to see many business partners, but this was exceptional. He is pleased that his team was delighted to see the retail store sites, which is one of the primary reasons we had flown in. Moreover, the whole team wants to congratulate Mr Prem Bedi on his victory in the court battle ...'

Prem glanced at me; I couldn't decrypt his expression.

'As discussed previously, we had come here to negotiate a deal better than the twenty-five per cent stake we were offered by Bedi & Sons ...'

Was it time now for Hyun to mention that the reputation of the stores had been tarnished due to the trial of Prem?

'However, Mr Lee, as a token of the long relationship that we wish to have with Bedi & Sons, and as a small token of gift for the recent victory, is willing to offer twenty-five per cent stake to Bedi and Sons in exchange for only twenty per cent of stake in your retail business. A small surprise gift from a friend to say we're not merely business partners.'

I couldn't have been more off the mark. Ashamed, I glanced at Prem, who just smiled, stood up and applauded.

'And Mr Lee also insists that tonight's party is to be hosted by him.'

The banquet hall roared with applause. As the two shook hands, Prem thanked Mr Lee. I felt a lump in my throat.

We finished at midnight. Mr Lee and his team left for their rooms. Prem had asked the Bedi & Sons' board members to stay back for a few minutes for an announcement. He was majestic in the way he clarified to all that he had taken the liberty of pervading into their personal lives without their permissions, but it was due to the exceptional circumstance that he had been pushed into. He unreservedly apologised and promised it would never occur again.

The directors went from shock to dismay to comprehension within minutes. None of them seemed to throw a fit, which was good.

'Mr Bedi, we are a team, and we are your family. An attack on you is an attack on all of us. Anyone in your position might have thought like you did. Please don't apologise,' Mr Bhandari, one of the directors, said. No one else said anything; everyone merely nodded. It demonstrated their honest allegiance towards Prem. The short meeting now over, everyone shook hands with Prem and me, assuring us of their cooperation, should anything like what had happened ever come up again.

Prem and I sat after everyone had left.

'Prem, let me apologise once again for doubting our directors and making you go against your principles,' I voiced my apology. It was at my instigation that he had prompted the whole search.

'It's okay, Tej. Everyone makes mistakes. Let's close this chapter and move on. Everyone seems to have forgiven us. We've got paperwork to get ready for tomorrow, which should be our immediate focus. It was quite generous of Mr Lee to make that offer, don't you think?'

'Oh yes, I felt humiliated and emotional. I saw that you were emotional too; I could feel it in your eyes.'

'My mother, as you know, Tej, was born into royalty. She had a noble upbringing and good education. One thing they taught all the kids in the household was never to renounce traditions and family customs. She followed all traditions until the day she passed away …'

He was reminiscing, and I let him carry on.

'She always said that whenever you are happy, really happy because you've achieved a new milestone, won something big or accomplished a goal in life, you should shed a tear or two to keep the evil eye away from you. These …' he pointed towards his eyes that were slightly moist again, 'sometimes I permit them to fall. For the last fifty-three years, it has always worked to keep the evil eye away from me.' He smiled and pulled out a silk monogrammed kerchief to wipe his eyes.

Did he just … ?

No, I told myself; the tears at Rea's bedside were most certainly not his. They couldn't have been his. Was I beginning to develop what they called clinical paranoia?

'I forgot to mention. Veena and I are going abroad for a week—it's been a while since I had a vacation, and Veena insists that it will be good for me, considering the tough time I've just been through,' he said.

'Of course, you deserve it, Prem. In fact, I considered suggesting that myself, after tomorrow's signing. Where do the cousins plan to go?'

'Veena is checking on that.'

'When do you go?'

'I left it to her too. But definitely after tomorrow, as Mr Lee is here. I didn't get to check with you, as we were engrossed in office affairs. Is that okay with you, as you would have to run the business for some more time due to my absence—only this time it's a vacation and not forced time off.'

'It's absolutely okay with me, Prem. I shall take care of everything. You should know that by now that you don't have to worry about anything when you're not in the office. We'll even take your email access away so you can enjoy your vacation.'

'Thanks. Thanks for believing in me, and standing by me when I needed you the most. Thanks for being such a great friend, Tej. This incident, and more importantly you, have opened my eyes in one respect—when I return from my short vacation, we should have a succession plan for Bedi & Sons.'

'Definitely.'

'And one more thing before I go, how much money did we make in stocks?'

'I haven't asked for statements yet, but the stock price hasn't stopped going up.'

'Tally up and we will announce a bonus to those people who held the stock when the world thought I was going down. There must be some way to identify the investors who owned our shares on June 10th and didn't panic all through the trial.'

'Of course we can find *that* from the records, but we cannot delineate and announce bonus for them—'

'I will mail them personal cheques if need be …' he smiled and walked away.

That was Prem Bedi.

That was the Mogul.

PREM BEDI

John F. Kennedy International Airport

New York

Veena and I had flown into New York from Mumbai, transiting at London. She had found some exclusive car hire firm on the internet that specialised in prestige and sports vehicles. No queues to stand in, the Corvette was waiting for us right outside the arrival terminal.

'Do you want to drive, Prem?'

'Of course.'

She took the keys from the concierge and passed them to me. The soft-top was already down. We packed our strolleys in the little boot and charted the route to our destination on the Satnav. We were to take the coastal I-95 up north and then east on to 1-195 to Woods Hole, and finally take the ferry to Martha's Vineyard. Veena owned a seaside property there and she had decided that we spend some time together to unwind.

I started the car and gingerly made our way out of the crowded airport. Driving in New York traffic was no better than Mumbai. It was only when we hit the expressway that I pressed the pedal to test the roar of the 6.2 litre engine, and it did not disappoint.

Oh, I had been yearning to drive.

There is an enormous difference between being acquitted as *not-guilty* and being absolved as innocent. I didn't want to end up another OJ Simpson. I didn't want to get a not-guilty verdict. I didn't want to live in the shadow of suspicion and shame for the rest of my life. I didn't want to be talked about and written about as someone who managed to escape justice. I wanted to be seen as someone who was persecuted because certain malicious group of people had an agenda against me. I wanted to give the investigators just about enough evidence that pointed towards me, to make it look like someone was framing me to malign me, to ruin my reputation, to devastate my business interests. The golf iron isn't the only weapon known to mankind; you would be spoilt for choice looking at the available selection of weapons in the black market in India. I wasn't exactly short of cash. I could pay for any weapon I wanted and a more-than-generous fee for the seller's lifetime silence. People who sold unlicensed firearms didn't squeal on their customers or blackmail them later, their whole business flourished on confidentiality. Golf iron wasn't an impulsive choice either; I chose to use the same. To make the whole thing look suspicious, like someone was trying very hard to make me the fall guy. I mean, I didn't leave behind any evidence whatsoever at the scene of crime, but I left an outsole shoe mark on my exit. I placed it there on purpose. I wanted the police to deliberate that the conspiracy against me was purported. I wanted them to take me to court with those weak discoveries and less than circumstantial evidence, and they took the bait. And yes, it wasn't an outright lie; I still believed in what my mother taught me. Whenever I was happy, whenever I achieved something that I set out to accomplish, I did ward off the evil eye. And that night I permitted my tears to descend, partly to give the forensics the final ammunition, albeit blank, to fire at me, and partly because, in the end, I was truly overcome by emotions to have had to carry out something so gruesome against the only woman I ever loved. It could be termed as a wave of guilt. I was quite disappointed that the discovery of teardrops did not come to the fore for a long time after the murders. It wouldn't have been a comprehensive victory for me had the DNA fingerprinting not been decreed by the Judge. Hence when His Honour asked for blood sample, I knew it was a home run—right on the money, as they say.

Of course, none of this had to happen.

I really loved Rea, but she had insisted on cheating on me, it was some kind of a visceral buzz for her. She loved the whole idea, not just the sex. I couldn't put into words, even if I tried, the pain and anguish and shame she caused me. I gave her several chances, but you could do nothing if the other person didn't want it. It had been instilled into me from the very beginning that marriages were sacrosanct, that they were made in heaven, and that they were meant to be for a lifetime. The vows must be respected.

I was patient for an obnoxiously long time. It got worse when people who knew me personally or professionally started talking, gossiping about my marriage and my life. And that hurt.

The will and insurance documents weren't put in place when we were madly in love. I hadn't been true to Tej about that. I had enforced them before Rea knew that I knew what she had been doing behind my back, and there wasn't a chance of her ever coming clean. Initially I assumed the thought of losing money might even cure her. It was an error of judgement on my part. Her appetite to cheat only got fuelled by the risk. She started blackmailing me, through random guys, for her own photographs.

Divorce can be a savage thing. Greed can be equally barbarous. Put them together and you create an insatiable monstrosity. At my age, you tend to ask yourself what was all this for? What was all this worth? What were you willing to pay to rectify the one vile mistake of your life? The answer wasn't easy and clean, but it was the only one. Anyone who passes a judgement on me should be made to get into my size eight-and-a-half shoes first.

We had driven for about an hour now and stopped for a break. We used the facilities, picked up hot coffees and came out and stood by the Corvette to enjoy the vista.

'Are you tired? Want me to drive?' Veena asked.

'Not at all, just enjoy the ride.'

It was country life all around us as we gazed across the little village that surrounded us in the middle of nowhere. Tractors, small plantations, rustic farm-workers and scattered rural dwellings.

We buckled up after the twenty-minute break and zoomed north again. I promised Veena I would let her drive when we stopped next, say after another hundred miles? She agreed and figured out how to connect her iPod to the car by now.

'What do you want to listen to, Prem?'

'I could turn it around and ask what music you have.'

'I've got twenty-five thousand songs on this. I'm sure you can't think of a track I don't have.'

'How many?'

'You heard that correct. Twenty-five thousand.'

'Put on some good playlist—blues and rock?'

'How about Queen's *We Are the Champions* …?'

I nodded.

'I have just the playlist you'll love.'

'Go on then.' Our tastes in music were similar, so her playlist would be good, I could tell.

Freddy Mercury's distinct vocal versatility came on vibrantly as we sped ahead. These American sports cars came equipped with some awesome music systems, I have to admit.

Veena and I were like two oceans. It would have failed the best geologists to discern where one culminated, where the other commenced.

Veena wasn't my cousin.

Veena was my twin.

She was exactly three minutes, eleven seconds younger to me. My parents had given their word to my mother's elder brother—as they were childless—that Mum and Dad would give their second child to them. If I were born after Veena, I had no reason to doubt that I would have been given and Veena would be a *Bedi*. At our births, our parents had realised that my mother could never bear another child, but that didn't make them renege on a promise that they had made earlier. We Bedis have always kept our word. My father used to tell me 'that a man was nothing if he didn't keep his word'. We were told this truth when Veena and I were eighteen. Both of us were sent to Britain to study. Both of us learnt driving there and got British driving licences. Veena, in time, got herself an Indian driving licence; I didn't bother. Mum once told me that when they had made our horoscopes at the time of our birth, a pundit had predicted that we had similar destinies. How eerily true his prediction would turn out to be. Both of us ended up losing our spouses early. She lost her husband to illness; I lost my wife to greed.

Queen's track was over. Bruce Springsteen came alive with *Thunder Road*.

And on that evening of the murders—7 June—Veena had driven me to Pali Hill. I could drive, but I couldn't risk parking the car somewhere around. The Mercedes S500 is a fairly conspicuous car, noticeable because of its uncommonness and sheer size. She dropped me about half a kilometre before the address and picked me up when I called her twenty minutes later—that's all it took me to get in and do my job. Though I was prepared, Rea and Mahesh hadn't even bothered to change the locks since the time they had won the property in the divorce battle, which made my entry a lot simpler and quicker. Both the phones we used that night were pay-as-you-go, the ones Veena had picked up from Delhi before she arrived, and they now sat somewhere in the depth of the Arabian Sea along with the golf club, the shoes, the gloves and my overalls, all bundled into a sack along with two metal bars to make them get to the basin and stay there. They might be found one day on the seabed or they might never be found. In any event, it would be too late by then.

No, Veena hadn't arrived when Tej met her. Veena came to Mumbai a couple of days prior to the murders. She stayed at Holiday Inn in Juhu under an alias—a discreet hotel away from anyone who could have possibly known her or me. We did the dry run on two consecutive nights before the final one. Sure enough, I had foolproof electronic gadgetry at my Altamount Road residence, but I also knew how to override it manually. It was merely one flick of a switch that turned it all off. Someone should have applied sheer common sense to ask if there was a manual override in case it was required; it was in the double garage on the side. If some of the staff in my household had knowledge of the same, they didn't ask or mention it. They were trained not to question since the days of my father. They weren't going to start breaking the rules now.

Life's Been Good, sang Joe Walsh in the car. I loved this playlist.

Instead of stopping at the Services, which we both thought were disgusting, synthetic eating holes, we drove into New London in Connecticut. Funnily enough, *New* London also had a *New* Thames River. We stopped at a café and organic shop that had a retro feel to it.

'How are you feeling, Veena?'

'Absolutely relieved. I can't describe how terrified I was all throughout your trial.'

That was the reason she hadn't come to court on any day. She was afraid her countenance might have given away something.

'But why, when you knew we had planned everything to the last T?'

'So many things could go wrong, Prem. What if you had accidently left any other evidence?'

'I know what you mean. But it's behind us now. And thank you for all the help.'

'Don't be stupid. You did it all for me.'

'For both of us.'

'I'm driving now, bhai,' Veena confirmed, in case I had any other ideas.

'Sure, why not.'

We left New London after lunch. Veena drove and I was left to manage the iPod, which wasn't my forte. But she gave me clear one-line instruction: 'Just press the play button.'

That wasn't so difficult.

Winning by Santana came on the stereo.

I reflected on what Veena had said at lunch. Of course all of this could have gone awry; even immaculate planning could fail. But then with Rea determined on conning me, it wasn't going on track anyway. I had to take the risk.

I had forgotten Rea, wiped her from my brain like a bad memory. I had been honest when I had expressed that to Tej. I had reached a point where she had become inconsequential. Despite living in the same city, we hadn't even as much as accidentally bumped into each other for twelve years. Mumbai, fortunately, afforded you that courtesy.

Rea perchance met Veena in Delhi earlier in the year. It could well have been a planned thing, as Rea knew the places Veena visited regularly, so I wouldn't rule it out altogether. She had been rude to Veena, and threatened her to convince *me* to sign off the damned insurance papers. After a dozen years, she had woken up when the insurance policy was about to mature and reap fifty crores. She and her husband wanted more money for some crazy venture. And she was willing to restart the long and despicable battle via her husband and his media connections. She didn't confront me directly, which she should have. Instead, since their *perchance* meeting, she incessantly called Veena and made her life hell. You had to give it to Rea and her husband for their tenacity though. The calls got more frequent and her tone more derisive. The insurance policies were identical, so she should have been happy with her share of fifty crores, but she wanted my part too. Rea had been more than copiously provided for in the divorce settlement. That money seemed to have dried up and she had no right to ask for more, but I guess you can't control greed. Her biggest grouse was that she had been relegated—she had actually used the word *relegated*—to a tiny bungalow in Bandra while my prosperity grew all the time. What she chose to ignore was that I worked like a dog for it. What she also overlooked was that the *tiny* bungalow was a small treasure in itself that most people couldn't buy with all the money they amassed in their lifetimes.

Signing away another fifty crores to her would not have bankrupted me, not at all. But that wasn't the point. Money wasn't my motive—Manish Desai got it wrong from the beginning. I needed to put an end to Rea's claims on my family money once and for all. And more than anything else, she had no right to be nasty to Veena.

The way I was brought up, I've been taught never to accept anyone walking over me. She thought she and her good-for-nothing husband could destroy me? She had been pining for a fight that I kept turning away from for more years than I cared to count. I wasn't some saint, but I sure as hell wasn't a chicken either. No way was I accepting another onslaught. Rea and Mahesh asked for it, they got it.

When Veena had called me to narrate her meeting with Rea, I could sense her throat choking with humiliation, with fear. Rea had crossed the line once again, spitting invectives at Veena. My dad used to say, 'Do not ever come between the lion and his pride, unless you want to end up as meat on the barbecue.' Rea had left me no alternative.

Now it was Elton John's *I'm Still Standing* playing.

Later I had played along with Tej's ideas and searches. I let him be suspicious of Mr Lee. I had proposed hiring a private detective to keep the momentum on for Tej and his son, to let them think that I was worried about further attacks. But I knew there wouldn't be any. My enemies were gone. And Manish Desai wouldn't dare to try anything again, not after his miserably failed attempt. I was confident that Freddy would go around in circles for a year and then eventually fess up that he had discovered nothing. It would turn to be an exercise in futility, a waste of time and money—his time and my money, but I didn't mind spending a bit extra to convince Tej that we tried our best. Tej had been a good friend, and his confidence in me was important.

Journey told us: *Don't Stop Believin'*—another brilliant song in Veena's playlist.

'How did you select all these tracks, Veena?'

'You like them?'

'Of course.'

'Do you want them?'

'I have them all, but not in any list as such.'

'Prem, you don't have an iPod, do you?'

'No,' I admitted.

'Okay, I'll buy you one when we get back to New York and then share this playlist with you.'

'Thanks.'

'When is your appointment with the doctor, Prem?'

'Monday morning, at ten.'

'We'll be back Sunday night then.'

Few years ago, my baldness hadn't been by design or for vanity. It was the result of clinical treatment of the illness people call cancer. Chemotherapy. I had been on a trip to US with Veena after my divorce when I was diagnosed. Veena had taken me to Sloan Kettering Cancer Centre. I had extended my vacation without telling anyone the reason. If anyone had looked closely when I returned bald, it would have been a slam-dunk giveaway. I had lost about ten kilos of weight. My skin looked paler and lacklustre. But I took precautions to make sure that no one ever did. I avoided golf for a couple of months by feigning a tennis elbow until I was certain I had regained my strength and colour, and no one could notice any change. It wasn't easy, but then few things in life are.

We were now turning east near Providence in Rhode Island, which is the smallest state in the US. Veena had been driving for almost an hour and I wanted the car back. She declined. Typical.

The track changed to *Eye of the Tiger.*

Sloan Kettering Cancer Centre

New York

The holiday at Martha's Vineyard had been relaxing, but now real life was here again, in the form of Marcia Miller MD. She was a second generation Mexican married to a Caucasian American. Tall, long and dark hair, she was a strikingly good-looking woman when I had met her first time over a decade ago, and ageing had been generous to her.

She had been the one who had treated me for leukemia when I was first diagnosed. You could call it sheer luck, but they had found a Human Leukocyte Antigen (HLA) match for cord blood—8 on 8 match. The stem cell had been taken for a patient with the same HLA, but unfortunately it had been too late for her; she had passed away before the transplant.

I had gone into the theatre within two days after arriving at the centre. They harvested me, which was nothing but draining all the blood from my body, removing the stem cells from my blood and then putting it back into me. I was intubated for two days. The next part of the process was to introduce the donor's stem cells into my body. That was the most painful procedure in the entire treatment. I was told it could take anything from thirty minutes to more than a few hours. My transplant took over four hours, and I still remember every one of those two hundred and forty six minutes.

Fortunately, my recovery had been faster than what they had expected, considering my age. Except for a severely upset stomach and loss of appetite, I had few side effects, and I was discharged after forty-five days with a strict warning that I had to return if there were any signs of infection.

For now, it was over. But I became a *chimera*.

What that meant was that the blood in my veins was no longer the royal one I was born with; it wasn't mine. It was the donor's engrafted stem cell that produced new blood and thus, the DNA in my blood was different to the DNA in the rest of my cells. The DNA typing of my hair, my skin, my sweat, my semen, and my tears would never match my blood DNA.

I wouldn't have been worried even if the forensic team had recovered my hair or skin residue from the scene of crime at Pali Hill. The DNA wouldn't have matched in any event. If the Judge had asked for a buccal swab, it would have been different, but I knew from past cases that the Judge would ask for a blood sample.

Now as I sat in her room, Marcia Miller gave me a full physical examination and asked me several questions.

'You seem to be in perfect health, Mr Bedi. The breathlessness seems to be on account of stress. Have you been through some severe trauma recently?'

'A lot,' Veena answered, I nodded.

'There you go, that's it. Relax and enjoy life, Mr Bedi, what's the point of being stressed? Whatever has to happen will happen, isn't it?'

I smiled.

'Thank you, Dr Miller. The new blood you gave me has now saved my life … twice.'

She looked perplexed. Veena gave me a stern look and took me by my arm. 'Come on, bhai, let me take you downtown. I have to buy you an iPod.'

AUTHOR'S NOTE

Caution: Spoiler Alert

Though I've made every effort to keep this short note ambiguous enough for a reader to not grasp the ending, I take no responsibility if you read it before the book and spoil your suspense. So, if you haven't read the book yet, I request you to STOP NOW.

You might have noticed that I have deliberately avoided dating this story. It is for a reason. What I've built the whole case on, is no longer possible; stopped being so after 2004-05. The point is that there was a time when this could have been fact, not fiction. The procedural changes happened only after the infamous case where Dr Abirami Chidambaram of the Alaska State Scientific Crime Detection Laboratory in Anchorage discovered that the semen found in the body of the rape victim matched that of a man who was in jail for some other charge at the time of the alleged rape. It was after that instance that the rules of criminal investigation and evidence collection changed in many parts of the world.

I wouldn't say anything more. I have mentioned the name of the doctor and the place, and provided reference to the crime in question. For those of you inclined to find out more—delve into it, and you shall find that I have kept strictly to the straight and narrow; if you don't wish to explore it further, I hope you still found the story enjoyable. But please do not try this at home.

Tears: I confirmed with a member of the forensic team in India that, theoretically, DNA can be extracted from dropped tears, but the probability is only between 10-15%. I could have easily switched the story around but the expert told me I shouldn't. His words: '*If it is possible academically, then you should go ahead and use tears for DNA, and no one should be able to contest it.*'

As we all know, there are over three *crore* (30 million) cases pending in Indian Courts. Which means: if I adhered to the true timetable on hearings of this trial, this book could go on forever. I have, therefore, fast-tracked the case to bring it to a swift conclusion, for which I apologise in advance.

Like always I thank my wife, Nidhi for being a partner in crime from the very beginning. I'd like to thank the entire Siyahi team for working with me to shape this story, and also the wonderful editors at HarperCollins India for giving the deft touches. My sincere gratitude to all my lawyer friends, officers in Indian Police Force and the Forensics teams for their timely help. Lastly I thank all my readers for reading my books.

Love, lots of it.

Vish Dhamija

Find me on:

Facebook: www.facebook.com/vishdhamija

Twitter: @vishdhamija

Email: vishdhamija@gmail.com